Up to now the work [...] cies have been known only to the highest government officials. Now one of Washington's most knowledgeable journalists has penetrated the inner sanctum of American espionage, and reveals in this book the inside story of spy organizations more powerful and more secret than the CIA.

The most important of these is the National Security Agency (NSA)—an army of anonymous government employees who receive, analyze and sift secret information gathered by electronically equipped spy planes, ships, and satellites. NSA uncovers such top secret information as locations of missile bases and confidential Soviet policies discussed in private conversations.

This fascinating book also reveals the operations of DIA, the highly secret branch of the Defense Department; INR, an arm of the State Department; and the intelligence branches of the Army, Navy and Air Force.

Unique, comprehensive, incisive, here, for the first time, are the facts about America's super spy agencies.

"Sure to make waves on the Potomac, *The Super Spies* is intriguing reading." —*Houston Post*

THE SUPER SPIES
was originally published by William Morrow & Co., Inc.

Also by Andrew Tully

White Tie and Dagger

Published by Pocket Books

 Are there paperbound books you want
but cannot find in your retail stores?

THE
SUPER SPIES

*More secret, more powerful
than the CIA*

by Andrew Tully

PUBLISHED BY POCKET BOOKS NEW YORK

To Frederick S. Wood
In Fair Elysium

THE SUPER SPIES

William Morrow edition published September, 1969
Pocket Book edition published November, 1970

Standard Book Number: 671-77211-2.
Library of Congress Catalog Card Number: 71-89012.
Copyright, ©, 1969, by Andrew Tully. All rights reserved.
This **Pocket Book** edition is published by arrangement with
William Morrow & Co., Inc.
Printed in the U.S.A.

PREFACE

Certain operational methods and locales have been fiction-
alized, for obvious reasons. Official positions held by foreign
defectors-in-place also have been disguised, and agents in the
field have been given fictitious names. Again for obvious reasons, no public credit can be given those many persons in
and out of Government whose assistance made this book possible.

ANDREW TULLY
Washington, D.C.

THE SUPER SPYMASTERS

Lieutenant General Joseph Francis Carroll, director of the Defense Intelligence Agency.

Lieutenant General Marshall S. Carter, director of the National Security Agency.

Major General Joseph A. McChristian, Assistant Chief of Staff for Intelligence, Department of the Army.

Rear Admiral Frederick J. Harlfinger II, Assistant Chief of Naval Operations (Intelligence), Commander, Naval Intelligence Command, Navy Department.

Major General Jack Eugene Thomas, Assistant Chief of Staff for Intelligence, United States Air Force.

Thomas L. Hughes, director, Bureau of Intelligence and Research, the State Department.

J. Edgar Hoover, director of the Federal Bureau of Investigation.

Dr. Glenn T. Seaborg, chairman, the United States Atomic Energy Commission.

CONTENTS

THERE is of course the Central Intelligence Agency. And then there are the other spies—the Defense Intelligence Agency, intelligence sections of the military services, the National Security Agency, the FBI, the Espionage Section [*sic*] of the Department of State and, yes, even the Atomic Energy Commission.

> *Excerpt from a lecture given at an espionage school in the Soviet Union.*

1

Saucers with Ears

When an official report reached the Pentagon one day in September, 1965, that a resident of Exeter, New Hampshire, had encountered a brilliantly glowing "Flying Saucer," an officer in Army Intelligence turned to a colleague with a remark familiar to men who have known battlefield action. "I hope it's one of ours," said the officer.

It is not known how much inside information, if any, this particular officer possessed. But in the years since June 24, 1947, when the first UFO (Unidentified Flying Object) was seen near Mount Rainier in the State of Washington, it had become common knowledge that both the American and Russian intelligence communities were launching unmanned aircraft electronically equipped to eavesdrop from the skies on each other's secrets.

Despite efforts by the military and the Central Intelligence Agency to debunk the flying saucer as a natural phenomenon, informed speculation had continued to maintain that it existed—as an intelligence device. This speculation was bolstered during the sixties by advances in the techniques of unmanned flight, especially by aerial reconnaissance aircraft and space satellites, and in the perfection of new and highly sophisticated devices for eavesdropping and the interception of coded radio messages.

The U.S.S. *Liberty,* which was fired upon by Israeli planes and torpedo boats off the Egyptian coast during the Arab-Israeli war in June, 1967, was loaded with gadgets which could listen in on communications more than one hundred miles away. So were the destroyers *Maddox* and *Turner Joy,* which came under attack by North Vietnamese vessels in the Tonkin Gulf in August, 1964, an incident which led to the first United States bombing strikes on North Vietnam and the massive commitment of American troops to the Vietnam war. So was the U.S.S. *Pueblo,* seized by a task force of North Korean patrol boats off the North Korean port of Wonsan in January, 1968. And it is significant that in 1953 the CIA had based its proposal for a survey aimed at debunking the flying saucer "myth" on the belief the saucers had been developed by a "hostile foreign power."

In fact, the United States Air Force at the time and for many years thereafter maintained a rigid silence on the matter because its experts were never sure who owned the flying saucers. Over the years, spy satellites have mysteriously "disappeared" after launching. That is to say, no wreckage was found. The official assumption was that they had crashed in the ocean after blasting off from the launching pad at Vandenberg Air Force Base in California, but even a military assumption has never been accepted as a fact. At any rate, no one in authority has ever categorically denied the possibility that a flying saucer observed in, say, Pocatello, Idaho, was a Soviet spy satellite that had gone out of whack.

Moreover, the sighting at Exeter was only one of many such reports considered to be highly credible by experts who had studied the phenomenon. Norman Muscarello, eighteen, was crossing a field at two o'clock in the morning of September 3 when he said he saw an object with red, pulsating lights coming toward him. He said he jumped into a ditch and watched, terrified, as the object then backed away and circled a nearby house.

Muscarello then flagged down a car and was driven to the Exeter police station. A cruiser patrolman was summoned by radio and when he arrived he told a story of having just left a distraught woman who told him a silent red object with flashing lights had followed her car for about nine miles. The patrolman returned with Muscarello to the field. There, the policeman reported, he saw a brilliant red, roundish object rising from behind two tall pine trees which bathed the area in a red light. Frantically, the policeman radioed the station: "My God, I see the damned thing myself!"

It is such verified sightings that have convinced the experts, notably Dr. J. Allen Hynek, head of Northwestern University's

Astronomy Department and an Air Force UFO consultant, and Prof. James MacDonald of the University of Arizona's Department of Meteorology. Dr. Hynek says he has never seen a UFO, "but too many reliable people have seen them to dismiss the phenomenon." The flood of reports, says Professor MacDonald, indicates that they "must be given extremely serious scientific attention."

Both in and out of Government, many of those who have given the flying saucer their scientific attention have concluded that they are mechanical creatures of the nation's most hush-hush espionage outfit, the code-breaking National Security Agency, and its Soviet counterpart. Ideally, these unmanned aircraft operate mostly in outer space, but because even modern science is not perfect they occasionally go temporarily out of control in the atmosphere, shortly after launching, and thus are sighted by the Norman Muscarellos of Exeter and—probably—by the Ivan Ivanovitches of Smolensk.

At any rate, it can now be revealed that a "flying saucer" was positively identified as a Soviet spy satellite after it crashed in a barren area of a western state on the night of October 16, 1967. Other "saucers," including a craft described by the military as "Volkswagen-sized" which crashed in Pakistan in 1963, had been identified tentatively as Soviet spaceships, but the 1967 find was labeled "certain."

The Russian spy satellite which crashed in October, 1967, was first sighted by two unidentified persons two hundred miles from the scene of the crash an hour earlier. They described the craft as apparently "afire." Presumably, the craft also was picked up by military radar, but no record of this has been disclosed.

The crash itself was seen by an Air Force gunnery sergeant who was driving down an otherwise deserted highway. He saw the spaceship explode and then hurtle to earth about four hundred yards from the highway. The sergeant inspected the wreckage and concluded that the craft had been unmanned. Then he returned to his base and reported his find to his superior officer.

Tight security was clamped down. The sergeant, with his permission in writing, was moved into his own private room in a special officers' barracks, where he was interrogated by no less than a brigadier general. Meanwhile, Air Force Intel-

ligence headquarters in Washington was notified. After the
sergeant's story had been transcribed, he signed the original
and three carbon copies, and also agreed in writing not to
divulge what he had seen.

Then the Air Force went to work in earnest. Part of a
company was dispatched to stand guard over the wreckage.
A special team equipped with a portable laboratory was flown
out from Washington. Details of their labors are unavailable,
but nine days after they went to work the team's scientists
announced that the pieces of wreckage without question were
the remains of a Soviet spy satellite.

From scattered bits of information, it is possible to conclude that fragments of electronic eavesdropping devices were
salvaged. For the rest, sophisticated photographic equipment
revealed markings in Cyrillic lettering that could be found
only on a piece of Soviet equipment, and by spectroanalysis
and chemical tests other experts determined that a certain
metal alloy in the wreckage was positively of Russian origin.

As in this case, intelligence investigations of flying saucers
have been cloaked in secrecy. But testimony has issued from
the horse's mouth that American counterespionage apparently
has met with considerable success in tracking down Soviet
efforts to turn exploration of space to military advantage.

Indeed, the prestigious Defense Intelligence Agency (DIA)
discovered evidence that some of the flying saucers reported
seen in various sections of the United States could be part of
a space-circling system of nuclear-armed satellites launched
by the Soviet Union. Former Secretary of Defense Robert
McNamara announced on November 3, 1967, that the Russians were working on the development of FOBS—Fractional
Orbit Bombardment System—designed to put nuclear bombs
into orbit.

McNamara was armed with knowledge provided by the
DIA, the Pentagon's spy shop. Through its agents abroad and
intelligence gathered by spy satellites in space, the DIA
picked up information on this new Soviet venture in the summer of 1966. Since then, the agency has reported a number
of incidents of Russian failure to get these satellites into the
stratosphere and has been successful in at least one instance
in recovering the wreckage. The Pentagon's detailed knowledge of the project also indicates that the DIA has intercepted and brought down one or more of these satellites.

Among other things, the DIA reported in late 1967 that the Russians' attempts to transfer one or more astronauts between spaceships is aimed at leaving the vacated ship in orbit as a "building block" for a future FOBS space station. Once completed, a network of such space stations would enable the Russians to launch a nuclear attack which would reach its target on earth in six minutes. Moreover, the Soviet tests launch warheads on an orbit that passes over the Pacific close to the South Pole, and the United States has virtually no warning system for detecting FOBS or missiles coming in from that direction.

If it matters, the Soviet project does not violate the U.S.-Russian treaty barring the military use of space signed in early 1967. McNamara admitted at the time of his FOBS announcement that such activities are exempt from the ban because the warhead is carried less than one orbit and there was no evidence the Soviets were using actual nuclear warheads. McNamara added that he was not "overly alarmed" because the Soviet launch vehicle would carry a much smaller payload than if used as an intercontinental ballistic missile and the longer flight would reduce the weapon's accuracy.

Nevertheless, the Russian program was of vital interest to the United States in terms of national security, and the DIA's success in exposing it was an achievement of spectacular proportions. Within the American intelligence community, it was also seen as another vindication of the modern spymaster's argument that there is no such thing as too much espionage.

Accepting this premise, the Main Street American is reminded of how far the United States' intelligence network has come since Nathan Hale faced a British hangman with the regret that he had but one life to give for his country. In the recent years which have seen the average citizen grow familiar with the necessity for spying, most of the publicity has gone to the Central Intelligence Agency, the nation's central espionage organization charged by law with correlating and evaluating *all* intelligence related to the national security. The CIA has not always enjoyed the headlines thrust on it and, in fact, most of them were undeserved as awarding a disproportionate measure of credit or blame to a single agency. For, despite television, there are other spies in Uncle

Sam's official house, and the CIA is not even the biggest or the most expensive.

The amount of money spent each year on the U.S. intelligence industry is classified—concealed in the budgets of various other Executive departments or armed service branches. But those whose guesses have been educated by experience in Washington estimate the bill at more than four billion dollars. Most of this money goes, not to the CIA, but to the Defense Department, whose spy empire includes the National Security Agency (NSA), the relatively new Defense Intelligence Agency—the intelligence branches of the Army, Navy and Air Force—and a sort of personal spook shop assigned to the Joint Chiefs of Staff. The NSA probably spends twice as much as the CIA, whose budget has been estimated at 750 million dollars a year. It employs more people than the some fourteen thousand who work for the CIA, and its establishment at Fort Meade, in the Maryland countryside fifteen miles northeast of Washington, is bigger than the CIA's sprawling complex in Langley, Virginia. In an earlier, less expansive day, this combination of military and civilian intelligence would have been deemed an indulgence, but since intelligence is knowledge and knowledge is power, the capital sometimes seems to be bursting at the seams with cloak-and-dagger organizations. Also members of the national intelligence community are the State Department's Bureau of Intelligence and Research (INR), which has existed in one form or another almost since the nation's founding, the Federal Bureau of Investigation and the Atomic Energy Commission.

What some CIA men call "the people across the street" may never achieve the same degree of celebrity, or notoriety, which has been the CIA's lot, chiefly because they lack the built-in glamour of a central spy agency. (From "across the street," members of this second half of the nation's espionage network like to refer to the CIA as the "Pickle Factory.") Nevertheless, during the past twenty years there have been increasing and important contributions made by the military agencies, especially the NSA, and by State's INR. The FBI, of course, has made its mark in the security branch of counterespionage. The Atomic Energy Commission is for the most part a consumer of intelligence, although it also produces intelligence such as announcements of nuclear explosions around the world through its worldwide monitoring system.

By comparison with the CIA, the work of these agencies has been virtually unknown to most Americans. Yet it is possible to tick off some of their successes:

• The NSA intercepted a message from North Vietnam President Ho Chi Minh to Soviet Premier Aleksei Kosygin in July, 1967, shortly after the summit meeting between Kosygin and President Johnson in Glassboro, New Jersey, in which Ho rejected Kosygin's offer to mediate the Vietnam war.

• The INR picked up from an Irish diplomat stationed in Vienna the first hard news that Great Britain was about to devalue the pound in November, 1967. Among other things, this piece of intelligence enabled President Johnson to prepare in advance a new plea to Congress for a tax increase based on the effect the British action would have on the dollar.

• An American diplomat in Moscow wearing a highly sensitized microphone and tape recorder under his jacket electronically overheard a conversation between two Russian officials in an office across the hall from the one in which he was sitting in a Kremlin building. The conversation, decoded by the NSA, concerned an embezzlement scandal in a heavy-machine plant in Kiev involving two prominent Ukrainian politicians.

• An Army Intelligence team, working out of Bangkok, in 1965, succeeded in sending two men into the jungles of Cambodia near the Vietnam border to photograph Viet Cong supply and rest and recreation bases in the Cambodian "sanctuary." Until then, the United States had no solid proof such bases existed.

Border clashes between Communist Chinese and Soviet troops, which reached a new height of violence in March, 1969, first were reported by INR agents in China several years earlier, long before the incidents first made headlines around the world. The 1969 headlines made no mention of copies of official Peking documents obtained through a Communist bank contact in Hong Kong which spoke of the "inevitability" of a military confrontation with the Soviet Union over the common frontier.

Events of early 1969 also reflected conflicts within the new

Nixon Administration over intelligence reports concerning the nuclear intentions of Red China and Russia vis-à-vis the United States. President Nixon's decision to go ahead with a modified anti-ballistic system (ABM) originally was based on intelligence which reported that the Peking regime was concentrating on an intercontinental system whose missiles could reach the United States. Pentagon intelligence had concluded that the Soviets were a secondary threat because their new SS-9 intercontinental missile—capable of carrying a warhead of 20 to 25 megatons—was built for second-strike, or deterrent, purposes.

But when Secretary of Defense Melvin R. Laird testified before the Disarmament Subcommittee of the Senate's Foreign Relations Committee, he chose to describe the SS-9 ICBM as a weapon designed to destroy America's retaliatory force in a surprise attack. In some intelligence quarters, Laird's testimony was viewed as a political ploy. Laird's reasoning, it was said, was that a harder case could be made for the ABM program by casting Moscow rather than Peking as the bogeyman.

At any rate, Laird had the support of most high officials of the Administration. While not denying a long-range Chinese threat to the United States, these officials—reportedly including Secretary of State William P. Rogers—argued that the Soviet Union was China's first target and that the Chinese logically were preoccupied with developing a medium-range missile system aimed at their Russian neighbors to the west. Meanwhile, the argument ran, intelligence analysts were firm in their conclusion that the Soviets had deployed more than 200 of the SS-9 missiles pointed at the United States. The conclusion was based in large part on reports from human spies within the Soviet orbit, and thus had special credibility for old-line military men who tend to distrust such intelligence gadgetry as unmanned flying machines and electronic eavesdropping.

As these examples indicate, a properly organized intelligence system still requires the services of human beings. No machine, for instance, could ever arrange a deal to buy information on the infighting in Mao Tse-tung's tight little politburo. But America's spies in the sky, including those "flying saucers" that get lost, provide more intelligence in a single day than any number of secret agents prowling the alleys and boulevards of the world could gather in a year or more.

Through a worldwide electronic espionage network, dominated by the machines and the scientific competence of the National Security Agency, the United States by early 1968 had detected and tracked every Russian adventure in space, whether a success or a failure. Working with various military intelligence agencies and the Atomic Energy Commission, the NSA almost casually predicts and reports on every nuclear bomb test by the Soviet Union and Communist China. The same cooperation enables the United States to locate missile bases in Cuba and the Soviet Union, listen in on conversations between Russian airplane pilots, and—by photographing harvest lands, with their flood and drought areas, and manufacturing complexes—to provide economists with the intelligence needed to produce an estimate of the productivity of any given country.

This material is partially the product of a screen of two thousand interception stations set up around the globe by NSA and the armed forces. The stations operate around-the-clock, manned by more than ten thousand soldiers, sailors, airmen and NSA experts, who eavesdrop and record the Morse and radioteletype messages of every country in the world. Most of the interception stations are located on U.S. military bases, but they also operate in the skies, on various types of aircraft, and at sea, aboard ships such as the U.S.S. *Liberty*. One of these flying interception stations became known in July, 1960, as the RB-47, which was shot down in the Barents Sea, bringing a Soviet protest that the United States had violated its territorial rights. Another was the U-2 piloted by Francis Gary Powers, which recorded Soviet radar signals.

But perhaps the biggest volume of intelligence is collected by SAMOS (for "Satellite and Missile Observation System"). SAMOS consists of satellites which eavesdrop on communications and photograph and televise military bases, airfields and missile installations from 150 miles up. SAMOS listens in on Communist radio transmitters, radar signals and microwave telephone lines, and transmits its findings to ground stations or ships at sea. By analysis of such signals and messages, NSA experts can locate rocket and other missile bases, and report verbatim radio or telephone conversations between, say, the Soviet Foreign Minister and a government official in Rumania. Through SAMOS, NSA analysts have compiled a catalog of conversations between Soviet pilots designed to pinpoint the locations of air squadrons and other air force bases. By studying the slang used in these conversations, they can find out where the pilots came from, and by noting the more personal remarks they can come up with an estimate on the state of morale in a given outfit. And, of course, SAMOS provides NSA cryptanalysts with bales of foreign codes to decipher. The measure of success enjoyed by these code-crackers is classified, but it is known to be substantial. Two NSA defectors who fled to the Soviet Union in 1960 told their interrogators that the agency had solved the codes of more than forty nations.

From the viewpoint of wartime security, the most important use to which this electronic intelligence is put is in devising ways of confusing Soviet radar installations which might detect and locate American bombers and missiles. These countermeasures are the sophisticated electronic bullets fired by planes loaded with radar-baffling equipment flying in advance of an aerial strike, and include rockets that explode tons of metal chaff, white-hot flares that decoy antimissile missiles, reflectors, electronic jamming decoys and instruments that emit false range and speed data.

In simple terms, SAMOS thus can best be described as an orbiting photographic and electronic eavesdropping spaceship which can go where man cannot and can seek out intelligence for which man's brain is not equipped. It spins around the world at 17,500 miles an hour for about a week, and even from 150 miles above the globe its photographic equipment can pick out individual aircraft parked at an airport. When all its pictures have been taken, the film cassette is ejected in a specific area as the satellite passes over the Pacific and is recovered in the air by a U.S. Air Force plane. Photographs at night and through cloud cover are taken with the aid of infrared devices.

Infrared systems also are used to photograph "heat signatures" left by Soviet intercontinental ballistic missiles (ICBM) as they take off from the launching pad. All masses, including human beings, leave such signatures behind after they move on, and the Air Force is now using these pictures of missile "ghosts" as part of the nation's MIDAS early-warning system, or ICBM alarm.

Meanwhile the military intelligence community, in collaboration with the Atomic Energy Commission, uses the two-satellite system, VELA, or Nuclear Test Detection Satellite, to place two satellites in orbit, fifty thousand miles apart, for the detection of aboveground nuclear explosions. It was this system that enabled United States intelligence to predict Communist China's explosion of its second atomic bomb on May 8, 1965, several days before it occurred. Peking did not announce the blast until May 14. Earlier, before China's first atomic bomb explosion on October 16, 1964, the U.S. intelligence community reported that a plutonium reactor was in operation near Paotow in Inner Mongolia. An estimate of the number of reactors contained in the installation was made by measuring the traces of argon and xenon gases given off during the production of plutonium—and routinely collected by one of America's flying saucers.

No Americans were present at the actual firing of either test, but they didn't have to be. The shock waves from the explosions were picked up by electronic ears and barometers. Magnetic eyes and radio direction finders spotted electrified particles emitted by the blasts. When all this had been studied, American experts were able to pinpoint the location of the explosions within a radius of a few miles. Meanwhile, Air Force planes equipped with special filters ingested the fallout from the radioactive clouds and a radio-chemical analysis of this debris told other experts the type of bomb exploded, its size, its design and its power.

Accomplishments of this kind and magnitude make worthwhile an in-depth look at today's American intelligence community. It seems safe to say that there are many more espionage agencies operating out of Washington and more Americans in the spy business than most citizens realize. In addition, numerous private agencies such as the Rand Corporation and many universities are engaged in research projects which in effect are scholarly excursions into espionage. Today's average spy never sees the "enemy." A product of the Cold War and the technological age, he is a physicist, a chemist, an engineer, a professor of languages, a counterfeiter, an electronics expert, a communications technician, an airplane pilot, a soldier, a sailor, a cryptologist, a translator of Sanskrit. There are jobs in the intelligence community for farmers and chefs, fingerprint experts and cloth weavers, photographers and television directors, makeup artists and female impersonators.

Bribes and blackmail are still used to obtain information, but such methods cannot compete wholesale with the specialists who can use satellites to map an entire country, or with sophisticated equipment aboard a ship or submarine listening to telephone and wireless conversations, or radar-tracking airplane, ship and troop movements. With hidden listening devices, the specialist can sit in an office and yet go to work and to bed with an official of a foreign country. Cryptologists crack the codes of friend and foe alike and translate secret messages. And behind all these operatives is another army of experts in a thousand fields who sit at government issue desks all day and evaluate the intelligence thus gathered.

Thus in the United States of the late sixties, there were more spies than there were diplomats in the State Department or employees of the Department of Labor. Herded together, the some sixty thousand employees of various espionage agencies would populate a city bigger than Reno, Nevada, or Rutland, Vermont. They would form more than three Army divisions. At seven thousand dollars a year, they would cost the American taxpayers 420 million dollars a year; it is a good bet that their total wages and salaries, but not their total expense accounts, add up to at least twice that sum.

2

Building an Empire

The empire by which the United States today seeks out information about the military, political and scientific activities of other nations is a far cry not only from Nathan Hale, but from the decrepit intelligence system discovered by General Dwight D. Eisenhower in the War Department as America entered World War II. Eisenhower bemoaned "a shocking deficiency that impeded all constructive planning," and reported that the basic requirement for needed intelligence, "a far-flung organization of fact finders," was nonexistent.

In effect, the nation's intelligence organization on the eve of Pearl Harbor consisted for the most part of the military attaché system. Eisenhower found the system virtually worthless. Of the attachés themselves, he would say only that "Usually they were estimable, socially acceptable gentlemen; few knew the essentials of intelligence work. Results were almost completely negative. . . ."

General George C. Marshall put it more bluntly. Our foreign intelligence prior to World War II, he said, was "little more than what a military attaché could learn at dinner, more or less, over the coffee cups."

The reason for this neglect, of course, was the aloof and inward-looking foreign policy pursued by the United States up to the very eve of World War II, a policy that bears the major responsibility for the tragedy of Pearl Harbor. Didn't we have the Atlantic and Pacific Oceans for protection?

That was the rationale prevailing when the United States became involved in World War I. On January 1, 1917, Army Intelligence was a stepchild of the General Staff, comprising

13

two officers and two clerks and shunted from cubbyhole to cubbyhole as more important sections sought expanded office space. The Office of Naval Intelligence (ONI) was a little better off; it had three officers and four clerks. Both services were served abroad by the military-naval attaché system, which not only was virtually useless but which was constantly under fire from Congress as a refuge for aging officers seeking vacations in foreign lands. Hastily reorganized at war's start, the Military Intelligence Division of the General Staff had been expanded into a staff of 1,200 officers and civilians by the time of the Armistice, but by the fall of 1919 it had been reduced to 88 officers and 143 civilians. During the subsequent peacetime years, the intelligence effort was cut back further; in 1934 the Office of Naval Intelligence had a permanent force of only twenty persons. The Army Intelligence budget in the twenties and the thirties seldom was more than $200,000 a year, compared with an estimated 560 million dollars in 1968, not counting the National Security Agency. For several years in the thirties, the Army was limited to 32 military attachés abroad.

Despite the attempts of some military men to build up national intelligence between the wars, it took Pearl Harbor to wake up the country to this crying need. This statement has become a cliché of the history books by now, but it remains a fact that despite the American success in intercepting Japanese messages that trumpeted the attack plans, the United States was caught completely by surprise. Harry Howe Ransom, perhaps the country's leading lay authority on intelligence, has called Pearl Harbor "a complete intelligence failure . . . a top-to-bottom failure of the intelligence system —or lack of system."

Ransom has emphasized, however, that the Japanese attack was "particularly a failure in intelligence communication and receptivity." That is to say, the commanders at the top failed to utilize efficiently the intelligence that was available, including the sinking of a submerged Japanese submarine in a forbidden zone near the entrance to Pearl Harbor at 6:45 A.M. on December 7, and the detection by an Army mobile radar unit of a cloud of Japanese planes at 7:02 A.M

The trouble was that the United States had no agency charged with or capable of collating and evaluating the bits and pieces of intelligence that flowed into Washington. There was no way for President Roosevelt to lay his hands on those bits and pieces immediately nor to appraise them with any degree of accuracy. Everybody was in on the act—Army and Navy Intelligence, military fliers, the FBI—but nobody was in charge. There was needed, as an older and wiser Henry Stimson remarked, "a sentinel on duty" at all times.

One of the misconceptions fed by the flood of reading matter on espionage during the sixties is that the Central Intelligence Agency was an immediate fruit of Pearl Harbor and engaged in all sorts of spectacular feats of derring-do during World War II. But the CIA was not created until 1947, a child of President Truman's irritation over the mass of conflicting intelligence reports flowing across his desk. America's wartime intelligence effort was dominated by the new Office of Strategic Services (OSS) under General William J. (Wild Bill) Donovan, whose contributions were supplemented by those of the hastily expanded existing agencies—Army and Navy Intelligence, the State Department and the FBI.

By the end of the war, OSS had twelve thousand employees engaged in every variety of espionage chore, from translating Urdu to blowing up trains in Germany. Any appraisal of its overall success depends on which critic is cited as an authority. With such a man as Wild Bill Donovan at its head—a man who moved so fast he created the myth that he often left one morning and returned the previous afternoon—the OSS was bound to get involved in wild-eyed schemes and over-elaborate plotting. Much of its work was "inefficient," according to Hanson Baldwin, the *New York Times'* military expert, "and some of it was stupid, and for a considerable part of the war we were dependent upon the British for much of our secret information." General Omar Bradley has said that early in World War II, "the British easily outstripped their American colleagues."

But once OSS got organized, it had its successes, due partly to its almost unlimited budget—57 million dollars in fiscal 1945—and its bloated personnel. Allen Dulles, who later would become director of the CIA, operated from Bern, Switzerland, a political action and intelligence network that reached into Germany, Yugoslavia, North Africa, Czechoslovakia, Bulgaria, Spain, Portugal and Hungary. Other OSS men scored brilliantly in the field of sabotage, commando raids and guerrilla warfare by joining forces with underground groups in Europe and Southeast Asia. OSS ran the intelligence operation for the invasion of North Africa, made a major contribution to the Allied invasion of Normandy in June, 1944, and all but displaced the British as the top operators in the Middle East.

But perhaps the most important contribution the OSS made to America's modern-day espionage establishment was its recruitment of academics for the less glamorous but vitally important work of research and analysis. The college professors, lawyers, Wall Street brokers and others who toiled in grubby little offices in Washington and abroad contributed most of the hard-boiled data on which successful operations were based. Of more far-reaching significance, their work convinced other members of the wartime intelligence team that there was an important place for the scholar in espionage activities. Toward the end of the war, the military was competing with the OSS for these professors and economists. Today the desk-bound specialist outnumbers the cloak-and-dagger operative in every government organization charged with the gathering and/or evaluation of intelligence.

One consequence of this assimilation of civilian experts into the intelligence community is the new esteem bestowed on intelligence by commanders in the field. In Korea, General Douglas MacArthur clung to the Old Guard view that the intelligence blokes were a necessary nuisance and largely went his own way regardless of their estimates. But by the time America became embroiled in Vietnam, fighting officers had learned something of the importance of their G-2, or intelligence, section. This contrasted with the situation during the Allied planning for the North African invasion when some operations officers ridiculed intelligence reports and substituted their own guesses as to how the enemy would react. Eisenhower, who must have had some doubts himself about the value of his fledgling intelligence staff, nevertheless was constrained to make it a part of the basis for all operations planning.

This, then, was the lesson learned from Pearl Harbor and World War II—that intelligence is vital to both the proper formulation and execution of foreign policy and to military operations. The lesson was the basis of the reorganization of American intelligence by President Truman, who recognized the need for a permanent policy to guide the national intelligence effort.

The first thing Truman did was to disband the OSS, partly because of pressure from the State Department, the FBI and the military services, but also because he wanted less derring-do and more scholarship in his spy shops. Upon its dissolution, OSS's excellent Research and Analysis sections were absorbed by the State Department and its covert operations were transferred to the Pentagon. Even after its staff had been whittled down to 350 in the late sixties, State's Intelligence and Research Bureau boasted that it still retained the best of the former OSS men, with the culls going to the CIA.

To the accompaniment of chortles of glee from Foggy Bottom, Truman also directed Secretary of State James F. Byrnes, who had strongly urged that his department have predominant control over any national strategic intelligence agency, to coordinate all interdepartmental intelligence. In other words, State was to be *the* central and *supreme* intelligence body. Truman appointed a Special Assistant to the Secretary of State for Research and approved a budget calling for 1,600 hired hands.

But Byrnes's day of glory was foredoomed. Both the armed forces and outside experts were appalled that the State Department should direct spying operations abroad. They pointed out that above all Foggy Bottom must keep its hands clean and thus should not be directly involved in international dirty tricks. The upshot was Truman's creation in January, 1946, of the National Intelligence Authority in which State, War and Navy were equal members. Operations were assigned to the NIA's Central Intelligence Group, which was succeeded two years later by the CIA. The State Department's intelligence unit was trimmed to 936 persons, with the remainder transferred to the military and the Central Intelligence Group, and, later, the CIA.

By 1947, therefore, the American intelligence community included the CIA, the State Department's Bureau of Intelligence and Research, the intelligence services of the Army and the Navy and the newborn United States Air Force, the FBI and the Atomic Energy Commission. To this lineup in 1949 was added the Armed Forces Security Agency (AFSA), which took over the strategic communications-intelligence functions of the three military services in order to provide unified access to all cryptologic activities and information. To make such services and intelligence available to intelligence units outside the Defense Department, President Truman in 1952 abolished the AFSA and created the National Security Agency. The Defense Intelligence Agency was established by Defense Secretary McNamara in 1961 to provide a centralized system of decision and command for the military's intelligence effort.

What was described by CIA types as "Bob McNamara's personal spook club" has from time to time seemed to have no other reason for being except to tighten the Secretary's control over the intelligence activities of the services. As such, of course, it is a reassuring symbol of civilian supremacy within the Pentagon. But some critics have suggested that McNamara built his own empire, which operated independently of the CIA in fields previously explored exclusively by the CIA. In any event, as will be seen, the Defense Intelligence Agency occasionally intruded upon the CIA's political-strategic preserve and over the years it has grown in size and influence far beyond its statutory functions—at the CIA's expense.

Indeed, during his tenure, McNamara frequently challenged the CIA's Presidential authority to "guide" the total intelligence effort. At one hearing in the House, McNamara was asked if he was "operating on the intelligence you get from the CIA."

McNamara's reply was not one to comfort the advocates of central control of intelligence activities. "No, sir," he said, "I receive information directly from the Defense Intelligence Agency, and that information is screened by no one outside the Pentagon." When John McCone was director of the CIA, he and McNamara would compete to see who could bring the President the latest intelligence reports. During the 1962 Cuban missile crisis, this rivalry approached the ridiculous, with McCone and McNamara rushing at all hours to the White House to show President Kennedy identical newly-developed pictures taken by American U-2 planes. The President usually had already seen them.

There are still many on Capitol Hill who wonder whether all this spying is necessary, or at least whether it is practical, or cost-effective. They cling to the notion that Harry Truman's idea in creating one central intelligence body was to eliminate some of the overlapping espionage operations and thus save the country a few dollars. Criticism is mounting that the American intelligence community is too expensive, too duplicative and exerts too much of an influence on the formulation of foreign policy. As for the average individual, he remains largely unaware of how much spying his government is doing.

Even the non-average individual is sometimes confused. At a Congressional hearing in 1965, for example, Senator Stuart W. Symington of Missouri, a former Secretary of the Air Force, had to confess that he had not known "until recently" that there was such an organization as the State Department's Bureau of Intelligence and Research.

3

So Many Spies

To the critics who complain that an American intelligence industry employing sixty thousand persons is an extravagance and probably a manufacturer of the redundant, the various spy bosses all offer a stock answer. It is a modern paraphrase of the Walsingham stricture that cost should never be a factor in the gathering of information about enemies and friends. In the language of the sixties, it is argued that duplication and overlapping of effort is a necessary luxury that serves special needs.

Although Congress has been derelict in not applying a more skeptical attitude to this argument, it is a fact that the case for the continued proliferation of the Republic's espionage effort has been strengthened by a number of Cold War incidents. During the Berlin crisis of 1961, for example, diplomats serving the State Department's Bureau of Intelligence and Research, plowing the same ground as the CIA, correctly concluded that Nikita Khrushchev was bluffing, while the CIA filled the official air with all sorts of ominous warnings about a coming showdown. Another and perhaps more striking example was the Cuban missile crisis of 1962 in which both the military and the INR collected surprisingly accurate intelligence, reported promptly the arrival of Russian arms, and insisted that Moscow was engaged in a serious attempt to intimidate the United States. Meanwhile, the CIA tended to scoff at any suggestion the Russians would dare to put American steadfastness to such a test.

At this time, unfortunately, military intelligence was in the bad graces of the Kennedy Administration. During the 1960 campaign, Kennedy had swallowed whole the wildly inflated Air Force estimates of Soviet missile and bomber production, and had gone about warning the country that there was a serious "missile gap" caused by the neglect of American missile production. Actually, the "missile gap" was in favor of the United States, but it did not look that way to Air Force evaluators combing reports of a spectacular "advance" in Soviet missile production. The Russians had skipped the so-called Atlas stage of their program and gone on to an 800,000-pound giant as the vehicle for their ICBM force, and this impressed the Air Force to the point of fright. By 1963, reported Air Force estimates, a missile gap favoring the Russians would hit its peak. But by 1961, the Russians had discovered that the big rocket was impractical as an effective weapon and reluctantly junked their grandiose plans in order to design a smaller and more streamlined missile. This set back their whole program almost a year.

It was Secretary of Defense Robert McNamara who finally arranged to set the Kennedy Administration straight on the true situation. He was skeptical of Air Force estimates almost from the moment he took office, and he demanded harder intelligence. For one thing, he could not reconcile Air Force estimates of as many as three hundred Soviet missiles deployed with some Navy estimates as low as ten. A combined Army-Air Force-Navy intelligence team was ordered to make an exhaustive check of all intelligence thus far collected and then to make its own surveys and studies. The team came up with the facts on Russia's major failure in the fall of 1961.

To get this information, the most closely guarded secret in the Soviet Union at the time, the intelligence team relied for the most part on the undercover services of a Soviet citizen —an old-fashioned, cloak-if-not-dagger, spy. He was what the intelligence community calls a defector-in-place, an expert in his field who had decided to betray his country in order to buy for himself eventual sanctuary beyond the Iron Curtain.

Igor is not his real name, but it must serve to protect his identity. He was an intellectual of the scientific breed, a physicist and an expert on guided missiles and rocketry. An American agent stationed in Moscow in a diplomatic cover post met Igor at a reception at an Eastern European embassy in the spring of 1960. During their conversation, the American sensed that Igor was subtly trying to leave the impression that he would like to continue their acquaintance. Since most Russians avoid prolonging even a casual conversation with an American, especially in their own country, the American was anxious to encourage him. Figuring he had nothing to lose, he suggested to Igor that they meet for a drink some evening.

Igor's face froze, and he shook his head. "I could not do that, I am sorry," he said. "I am much too busy." Then he walked away.

The American feared that was the end of that. And yet there had been something unusual about Igor's manner. He couldn't help feeling that the Russian *did* want to pursue their acquaintance, for whatever reasons of his own.

Certain lines of research produced the information that Igor was an administrative official in a department charged with procurement in the Soviet ICBM program. He was enormously worth cultivating if there was the slightest chance he was interested in even a social relationship with someone in the American camp. With his access to secret information, there was always the possibility that in the most innocent conversation he might suffer a slip of the tongue and let fall a word or a phrase that could be combined with another word or phrase gathered elsewhere to reveal something important.

However, the American was well aware that he dare not approach Igor, in any fashion. So he waited, in the meantime making sure to be seen at every diplomatic party to which he could wangle an invitation. Three times during a period of five months he encountered Igor at various receptions, and three times he made it a point to greet the Russian only perfunctorily and then move on.

Almost seven months after their first meeting, the American picked up his topcoat in the cloakroom of an Asian Embassy after a party. When he got home, he discovered a note in his coat pocket. The note was unsigned, but it suggested that "we might have that drink" the next evening at a *pivnoyzal,* or beer parlor, in a so-called working-class section of Moscow.

The American showed up at the appointed time. The *pivnoyzal* was crowded, and he had to drink his beer at a communal stand-up table for fifteen minutes before he found a free table for two. He had just sat down, when Igor appeared and plumped down on the other chair.

The Russian wasted no time. He had, he said, certain information the Americans should be interested in. He was prepared to sell it and other information to the Americans over a period of time in exchange for regular sums of American cash deposited in a Swiss bank and the promise that he would be assisted eventually in leaving the Soviet Union for good. The information, said Igor, would concern the Soviet ICBM program, especially as it concerned new and more sophisticated equipment. Igor rose. "You'll hear from me," he said, and left.

During the next month, the American found rolls of microfilm in his topcoat pocket whenever he reached home after a diplomatic reception. Twice the films were dropped in his pocket while he was in a restaurant. Igor made no attempt to contact him; obviously he was waiting for the Americans to check out his information. It checked out as both authentic and valuable; Igor knew what was important. But Igor also was a patient man. It was not until one night in April, 1961, that he arranged to meet the American again. This time, he was told certain monies already had been deposited to a Swiss bank account in his name, and that his employers were satisfied with his work.

By this time, the United States' combined military intelligence team had embarked on its study of the Soviet Union's missile production. The National Security Agency already had come up with some valuable interceptions of Soviet communications bearing on the program, and would come up with still more in the months ahead. But Igor was offered a bonus of $100,000 if he could deliver a comprehensive, expert and detailed analysis of the Russian missile program. His employers, he was told, were particularly interested in numbers. Was the program on schedule, or ahead of schedule, or behind schedule?

Igor delivered. What seems incredible, but is not, is that he delivered the package—in three installments of microfilm— in less than two weeks' time. It was all there: the number of missiles deployed, highly technical information on the difficulties the Russians had encountered with their giant rocket, excerpts from the minutes of the top-level meetings at which it was decided to scrap the giant, and, finally, the admission from official records that the program was "ten months and 13 days" behind schedule.

Here, President Kennedy decided to invoke the intelligence

tactic of informing the enemy of the truth. Politically, it was a bitter pill for Kennedy to swallow, but he insisted the U.S. had to let the Russians know that we knew they were lagging behind us, in order to try to prevent them from miscalculating their chances of playing the bully. Khrushchev was assuming a belligerent air, and if he were allowed to continue to believe the U.S. still thought its own missile effort was lagging he might indulge himself in new adventures in brinksmanship. In due course, then, the truth was told in a speech by Deputy Secretary of Defense Roswell Gilpatric in November, 1961.

Shortly, reports from contacts abroad disclosed to the INR hierarchy that Gilpatric's speech had been a horrible shock to the Soviet leadership. Khrushchev and his colleagues now had to live with the knowledge that the United States not only had military superiority, but knew it. Thus it was obvious that American intelligence had managed somehow to locate and count the deployed Soviet missiles, an almost unthinkable thought in the Soviets' closed society. The Soviet leaders knew, as did the Americans, that an ICBM missile system whose various locations were known to the enemy was effective only for a first, surprise strike. After that, the enemy could be expected to destroy it.

But such serious disagreement among intelligence agencies, military and civilian, posed two questions heard with increasing frequency in the years that followed: 1. What are all these spy organizations *doing?* And 2. Why are so many of them needed when, in a given situation, they sometimes come up with different interpretations of the same intelligence? To understand the official rationale, it is necessary to examine the backgrounds of these agencies and their distinct and peculiar objectives.

Before the Defense Intelligence Agency was established in 1961, each of the military departments operated a separate, vertical intelligence organization in which all of the intelligence functions—collection, production, dissemination, covert operations—were performed in support of the headquarters of the particular service. Such a compartmented system was inherently duplicative. Moreover, it had been designed to work along departmental and service channels, and thus was in basic conflict with a unified Department of Defense.

The cost-conscious Robert McNamara was appalled at the waste in manpower and money involved. Furthermore, Mc-

Namara had noticed that the intelligence gathered did not always automatically find its way through channels to the office of the civilian who was charged by the law with responsibility for the Defense establishment.

In July, 1961, therefore, McNamara established the Defense Intelligence Agency as the Defense Secretary's own centralized command headquarters over all military intelligence. His directive made the DIA responsible for "the organization, direction, management and control of all Department of Defense intelligence resources assigned to or *included within* the DIA." (Italics added.) More to the point, the DIA was ordered to "provide military intelligence" to the Secretary of Defense, the staff assistants to the Secretary of Defense, the military departments, the Joint Chiefs of Staff, specialized Department of Defense agencies and unified and specified commands. In short, hoarding intelligence was made illegal.

However, the McNamara directive also made of the DIA another spy shop. Among other things, it was assigned to "provide all Department of Defense current intelligence," which means it conducts its own espionage operations and evaluations above and beyond those conducted by the service agencies. It also conducts "such technical and counter-intelligence functions as may be assigned," and provides "plans, programs, policies and procedures for Department of Defense *collection* activities." (Italics added.)

CIA men pointed out at the time that there was nothing the DIA could do that the CIA wasn't already doing. Moreover, the three service arms continued to exist, so the DIA really didn't save the taxpayers any money. McNamara ignored this cattiness, but the implication of the DIA directive was clear: The DIA would engage in whatever specialized spying its specialized needs required, which was to say that it would intrude frequently on the CIA's broad field. Meanwhile, McNamara claimed the DIA would save the Treasury up to 100 million dollars a year by eliminating duplication. In the spirit of the secret world in which the spying industry operates, he gave no details.

Lieutenant General Joseph Francis Carroll, a former FBI special agent and a onetime salesman for Swift and Company, was named director of the DIA in October, 1961, two months after its creation by McNamara. A handsome, businesslike

Irishman with five children, Carroll has a facade of amiability but he still retains much of the careful reticence of the typical FBI man. He is, at any rate, a kind of career policeman. While with the FBI in Washington, where he rose to first assistant to the Assistant Director, he was twice loaned out, first to direct the Compliance Enforcement Division of the Surplus Property Administration after World War II, and then to organize an agency for investigative and counterintelligence functions for the weanling United States Air Force.

Carroll never returned to civilian life. He was ordered to active duty as a colonel in the Air Force Reserve in 1948, and rose to his current rank when he became the Inspector General of the Air Force in February, 1960.

A Hoover Commission Task Force report in 1949 noted that Army Intelligence apparently was still a stepchild of the brass hats, since it had had "seven chiefs in seven years, some of them with no prior intelligence experience whatsoever." But during the Korean War, and particularly during McNamara's tenure at the Pentagon, the Army's so-called G-2 raised itself to the level of a professional organization which is attracting more and more career officers of superior competence.

One of these is G-2's boss, Major General Joseph A. McChristian, a rugged former tank officer, whose title is Assistant Chief of Staff for Intelligence. McChristian, a competitive swimmer and tennis player, rose from the ranks, winning appointment to West Point in 1934 after two years in the Regular Army. During World War II, he served with the 10th Armored Division as commander of its 61st Armored Infantry Battalion and as divisional chief of staff.

Shortly after V-E Day, McChristian served as Chief of Staff for Intelligence of General George S. Patton's Third Army, and then as Deputy Director of Intelligence, Headquarters U.S. Forces, Austria. He pursued his career in intelligence with the Intelligence Division of the Army General Staff and as a member of the military assistance group in Greece during the Communist civil war of 1949. He has also served in the office of the Army's Assistant Chief of Staff for Intelligence, where he was Chief of Western Division of Foreign Intelligence, and as Assistant Chief of Staff, Intelligence, U.S. Army, Pacific. McChristian was appointed boss of Army Intelligence on August 5, 1968.

In a nutshell, G-2's mission is the collection, evaluation and dissemination of information pertaining to the war potential, topography and military forces of foreign nations. In addition, G-2 regularly appraises the capability of the United States to defend itself.

The Army attaché system is still one of its major sources of foreign intelligence, with attachés serving as representatives of the Army Chief of Staff to the governments of foreign countries. Officially, the attaché is under the control of the American ambassador or other chief of mission, but he does a great deal of freewheeling which never comes to the official attention of his boss. Army Intelligence also includes the Army Intelligence Center, which is the administrative unit for the Army Intelligence School, the Central Records Facility, the Army Intelligence Board, the Photo Interpretation Center, the Strategic Intelligence School, a joint Army-Navy-Air Force venture and the Army Security Center.

Few of these organizations ever come to the attention of the citizen, who has little interest in the knowledge that the Central Records Facility is a depository for more than six million personnel security investigation files from all Army commands, or that the Army Intelligence Board investigates, develops and tests special devices used in espionage operations. But G-2's Counter-Intelligence is better known, largely as a result of its operations during World War II.

The CIC is the Army counterpart of the FBI. That is to say, within the military it is charged with the prevention and detection of acts of treason, espionage and sabotage, and the policing of such problems as gambling, black market activities and prostitution. The CIC was in charge of security for the famous Manhattan Project, which developed the atomic bomb. During World War II, its activities overseas ranged from the location of mine fields in the invasion of Sicily to the capture of the complete records of the Italian Secret Service and the German lists of Axis sympathizers during the North African landings of 1943. In occupied Japan, the CIC's investigators kept in touch with local opinion and regularly briefed General Douglas MacArthur on political and subversive matters.

Army Intelligence spends about 75 million dollars a year producing and distributing maps of every country in the world. It makes studies of terrain and topography and of

geodetic data. The Intelligence Branch of the Army Trans-
portation Corps prepares periodic reports on highways in the
Soviet Union. The Intelligence Branch of the Signal Corps
does the same for the Russian telephone network. Some of
this work undoubtedly overlaps that done by the various
research branches of the CIA, but the Pentagon has always
argued that it is better to have a bit of overlapping than a gap
in information.

Like its Army counterpart, the Office of Naval Intelligence
(ONI) has as its main responsibility keeping naval planners
informed of the war-making capabilities and intentions of
foreign nations and supplying the information needed for
plans and operations. Also, like Army Intelligence, ONI has
its Naval attaché system. In recent years, ONI's emphasis
has been on Soviet submarine capabilities and deployment; it
was undoubtedly the busiest branch of any of the three services during the brief Arab-Israeli war of June, 1967. Over the
years, ONI has built up a bulky file on port, harbor and
beach facilities around the world and on potential targets
for amphibious operations. Considering the amount of money
and effort expended since World War II on these intelligence
surveys, it would be inexcusable for the Navy to be confronted with a problem similar to that posed during preparations for the North African landings of World War II. At that
time, the Government was forced to call on the American
public to send in snapshots or movie film taken during foreign
travel. What was needed was information about beaches and
sea approaches along the Barbary coastline, but the information was never forthcoming.

Rear Admiral Frederick J. Harlfinger II was the first to
receive the title of Commander Intelligence Command when
he was named chief of the ONI in May, 1968. A former
commander of the South Atlantic Force, U.S. Atlantic Fleet,
Harlfinger is a graduate of the U.S. Naval Academy and an
old submarine hand. Within the Navy, he is famous as the
man who conceived the plan by which the submarine *Trout*
during World War II brought out of the Philippines a substantial amount of that Commonwealth's gold, silver and
securities.

At the start of World War II, the Army Air Corps was
described by the historians, Wesley F. Craven and James L.
Cate, as "probably more deficient in its provision for intelli-

gence than in any other phase of its activities." The main
reason for this was that the Air Corps was a branch of the
Army and was low man on the totem pole of appropriations.
Gen. Henry H. (Hap) Arnold, wartime commander of the
flying arm, complained there were "American journalists and
ordinary travelers in Germany who knew more about the
Luftwaffe's preparations than I, the Assistant Chief of the
United States Army Air Corps." One study called the air
intelligence product during World War II "little better than
the product of a sincere adolescent."

Today, Air Force Intelligence, reorganized several times,
is a highly professional organization which operates radar
tracking stations spanning the globe, helps to track Russian
missile tests and generally prepares itself for the mission of
carrying the attack into the enemy's interior in case of war.

Air Force Intelligence produces bales of photo intelligence
from its air reconnaissance missions, including those flown by
U-2 planes, and collects the raw material for air maps and
charts. Its Target Directorate analyzes potential targets and
assesses them according to military, political and economic
considerations. Relative vulnerability of various targets is
also appraised and weapons requirements set down in the
unit's Bombing Encyclopedia. The Directorate of Estimates
maintains a worldwide surveillance for evidence of possible
hostile action or unusual movements of troops or aircraft.
The Air Attaché system serves as a major collector of information on the military capabilities of both Communist and
Free World governments.

Head of Air Force Intelligence is a former Salt Lake City
newspaperman, Major General Jack E. Thomas, U.S.A.F.
Thomas served sixteen months in Italy during World War II
as an intelligence officer and won the Legion of Merit. As a
staff officer in the Office of Military Government, he took
part in discussions with Soviet, British and French representatives at the close of the war, and reportedly did considerable
extracurricular spying on the side.

The National Security Agency comes closer than any other
Government organization to being completely anonymous. Its
operations are a much more closely-guarded secret than those
of the CIA, and as a semiautonomous agency of the Department of Defense it goes its own way, largely undisturbed
by bureaucratic nosiness. Established in 1952 by President

Truman, the NSA serves all the other intelligence agencies as a fabulous electronic spying factory.

Even today, Government manuals describe the NSA crisply and esoterically as "established pursuant to Presidential directive in 1952" and note only that it "performs highly specialized technical and coordinating functions relating to the national security." These functions, it is known, consist of intercepting, traffic-analyzing and cryptanalyzing the messages of all other nations, our friends as well as our enemies. The NSA also is charged with protecting the security of American messages and cryptography.

Lieutenant General Marshall S. Carter, U.S.A., is a West Point graduate who specialized in both political and intelligence fields before his appointment in 1966 as director of the NSA. He came to the NSA from the post of deputy director of the CIA, and before that he had served as a special assistant to the Secretary of State and Assistant Chief of Staff for G-5, in the headquarters of the China Theater. He held the personal rank of minister in various posts with the Military Assistance Program for Europe, before taking time out from his military-political duties to serve as Chief of Staff of the Eighth Army in Korea from 1959 to 1961.

Although Government manuals describe NSA as "an element of the Department of Defense," this ultra-secret establishment is not subject to military rule. General Carter has said that it is "within but not a part of the Defense Department." Unlike other Pentagon appendages, the NSA does not fall under the Joint Chiefs of Staff but is responsible directly to civilian supervision—through the Assistant Secretary of Defense for Research and Engineering to the Secretary of Defense, the National Security Council and the President. Thus its highly sensitive activities are not subject to the pressures which constantly arise from inter-service rivalries.

This exclusion of the career military has caused grumbling in some Pentagon offices about "professors playing with secret codes." The reference appears principally aimed at the NSA's Scientific Advisory Board, composed of leading figures in fields related to cryptology, such as mathematics and electronics. The board is advised by panels of specialists and also receives the product of an independent research organization, the Institute for Defense Analyses, which occupies a 1.9 million-dollar building on the campus of Princeton University. And, of course, most of NSA's own personnel necessarily is of the professional breed.

However, there seems little danger that the military will be taken over by a band of myopic scientists. Overseeing the entire intelligence effort is the United States Intelligence Board, headed by the director of the CIA. Then there is a sort of bureaucratic policeman, the President's Foreign Intelligence Advisory Board. This is composed of six civilians from outside the Government and was set up in 1961 to "conduct a continuing review and assessment" of all intelligence functions. President Kennedy created this board after the 1961 Cuban invasion fiasco when it became evident that the CIA, out of sheer enthusiasm for the plot, had overstepped its constituted authority.

The preoccupation of recent Presidents with providing close supervision of the nation's intelligence industry might be said to date from the Bay of Pigs. That failure made plain the dangers that accrue when a member of an intelligence community, charged only with the collection and evaluation of information to help *guide* American foreign policy, engaged in covert activities aimed—wittingly or not—at *directing* foreign policy. The sensitivity of any government to the pressures of intelligence findings is one of the reasons the State Department puts forward to justify its continued maintenance of its own intelligence operation.

Visitors to the office of Thomas Lowe Hughes, director of the INR, usually are surprised to discover that Hughes is not a career State Department man. Perhaps it is because Hughes is an authentic egghead and is known in State's cubbyholes as "the quiet man." At any rate, Hughes is a Minnesotan who graduated summa cum laude from Carleton College and went on to earn his Ph.D. in politics as a Rhodes Scholar at Balliol College, Oxford. But he came to State from the snakepit of politics. He was an assistant to then Senator Hubert Humphrey, a staff assistant at several Democratic conventions and staff director of the 1960 Democratic Platform Committee. He was President Kennedy's personal choice as deputy director of the INR in 1961, and succeeded to the top job in 1963.

State's Bureau of Intelligence and Research consisted of only 350 persons in 1969. Curiously, however, none of its directors has ever made a serious effort to acquire more bodies. The reason advanced is that the State Department is in daily need of highly specialized information whose special relevancy can only be evaluated by a relatively few persons within the department with a special knowledge of the department's problems and demands. Or, as explained by Allan Evans, Deputy Director for Research, the INR's daily briefings to the Secretary of State and other high department officials are marked by an "essential characteristic" in that they "lend perspective to up-to-the-minute information through the application of deep background knowledge."

At any rate, INR had become firmly established by 1969 after a long hiatus stretching from Colonial days to its creation by President Truman in 1945. In 1909, for example, the State Department had only four employees whose functions were classified as intelligence. There were only five of these elegant spies in 1922, and only eighteen in 1948. In 1945, when Dean Acheson was Under Secretary of State, he told Congress that until World War II, State's "technique of gathering information differed only by reason of the typewriter and telegraph from the techniques which John Quincy Adams was using in St. Petersburg and Benjamin Franklin was using in Paris." And yet the State Department always has been inherently a collector and user of intelligence. Diplomacy, as Harry Truman once remarked, "is spying in striped pants." Indeed, the State Department was born as a "Committee on Secret Correspondence" to handle communications between the colonies and friendly European countries.

Today, all of the basic "research" inside the State Department is done by the INR. On a day-to-day basis, the bureau is responsible for the rapid alerting of the Secretary of State to any new crisis or any new developments which demand quick attention. A watch office is manned around the clock, seven days a week. The INR receives all communications that come into the Department, including all incoming embassy telegrams and foreign policy information from agencies charged with reporting to the United States Government. Much of this material, of course, goes simultaneously to other offices of the Department, but no one office receives as much information as the INR. The INR also does a certain amount of collecting of intelligence, although bureau officials tend to be mute about this activity. But the bureau staff spends most of its time producing research and analysis papers on subjects varying from Soviet Premier Aleksei Kosygin's general state of health to a boundary dispute in the Middle East. Perhaps most important from the Department's single-minded view of other intelligence organizations, the INR sticks its nose into the operations of these organizations to insure that their activities abroad accord with United States foreign policy objectives.

Although the FBI is a member of the intelligence community, its production of foreign intelligence is only incidental, since it has been barred from operating abroad since 1946. This exclusion, resulting from the post-war reorganization of the country's intelligence network, did not set well with FBI Director J. Edgar Hoover, who pointed with pardonable pride to the superb job the FBI's Special Intelligence Service performed in the Western Hemisphere during the war. But President Truman foresaw a conflict between the prima donnas of the CIA and the equally temperamental Hoover and ruled that in the future the FBI should operate largely as an agency for domestic counterintelligence.

Nevertheless, the FBI stations agents in most of the world's capitals and many other foreign cities, ostensibly in pursuit of the bureau's counterintelligence mission. Both CIA and DIA officials often have complained privately that Hoover's cool corps also intrudes upon the pure intelligence field around the world, and tell the story of the embarrassing moment when a DIA operative shadowed a "subject" for eleven days, finally to discover that the man was an FBI agent working on the same project.

Hoover undoubtedly is the member of the intelligence community with the most personal prestige across the country. At the end of 1968, he was completing his forty-fourth year as boss of this prestigious investigative principality. A man of tremendous efficiency, occasionally marred by intemperate public statements, Hoover made an honest woman of the FBI. He also made the bureau a glamorous public institution with which neither Presidents nor Congresses have dared to tinker. For that reason alone, he is one of the dominant figures in American intelligence. Within the national spy shop, he is also probably the most unpopular because of his stern, uncompromising, no-nonsense—and provincial—approach to even the most sensitive foreign policy matters.

The Atomic Energy Commission rates membership in the

intelligence community only through its special status, since it is primarily a consumer rather than a producer of intelligence. But on occasion it provides information vital to the formulation of foreign policy when it monitors nuclear explosions abroad and produces estimates of the nuclear weapons capabilities of foreign powers. Its announcements of nuclear blasts in the Soviet Union and Communist China—sometimes reported only to the intelligence community—are "must" information for both policy makers and those concerned with protecting the national security. From the AEC, for example, the military receives vital information on the progress of the Russian program to develop more sophisticated hydrogen warheads for ballistic missiles.

Dr. Glenn T. Seaborg, former chancellor of the University of California at Berkeley, was named chairman of the AEC in 1961 to fill the post vacated by John A. McCone, and subsequently was reappointed twice to five-year terms. He is recognized as one of the world's outstanding nuclear scientists, and won the Nobel Prize in chemistry at thirty-nine for his work in the discovery of numerous new elements, including plutonium. He also won the $50,000 Enrico Fermi Award in 1959. A jovial, second-generation Swede, Dr. Seaborg is fond of teasing his colleagues in the intelligence community about their sobersided preoccupation with the secrets they share. "Come now," he once told Allen Dulles, then head of the CIA, "you mustn't be so solemn. It's the secret that is the serious matter, not oneself."

Lyndon Johnson, who always had a keen appreciation of intelligence, might have echoed Dr. Seaborg's dictum. He once remarked to his then Press Secretary, George Reedy, that "some of this stuff gives me a belly laugh." Johnson also was wont to complain about the sheer mass of raw material produced by the Republic's far-flung and bloated espionage network. "God knows we can't neglect this business," he told a visitor, "but I sometimes wonder whether we need every last scrap of intelligence that flows into this town."

Johnson might have made note of the fact that much of this mass is not only duplicative but at times perilously misleading. He could have pointed out that during the Kennedy Administration the file of reports devoted solely to "Soviet Missiles in Cuba" for the year 1959 was five inches thick, although at that time the Russians had sent not so much as a handgun to Fidel Castro or anyone else on the island. But his intelligence people would have shrugged off Johnson's complaint. In the Bible of espionage, today's wild rumor is apt to become tomorrow's hard fact.

4

Espionage by Gadget

Lyndon Johnson's complaint that the flood of intelligence pouring into Washington sometimes would appear to be too much of a good thing would not have been endorsed by a Defense Intelligence Agency operative newly arrived in Saigon during the winter of 1966. The DIA agent, an Air Force colonel working in civilian clothes, discovered a scrap of knowledge that had been buried in his memory for more than a decade and used it to expose and bring before a firing squad a North Vietnamese *agent provocateur* who had wormed his way into the confidence of South Vietnam's high command.

The story is at once an important morsel of justification for the intelligence premise that no piece of information can be discarded out of hand, and an example of how the untidy business of espionage has been altered by the development of awesome—and frightening—electronic gadgets employed to eavesdrop on the individual.

Here, the colonel shall be known as Adams and the North Vietnamese secret agent as Thuc to conceal their true identities. Adams's involvement in the story began in a Pentagon office several months after the Geneva Conference of 1954 had partitioned French Indochina into North and South Vietnam. Scanning a sheaf of intelligence reports from Hong Kong, he encountered the name Thuc. The reference seemed unimportant at the time; Thuc's name was merely mentioned in passing as having been seen leaving a house in Kowloon where some politicians from Hanoi had been enjoying a dinner party. Indeed, the emphasis in the report was on efforts by the North Vietnamese delegation to arrange an agricultural loan from a group of Hong Kong financiers. There was no suggestion that Thuc's attendance at the party was anything but social.

Several days after his arrival in Saigon, Colonel Adams attended a routine intelligence briefing. The briefing was conducted by a Major Thuc, who had been described to Adams as one of the leading figures in South Vietnam's state intelligence organization. At the time, the name Thuc seemed naggingly familiar to Adams, but he had other things to think about. It was not until Thuc was well launched into the briefing—delivered in French—that a bell rang in Adams's memory.

Now he remembered that flimsy sheet of paper he had seen in Washington. Routinely, it had described the Thuc who had been seen leaving the North Viet party as short, fat, pockmarked, mustached and wearing black horn-rimmed glasses. The Thuc who was giving the briefing was short, fat, pockmarked, mustached and wearing black horn-rimmed glasses. The 1954 intelligence report had noted that Thuc spoke French with a Norman accent; so did the Thuc conducting the briefing.

After the briefing, Adams returned to his office and launched a discreet investigation that took more than a month. At the end of that time, for additional reasons which have never been disclosed, he was satisfied that the Major Thuc who was a respected member of the South Vietnamese intelligence community was the same Thuc who had hobnobbed with the North Viet politicians in Hong Kong. Moreover, Adams's investigation strongly indicated that Thuc was a double agent, serving Hanoi. His movements and associations and certain apparently innocuous inconsistencies in some of his intelligence reports could not be disregarded in the light of his history. There were even hints that Thuc had used South Vietnamese agents planted in North Vietnam to pass innocent-sounding messages to the Hanoi regime through other Saigon operatives known to have been compromised by the North Vietnamese secret police.

Adams got the go-ahead from on high to pursue his detective work. He was warned, however, that the American establishment would take no action unless and until he provided hard, jury-convincing evidence that Thuc was a traitor.

Adams went to work with a team of four handpicked

American intelligence operatives and three South Vietnamese. His task was to find out everything he could about Thuc's daily, and nightly, routines, through careful surveillance and the collection of scraps of trivial information. Adams's sources ranged from other South Vietnamese intelligence officials to waiters in the fancier Saigon restaurants and a lady of liberal moral outlook who was known to supply comely females for groups of South Vietnamese military officers seeking *divertissement*. All this information, of course, was to be gathered in the most casual manner, as the sort of juicy material relished by gossips.

There was also an immediate bonus. Adams's superior officer introduced him at a party one night to a Viet captain who wanted Thuc's job, and whose chances of getting it seemed almost nonexistent. The captain, here given the pseudonym Kanh, listened attentively and politely while Adams explained that his mission was to study the efficiency of the joint American-Vietnamese intelligence effort. Perhaps he believed it. In any case, he didn't have to be told that here was an opportunity to take the hatchet to Thuc.

Shortly thereafter, Thuc's body servant fell ill. A few days later, Captain Kanh reported to Adams that as one of his routine housekeeping duties in Thuc's section he had replaced the ailing servant with one of his own personal agents. Thuc, who knew nothing of Kanh's ambitions, was unsuspecting; he thanked Kanh profusely for finding a substitute so promptly.

For more than two months, however, Adams's task force was unable to dredge up the slightest clue that Thuc was working with Hanoi. It learned much about Thuc's love life and his predilection for certain unorthodox sexual antics, and discovered he could hold his favorite liquor—Old Fitzgerald bonded bourbon. But otherwise he was clean. The new body servant eavesdropped on Thuc's conversations with his bibulous friends at parties and over the telephone with no results. Indeed, it appeared that, despite his after-hours pleasures, Thuc was one of the hardest-working officers in South Vietnam.

But by now Adams was convinced that some of the people Thuc saw and talked with, both by day and by night, were involved with him in a treacherous conspiracy. False intelligence planted in Thuc's section had found its way to Hanoi.

The evaluation of other intelligence gathered by the section was becoming increasingly faulty.

It was then that Adams turned to the new electronic science which has made eavesdropping almost as easy as reading a newspaper. He wanted to listen in on the conversations Thuc had when the body servant could not be present. This could only be done by the use of ubiquitous devices which would accompany Thuc wherever he went and eavesdrop on him in places where he felt safe from surveillance.

Adams checked with some experts in an obscure little corner of the National Security Agency. He discovered they could provide him with tiny microphones and radio transmitters in the form of tieclasps, wristwatches, cuff links, fountain pens and coat buttons. He could choose from a variety of tape recorders so small they could be carried in a cigarette package. Adams hit on the idea of making Thuc a walking, talking radio station—without his knowledge, of course.

Captain Kanh and the agent-body servant he had placed in Thuc's household managed this. Kanh provided the electronics experts with a number of buttons for South Vietnamese officers' uniforms. The experts tinkered with the buttons for a few hours and then returned them to Colonel Adams who in turn returned them to Kanh who in turn gave them to the servant. The servant then replaced three buttons on the jacket of one of Thuc's uniforms with three doctored buttons. The new top button, in fact, was a microphone, the second button a transmitter and the third a small extended light battery unit. A length of ultra-thin wire which the servant sewed into the jacket's lining became an aerial. Also concealed in the lining was a long thin device weighing less than two ounces. This was a tape recorder with eight hours of tape.

Other tiny microphones were woven into several of Thuc's ties; they would broadcast whatever Thuc was saying to eavesdroppers trailing him a block or so away. Microphones were installed in picture frames in Thuc's house and connected to tape recorders by hair-thin wiring brushed into the varnish or paint of the walls. Woven microphones were concealed in the three pillows on Thuc's bed for the convenience of the servant listening in the next room.

During the next three weeks, the servant was busy sewing

new buttons on Thuc's other uniforms and changing the various batteries and tape recorders. On the twenty-second day, Adams donned earphones and flicked a switch that would enable him to listen in on a conversation between Thuc and three South Vietnamese businessmen in the home of one of the businessmen.

What Adams heard, through an interpreter translating simultaneously, was the ball game. In the businessman's cozy dining room, the four men were discussing a top-secret project—the operation of a plant set up in the countryside near Go Vap to counterfeit American currency. Two nights hence, the counterfeiters planned an official visit to the plant to check on the progress of their hired hands.

It took Adam's men only five hours the next day to locate the plant. It was in a farmhouse set among rice fields and reached by a narrow rutty road. Two farmers in the neighborhood told of having seen men unloading pieces of equipment, recognizable by intelligence as printing press parts. The farmers were given fifty dollars apiece. Then the farmhouse was put under 24-hour surveillance against the possibility the farmers might decide to sell what they knew to the funny money makers and, of course, the chance Thuc and his friends might show up ahead of schedule.

Shortly after Thuc and his friends arrived the next evening, Colonel Adams led a force of Vietnamese and American special agents against the plant. The three businessmen were shot and killed by Vietnamese soldiers while attempting to escape, a development that by happy coincidence spared the Saigon authorities the necessity for a civil, public trial which would have produced publicity advantageous only to Hanoi. But Thuc turned timid and surrendered meekly. He was executed by a firing squad after a brief, perfunctory and secret court-martial three days later. By informal agreement between American and Vietnamese diplomats, the counterfeiting plant and eight hundred dollars in fresh, bogus ten-dollar bills was turned over to the custody of a United States Treasury representative.

Colonel Adams's employment of miniaturized electronic snoopers to trap Major Thuc was not the far-out example of scientific espionage it might seem to the layman. Spies of all nations use such gadgets every day, thankful for the technological advances which have made their chores easier, if a trifle more esoteric. They are part and parcel of the communications revolution of the fifties and sixties which has assigned a lion's share of the mission of intelligence-gathering to mild-looking, highly cerebral scientists. Adams's bugging devices were small-scale prototypes of some of the complicated devices and processes used by the National Security Agency to eavesdrop from the stratosphere and to protect the secret communications of the United States Government.

One of the most fascinating of these electronic instruments, and certainly the most important—perhaps in the world—is the President's Black Box. This is the slim black case that contains the codes that would be used to transmit the Presidential order to launch a nuclear attack. It goes wherever the President goes, day and night, carried by one of five warrant officers assigned to the duty alternately, around the clock. When the President is working in his office, the officer on duty is in the next room. At night, he sits outside the President's bedroom in the White House, or at the Nixon vacation stockade in Key Biscayne, Florida, or the Waldorf-Astoria Hotel in New York. At the beach, the warrant officer on duty wears swimming trunks and a sports shirt; aboard ship he wears the dress of a deckhand. When Richard Nixon plays golf at the Burning Tree Club in Washington or elsewhere, the warrant officer wears slacks and sports shirt. The Black Box followed President Nixon to Europe in February, 1969. Indeed, Pope Paul asked the President if he had it with him. Nixon said he did, and with His Holiness's permission, invited the warrant officer—dressed in a conservative blue suit —to come in and meet the spiritual ruler of the world's Catholics.

These officers are not merely custodians of the Black Box. They represent authentication to the command receiving the attack order. They certify to the officer who pushes the nuclear button that the message does, in fact, come from the President, that it is indisputably genuine.

The Black Box codes consist of several layers, to make sure that only a valid message gets through. The President transmits his order in this layer-cake, electronic jumble, knowing that at least one copy of the message will get through, whatever destruction may have fallen on the nation. For the Air Force has dispersed its communications, fortified others, sent others into the skies as flying command posts, provided alternate routes and arranged various transmission methods, including radio, telephone and teletype.

From the President, the order goes directly to two officers in a concrete missile-control shelter deep underground. The officers each have a 3 by 5 inch card with a plastic coating bearing the key to the nuclear attack code which they must wear on a chain around their necks at all times when on duty. When the message comes in over the red telephone of the Primary Alert System, each officer must take down the message, decode it and then confirm each other's reading before starting the countdown. Different codes transmit the "Go" order to manned bombers, who speed toward preassigned targets at the sounding of the alert. However, they may not proceed past a certain point—the "fail-safe" point—until they receive further instructions. These come in code from the Red Box on the wall of Strategic Air Command headquarters at Offutt Air Force Base and in the flying command posts. The pilots then must match these "attack" instructions with the separate pieces of code they carry aloft with them to verify that it is the real thing. Three members of each crew must do this matching individually; the attack proceeds only if they agree on verifications.

Similarly, the NSA provides protection for the less solemn communications systems which must, figuratively, always be at the President's elbow. It does this through the Defense Communications Agency and its subordinate branch, the White House Communications Agency. When the President travels, his communications facilities are set up wherever he stops. These include a telephone scrambler and a cipher machine, and, of course, the Black Box. The radiotelephone in the President's personal limousine has a scrambler attachment. A scrambler attachment and cipher machine are part of the standard equipment of the Presidential plane, Air Force One. During his round-the-world trip of December, 1967, President Johnson talked with a State Department official in Washington by radiotelephone while being driven from the airport to the Vatican.

Another NSA contribution to the security of Presidential communications is the so-called "hot line," a teletype connection between the White House and the Kremlin. Messages transmitted on this line are sent in what cryptologists call "one-time type." That is to say, there is a random key used only once in order to frustrate attempts to break the code. (Any repetition of any kind of a key, no matter how ingenious or complicated, makes its eventual solution by unfriendly or even merely curious cryptologic experts inevitable.) The Soviet Union provides keying tapes for reception of messages from Washington. Moscow and Washington have four teleprinters each, two with the English alphabet and two with the Russian. Operative since August 30, 1963, the hot line has been used on various occasions, including the morning of January 24, 1968, when President Johnson asked the Soviet Union to use its influence to secure the release of the intelligence ship U.S.S. *Pueblo,* boarded and captured by North Korean patrol boat crews.

The telephone scramblers used in the White House, the State Department, the Pentagon and other sensitive Government establishments probably are what is known in the trade as PCM's. These are electronic devices that convert the voice signal into a series of "pulses" and "nonpulses," which somewhat resemble a teletype signal. Voice frequency determines the number of pulses per second; and this in itself helps to mask the conversation. Special PCM (or "pulse code modulation") equipment is needed to reconvert these pulses to voice form, probably with the aid of machine-operated electronic cipher breakers. Since two and a half minutes of PCM will encipher a million pulses—at the rate of eight thousand pulses a second—the pulses can be stored on magnetized tape or on film and deciphered at the receiver's convenience.

One of these scramblers is considered sufficient for White House traffic, since they cost $100,000 apiece, including installation. But the State Department has seven in Washington, plus nine more in European cities and at the U.S. mission to the United Nations in New York. Flying command posts all carry scramblers to direct and control U.S. nuclear retaliatory forces in the event a missile attack destroyed the Air Force's underground headquarters.

Scramblers also are employed on the battlefield by Army armor and reconnaissance units. One type scrambles voice messages by mixing them with teletype signals transmitted on a lower frequency. The receiver merely uses a feedback line to excise the teletype signals, thus leaving the speech clear. A lighter scrambler system also has been devised for attachment to portable telephone and radio systems used by officers in front-line combat and for field action against hit-and-run guerrilla forces.

With all these fascinating gadgets to play with, there is yet a lot of traditionalism—a reliance on methods tried and true —in the spymaster. The fine art of blackmail is still effective in certain cases where information can be obtained only from a particular source, and the more sinister types continue to catch innocent officials in homosexual traps as though they invented a practice which was aging in Julius Caesar's time. And, of course, pretty girls and even girls who are merely compliant will never go out of style.

A nubile female who is known only as Ingrid except in a certain group high in Defense Department intelligence circles proved once again the efficacy of properly applied sex in the fall of 1967. Moreover she did so by employing a trick of strategy that undoubtedly was first used by one of Eve's daughters. In point of fact, Ingrid's act was identical with one used by another, British, Mata Hari during World War II, as was the locale—Washington, D.C.

Ingrid was employed by an old-fashioned cloak-and-dagger agent in the Defense Intelligence Agency to steal some code books from the home of the head of a purchasing commission of a neutral country permanently stationed in Washington. She manipulated a meeting with the man by posing as a free-lance writer, not an outlandish disguise in a city teeming with wordsmiths of all descriptions. But her prey was not the commission's boss but a handsome young aide with a reputation for womanizing. Ingrid was a tall brunette of considerable beauty, and during the course of preparing a "personality sketch" of his chief managed to spend a considerable amount of time with the young man. Predictably, and with all assistance from Ingrid, he fell in love with her.

The two became what one intelligence officer called "instant bedfellows." Within a few weeks, Ingrid's age-old womanly wisdom told her that this man would do anything for her. Since that was how she wanted it, she put her lover bluntly to the test.

As she later told it, she turned to him one night in bed and told him: "I want those code books in the office safe."

He acquiesced, figuratively speaking without blinking an eye. Ingrid, he said, should have anything she wanted. Nothing mattered to him but their love and her happiness. His response was not farfetched at all; intelligence files all over the world bulge with the cases of young men who, in these modern and cynical times, still betray their countries for romance's sake. In one case which never made the newspapers, two attachés at an Iron Curtain embassy in Washington were trapped by the FBI at their espionage chores in the same week as the result of information furnished by their girl friends, both naturalized Czechs.

At any rate, Ingrid's young man fell in with her plan. The purchasing chief was to leave within a few days for six weeks' home leave. A watchman, a national of the country to which the commission was accredited, would guard the chief's home in Georgetown, but Ingrid was sure he could be handled.

Thus, a few days after the chief's departure, Ingrid and her young man showed up one midnight after obviously having looked upon the wine at its reddest. The young man gave the watchman a wink, and explained that they had nowhere to go, alas. The young woman, the watchman should understand, was married, and they could not go to the young man's apartment because a girl to whom he paid occasional court and who was insanely jealous lived in the same building. Since the young man was a familiar visitor to the residence as a member of the commission, the watchman returned the wink and opened up.

Ingrid and her lover spent several nights in the house over the course of the next two weeks until the watchman, always tipped generously, grew accustomed to their romantic vagary. Then one night they arrived in a cab instead of in the young man's Jaguar. Ingrid staggered out of the cab waving a bottle of champagne and insisted on pouring the watchman a drink. He managed to persuade her that it would be more discreet for him to do his drinking in the kitchen rather than in the street, and subsequently downed not one but two glasses of the bubbly. He dropped off almost immediately into the heavy sleep induced by a Mickey Finn.

The young man forthwith summoned the cabdriver, an expert locksmith in one of the many classified crannies of the Pentagon. This craftsman solved the combination of the safe within an hour, and Ingrid left him and her young man to tidy up while she hurried off with the code books. Ingrid carried on their affair for another three months and then introduced him, by prearrangement, to a stunning blonde who proceeded to take him for her own, again by prearrangement. Ingrid was tearful but philosophical when the young man bade her farewell. "I knew it would happen," she said. "You were just too beautiful to last." So far as is known, the young man is still working for his country, back home.

These days, Ingrid's old-fashioned exploit is of a piece with the continued use by most espionage agencies, including American, of the microdot, a bit of film the size of a printed period which can be enlarged to show the message on a sheet of 8 by 11 typewriter paper. Microdots are almost as old as photography itself and were used in the latter part of the nineteenth century to carry messages between cities in time of war, although the "dots" were much bigger than they are today.

German intelligence perfected the microdot to its present size during World War II and used it successfully all over the world. One microdot message which caused the FBI particular anguish asked a German spy in New York in 1941 to find out "Where are being made the tests with uranium?" That launched a stepped-up campaign against almost every typewritten syllable arriving from abroad after an FBI laboratory technician pried it off an envelope carried by a suspected German agent.

Today, microdots are still produced mechanically in a Zapp Cabinet invented by a German photographic expert in 1943. The mechanical process in effect merely speeds up the original handmade system, by which the final in a series of photographs was made through a reversed microscope to bring the print down to less than 0.05 inches in diameter. When the negative had been developed the agent or technician used a hypodermic needle, whose point had been clipped off and its round edge sharpened, as a cookie cutter to dip into the emulsion and lift out the microdot. The microdot then was cemented onto an innocuous letter or businessman's brochure and pressed down further by the "period" key of a typewriter. A relatively cheap and uncomplicated means of carrying secret messages, the microdot is still employed with businessman-couriers and others who are known not to be under suspicion.

As a matter of fact, the simplest of codes often are used to transmit messages concerning most important matters because they are thus unlikely to attract suspicion. They are, of course, only used once, to avoid the risk entailed by repetition.

Perhaps the best example of a simple code used to report a development of great significance was the informal jargon which masked a message from Washington to Secretary of War Henry Stimson, then attending the Potsdam conference, announcing the first atomic bomb explosion. A special consultant to Stimson, George L. Harrison, reported on the visibility of TRINITY—the code name for the bomb—by relating it to the 250-mile distance between Washington and Stimson's country home, Highhold, on Long Island. The noise the bomb made was compared to the sixty miles between Harrison's farm in Virginia and Washington. LITTLE BOY referred to the bomb just exploded, BIG BROTHER to the uranium bomb to be tested later, and DOCTOR to General Leslie R. Groves, head of the Manhattan District.

Harrison's message to Potsdam read:

DOCTOR HAS JUST RETURNED MOST ENTHUSIASTIC AND CONFIDENT THAT THE LITTLE BOY IS AS HUSKY AS HIS BIG BROTHER. THE LIGHT IN HIS EYES DISCERNIBLE FROM HERE TO HIGHHOLD AND I COULD HAVE HEARD HIS SCREAMS FROM HERE TO MY FARM.

Stimson had no trouble understanding it the first time he read it.

5

Inside NSA

George Harrison's code message to Secretary of War Henry Stimson announcing the explosion of the first atomic bomb was a simple matter, but it was also a symbol of a new era. World War II had ushered in the age of communications, by which military commanders and statesmen are assured of virtually instantaneous and secure receipt of intelligence. It was of vital importance that the American negotiators at Potsdam be informed immediately, and secretly, of the results of the bomb test in order that this information might be used as a weapon in the negotiations with Josef Stalin. The waging of war and of peace, of course, always had depended to a great extent on communications, but World War II had raised the art to the status of a science. All over the world today, presidents, premiers and dictators are able to wield their power more effectively because of the speed and security with which they receive information and issue their orders.

In the United States, the center of this network of communications is the empire of men and electronics known as the National Security Agency. With assists from the cryptologic sections of the three armed services, the NSA undoubtedly is the greatest organization of its kind since the Biblical Israelites crossed over into Canaan.

The NSA is sequestered on eighty-two acres at Fort Meade, Maryland, in a 47-million-dollar complex of two buildings which together make up the biggest Government installation in the Washington area. Its 1,900,000 square feet of space dwarfs the CIA's 1,135,000, and its Operations

Building has the longest unobstructed corridor in the country —980 feet. Like the CIA complex in Langley, Virginia, the NSA installation has many of the conveniences of a suburban shopping center, including a cafeteria, an auditorium seating 500, a post exchange, eight snack bars, a hospital complete with operating room and X-ray laboratory, a dentist's office, a branch of the State Bank of Laurel, a dry-cleaning shop, a shoe shop and a barber shop.

What David Kahn in his book, *The Code Breakers,* called "This cathedral of cryptology" is supposed to have more electric wiring than any building in the world. It is fully air-conditioned, and has what one Army general described as an "utterly secure public address system," whatever that means. It also has a German-made pneumatic tube system that can accommodate 800 containers an hour at a speed of 75 feet a second.

Basically, the NSA's espionage field is cryptography, which is the science of communications intelligence employed to protect the security of governmental messages, especially those of a military or diplomatic nature, and to break the security of the communications of other nations. Given the weaknesses and complexities of human nature, the cryptographer and his awesome machines probably will never replace the cloak-and-dagger operative, but they have relegated the human spy to a secondary and sometime role in the gathering of intelligence.

Secret or classified governmental messages are sent in code or cipher. A code involves substituting a word, symbol or group of symbols for a whole word, a group of words or a thought. The letters ZTPLN might stand for the word "attack." Or, if a number code is used, the symbol might be 86432. In a cipher, a letter or a number stands for a single letter in a word. There are simple ciphers, in which the same symbol—letter or number—always stands for the same letter. But in the complex ciphers used today the same symbol can stand for a different letter each time it turns up. Thus, "e" or "7" could stand for "b" the first time it is used, for "w" the second time, and so on.

Often a message is put first into code and then into cipher, further to confuse the interceptor. In his book, *The Craft of Intelligence,* the former CIA director, Allen Dulles, recalled that in some instances during World Wars I and II such precautions were made unnecessary by the use of a code based on the Navajo language, which has no written forms. Dulles pointed out that "neither the Germans nor the Japanese had any Navajos," and besides the language was relatively unknown to foreign scholars.

A cryptogram or cryptograph is any message in code or cipher. Cryptography, in its purest sense, means the devising of codes and ciphers for a government's own use. Cryptanalysis is the science of "decrypting" or breaking the codes and ciphers of a foreign government. Despite an earlier stricture by Henry Stimson that "gentlemen don't read other people's mail," U.S. intelligence agencies do so whenever the opportunity presents itself, but mostly they depend on their experts' readings of the airwaves and their translation of foreign codes and ciphers by mathematical analysis. Since the development of electronic brains, most of this cryptanalysis is done by machine.

There is no longer such a thing as a simple code or cipher, but a simple illustration of how the science is used by most experts will give the layman some idea of what it is all about. Take the word SECRET. In transposition, this becomes ETCRSE; the letters are the same but their order is jumbled. In substitution, SECRET might become 19 5 3 18 5 20; the letters are in the same positions but wear a disguise. This disguise can be made more effective if a different number is assigned to a letter each time it is used in a message. Thus the "e" in SECRET would appear the first time as "3" and the second time as, perhaps, "34," and so on. But, of course, NSA's experts tackle codes and ciphers a thousand times more difficult, using electronic code machines and computers.

Although its operations and secrets are more closely guarded than those of any other American intelligence agency, it is possible to look in on the NSA's enormous headquarters building at Fort Meade and observe the working habits of its employees—experts and spear carriers. It is not a glamorous scene, despite NSA's preoccupation with such esoteric raw material. Except for the highly sophisticated machines and computers in various cubbyholes, NSA headquarters might be the main office of a big seed and grain company.

Like office employees everywhere, NSA people work in big

open rooms crowded with desks. There, the cryptanalysts receive the so-called raw intercepts picked up by space satellites, spy ships, land listening posts, submarines, aircraft. Traffic analysts determine the location of the sending points and their routing, in order to label them with a classification which could be of assistance to the cryptanalyst. Besides, traffic patterns often reveal the locations of military and technical installations.

Cryptanalysts work in teams, under a chief who makes assignments and recommends the method to be used in seeking to break and translate a coded or enciphered message. They also work in three shifts—from 7:20 A.M. to 3:50 P.M., from 7:40 A.M to 4:10 P.M. and from 8 A.M. to 4:30 P.M. Most of them are attached to the Office of Production, or PROD, which is the largest of NSA's three operating branches and which is engaged in the production of communications intelligence. PROD is responsible for the operation of NSA's net of two thousand intercept positions around the world, which is described as "one man listening in to one radio set"; so-called "ferret" airplanes; spy ships and submarines, and such spy satellites as the SAMOS, which carry a 400-pound package of listening instruments. Using such electronic espionage agents, the NSA was able to begin monitoring Soviet missiles in 1958, only a year after the Russians launched their history-making Sputnik.

Time means everything—and nothing—to NSA's cryptanalysts. A team may work for as long as three years on a foreign cryptographic system, although there is constant pressure to break a system "yesterday." The experts seek to break and read all cryptosystems of all countries, but from a practical viewpoint this is impossible. There is not enough manpower nor enough money. Indeed, the probability is that NSA experts read only about 15 percent of the total volume of intercepts received. Predictably, they concentrate on intercepts from the Soviet Union, Communist China, other Communist countries and certain neutral nations. Solutions are dispatched to the various departments and agencies of the United States Government requiring the information. In addition, a military aide brings to the President every morning the NSA "Black Book" containing the more important solutions and translated messages.

Naturally, the Government is most interested in military

and diplomatic intelligence, but frequently there are interesting, and amusing, bonuses. For example, one intercept in the spring of 1968 revealed a radio telephone discussion between the heads of state of two European Communist bloc nations about the Broadway play, *Hair,* which featured a scene in which the players appeared in the nude. One of these tribal chieftains had read a review in a Communist magazine of the play, and their discussion was concerned equally with the deterioration of capitalist morals and lip-smacking comments on the production.

Intercepts also provide information on private foreign reaction to developments and incidents in the United States. Thus President Johnson was able to learn from the "Black Book" that France's Charles de Gaulle looked with favor on Robert F. Kennedy's bid for the Democratic Presidential nomination. De Gaulle praised Bobby's "European, sophisticated intelligence," while deploring his "youthful arrogance." He dismissed Richard Nixon as a "chauvinist," a curious criticism on the part of a man who has always been a towering symbol of his own country's claim to *la gloire.* De Gaulle found Hubert Humphrey a "nonentity" and expressed apprehension over Senator Eugene McCarthy's unconventional approach to power politics.

Another intercept reflected the influence the 1968 election in America had on international politics. This was a message from Hanoi to the North Vietnamese peace negotiation team in Paris, a rather aimless and disjointed philosophical discussion of the relative qualities of Nixon and Humphrey and the probable posture the winner would take toward the negotiations.

The message, signed by a Foreign Office official, might have been composed by an American political pundit engaged in the time-honored pursuit of dissecting the rival candidates. Humphrey, it said, was more liberal and had the instincts of a man of peace, but this did not necessarily mean he would take a softer line. As a liberal, the message continued, Humphrey might be fearful about making any new concessions lest he encounter trouble with a more conservative Congress. Nixon was described as a reactionary at heart, but a politician seeking to improve his image. Since he was campaigning on an end-the-war platform, the peace negotiators were told, he might find it necessary to adopt a more

conciliatory stand than Humphrey's. The message likened
Nixon to Lyndon Johnson, when the latter took over after
the assassination of President John F. Kennedy, and showed
a determination to be more liberal than his predecessor in
order to prove his critics wrong. Thus, the message concluded, Hanoi might well get a better deal from a President
Nixon than from a President Humphrey. In the meantime,
nothing should be done to break off the negotiations because
President Johnson might be forced to take a softer line in
order to bolster Humphrey's chances of election.

After the assassinations of Robert Kennedy and Dr. Martin Luther King, messages exchanged by the governments of
East Germany and Bulgaria agreed that a revolution was
"imminent" in the United States, with the Negroes and
liberals forming a coalition to take over the nation by force.
Violence at the Democratic National Convention in Chicago
was hailed unanimously by Soviet satellite governments in
Europe as the beginning of the destruction of the two party
system in America.

Such intercepts and others providing intelligence of somewhat more vital importance are processed with the help of
some 3 billion dollars' worth of assorted decoding machines
and high-priced computers. Among the computers used are
a $3,300,000 I.B.M. 7090, which can perform 230,000 addi-
tions per second, other I.B.M. models, a group of Univacs
and an Atlas specially built to NSA specifications. The messages are collated according to origin and pattern, punched
on cards by key-punch operators and fed into the computers
by other technicians. Special computers are used to run special restricted tests in order not to waste the time of the
all-purpose computers.

Thus the machine handles a great deal of the drudgery man
used to do. But the cryptanalyst is still indispensable. No
machine has been devised that can think like a human being,
nor employ experience so effectively, nor resort to human
instinct, combined perhaps with a vague recollection of a
previous cipher broken. In the tough going, the expert must
call on his expertise, no matter how indistinct toward a particular problem, to work out whether a given symbol means
"x" or "y." Moreover, it is the human expert who decides
how a problem must be programmed for the machine.

There is no doubt, however, that these electronic marvels

have helped make the NSA the world's most efficient guardian of its nation's codes and the most successful at breaking the codes of other countries. One reason is that the United States can afford the best and the most advanced machines. Another is that this country has the greatest reservoir of technological talent, the boasts of the Soviet Union to the contrary notwithstanding.

Nevertheless, it is a fact that the NSA and other U.S. cryptologic agencies encounter their greatest difficulty in breaking Russian codes and ciphers. For their most important secret messages, the Russians use the so-called "one-time pads" or "gammas," and they are 95 percent secure because each "pad" is entirely different from every other and is used only once and then destroyed. This system accepts the premise that any repetition of any kind in the keys of cryptograms under analysis probably dooms them to solution. If a good analyst has enough time and enough text, he can break any cipher. The "one-time pad" deprives him of both, since he sees the cipher key only once.

One-time keys are used in machine-encoded messages and also are given to secret agents. A Soviet spy in the United States, for example, may carry a pad no bigger than a postage stamp, containing as many as 250 pages. A duplicate copy of the pad is in Moscow. There are dozens of five-digit groups printed on each page. When the spy has used a page to decipher a message from Moscow he burns it, and uses the next page to decipher the next message. Since the numbers vary on each page, however, and are never repeated, they are meaningless to any analyst.

Yet one-time Soviet keys *have* been cracked. No one will say how, but probably some of the solutions have been achieved as a result of errors by encoding clerks. More ciphers are solved through such accidental circumstances than intelligence men will admit. And since the experts are unanimous in proclaiming the "one-time pad" system all but absolutely secure, it's a good bet that any other solutions have been the result of sheer chance.

It may seem curious to the layman that the "one-time pad" has not been universally adopted. But even allowing for the immense sums granted intelligence agencies, no nation—not even the United States—could afford to do so. One intelligence authority has estimated that it would require the em-

ployment of at least thirty thousand more persons to operate
an exclusively "one-time pad" system in the Defense and
State Departments alone. Besides, the task of producing and
distributing such enormous quantities of keys is insuperable.
So much time would be spent devising and circulating the
pads that all messages would be seriously delayed, some of
them for weeks.

The protection of secret American Government communications is the responsibility of the second of NSA's three
operating divisions, the Office of Communications Security,
or COMSEC. It is the smallest of the divisions, with about
1,700 employees, compared with 8,200 for the Office of Production (PROD) and 2,300 for the Office of Research and
Development.

COMSEC dictates the cryptological systems used by each
department of the Government and places restrictions on
their use, lest a volume of inconsequential material provide
the "enemy" with opportunities to break the systems. COM-
SEC also furnishes some of the enciphering machines and
does the contracting for others. It also is responsible for the
production of scrambling machines, which keep voice communications private. But COMSEC's principal function is to
devise new systems of encipherment and get them installed
in new machines. COMSEC cryptologists work closely with
Government departments and agencies, including the intelligence branches of the three armed services and the Defense
Intelligence Agency, to make sure they don't demand expensive systems and machines not required by their particular
needs. COMSEC also produces and supplies the enciphering
keys. A special COMSEC board evaluates suggestions, which
pour into the NSA at the rate of more than four hundred a
year, for new systems. Unfortunately, the NSA is not obli-
gated by law or even by an informal promise to pay compen-
sation for ideas accepted, and undoubtedly this opaque position deters many inventors from submitting ideas. History
affirms the near-sightedness of this policy, since most of the
really spectacular discoveries or inventions in the cryptographic field were the contributions of persons with no technical or scientific background.

COMSEC can protect the quality of American cipher systems, but obviously has no means to safeguard them once
they leave NSA headquarters. That is to say, they can and

sometimes are captured by the "enemy." A $1,400 Hagelen enciphering machine was seized by North Vietnamese troops near Khesanh, South Vietnam, in the fall of 1967; two American soldiers were killed trying to carry it to safety during a general retreat. An American diplomat stationed in a European capital was forced sheepishly to confess that another enciphering machine was "lost" sometime during a six-hour period when his office was being moved from one building to another.

NSA's third operating office, the Office of Rearch and Development (R/D), consists of three sections—Research, Engineering, Mathematics, Physics; Standard Technical Equipment Development, and Research and Development. The titles only seem redundant and duplicative.

The first section does basic research aimed at discovering new tests and techniques to solve ciphers. Its technicians also work at improving the capabilities of computers—getting more speed and more data-handling capacity. Standard Technical Equipment Development conducts basic research into new methods of encipherment. Research and Development actually is almost entirely preoccupied with basic transmission research in a constant effort to increase the sensitivity of NSA's intercepting receivers and strengthening the security of transmission methods. Among other achievements, it has developed a technique which reduces secret radio transmissions to a barrage of static in the ear of the interceptor lacking an unscrambling key.

Other units of NSA are the Office of Personnel Services, the Office of Training Services and the Office of Security Services, which, as will be seen, is Big Brother to NSA employees. There is a superb library, crammed with works on a variety of esoteric cryptological subjects, and a collection of 673 mathematical and physics publications in nine different languages.

NSA also is served by the Institute for Defense Analyses, an independent research organization supported by government contracts which is renowned in the so-called "think tank" field. The IDA was formed in 1956 by five universities to make available to the Government academic evaluations of national defense projects. From its headquarters on the campus of Princeton University, IDA pours forth a mass of information compiled by communications mathematicians who are permitted to work on any basic research project that interests them. Much of this information goes directly to the military intelligence branches, which still maintain their own separate cryptological agencies.

All this may seem staggeringly grandiose, and perhaps it is, but NSA defends itself by pointing to the size of modern American Government communications. Within the world-wide strategic network called the Defense Communications Systems, for example, the military transmits more than 300,-000 messages every day of the year over channels that add up to more than 10,000,000 miles. Because the network is operated by members of the armed forces, the cost of operating is "held" to about one and one-quarter million dollars a year, but the network's equipment is now appraised at 2.8 billion dollars and new, more sophisticated and more expensive electronic hardware is added every year.

This system, of course, serves all Government departments and agencies, whether for purposes of espionage or more casual communications. In turn it is served by the cryptological deep thinkers of NSA. To handle this work load, as well as transact its espionage business, NSA employs sixteen thousand persons. Most of them are at its Fort Meade headquarters, but others are scattered around the world with its intercept net and other communications surveillance units. In an agency which is a monument to the machine, human bodies are just as essential as they are in a baseball game.

NSA both hires experts and trains its own. For the most part, its personnel flows in from a nationwide recruiting campaign in the country's colleges although it pirates as many geniuses as possible from private industry. Applicants need not have majored in the fields in which they will work; the agency prefers to put its younger employees through the mill of the Office of Training Services. It recognizes no substitutes for its own courses in cryptology and cryptanalysis. Language majors are always required to become proficient in still a third tongue.

Besides a Professional Qualification Test, applicants must submit to a rigorous security check. No person with close relatives living in a Communist country can get a job with NSA. An applicant is investigated by several agencies, including the FBI, with particular attention paid to any information which might bear on his loyalty. His birth, education and employment records are verified, his credit rating checked, his reputation with friends, neighbors, former co-workers and employers inquired into. He must pass a lie detector test, and if he gets the job must do so periodically during the period of his employment. Follow-up checks are made every four years.

Conditional employees are denied access to sensitive material until they are fully cleared. Only the director, General Carter, may grant interim clearances. Supervisors must notify the personnel and security offices within two hours of any employee's unauthorized absence from work A board of psychiatric consultants works constantly to tighten the agency's psychological assessment program. Special permission is required for an employee to enter an area in which he does not work, and he is barred even from his own area unless he is wearing his own special colored badge. Restricted areas are patrolled by armed guards. Other guards patrol twenty-four hours a day those offices where the most secret documents are stored in special safes, and employees are required to travel in pairs when taking secret papers from NSA to other agencies. Papers may never be taken home; they must be locked up either at NSA or at another approved agency.

At the State Department, the Pentagon and the United States mission to the United Nations in New York, cryptologic material is kept in code rooms protected by solid steel doors three and a half inches thick. The rooms have their own pantries and toilets, to reduce unnecessary coming and going, and guards are stationed outside. Ceiling domes sound an ultrasonic ray warning if there is any movement in the rooms after hours.

NSA headquarters itself is protected by three fences encircling the complex. Two of the fences, the inner and outer rings, are Cyclone fences with a topping of barbed wire. The other is of five-stranded electrified wire. Throughout the complex, numerous checkpoints keep visitors under tight control and employees out of unauthorized areas. Unclassified letters to private citizens are protected by an imprint on the inside of the envelopes that makes it impossible to read the letter through the envelope. Personal letters to employees addressed to them at the agency are opened and read.

The point can be made that NSA employees are denied the guarantees of the Bill of Rights. Under the 1964 law, the NSA director is empowered to discharge any employee if he considers it "in the interest of the United States," without giving the employee an opportunity to defend himself. It is a bad law which puts every NSA employee at the mercy of any personal enemy capable of writing a smear letter to his employer.

In 1919, an economy-minded Administration grumbled over allotting a budget of $100,000 to new permanent code and cipher organization set up by Herbert O. Yardley, "the father of American cryptology." In the fiscal year 1969, the classified National Security Agency's budget was estimated by experts at upwards of 2 billion dollars. This includes the cost of launching satellites to spy on the communications of other nations, but excludes the appropriations for the intelligence branches of the service agencies. It amounts roughly to seventeen dollars a year for every family in America.

Whether NSA's cryptologic achievements are worth this kind of money to the taxpayer pretty much depends on whose opinion is sought. When General Carter moved from his post as deputy director of CIA to the directorship of NSA, he remarked that "I've seen some beauts, but this beats them all."

Main Street, however, could be excused for nursing some doubts had it been privy to a conversation between then Soviet Premier Nikita Khrushchev and the American Ambassador to the United Nations, Henry Cabot Lodge, during Mr. K's 1959 visit to the United States. Khrushchev boasted that he had seen a coded message President Eisenhower had dispatched to Prime Minister Nehru of India concerning border trouble with Communist China, and a message to Eisenhower from the Shah of Iran. Since Khrushchev was able to quote from the texts of the messages, it seemed obvious that at that stage of its development NSA had not succeeded in making all its codes unbreakable.

6

The Czech Crisis

Gottfried was a long way from the scholarly cryptologists and the electronic servants of the National Security Agency at Fort Meade, Maryland, U.S.A., as, hunched over on knees and elbows in the dripping German forest, he beamed his flashlight briefly on the penciled map. Gottfried was an American Army sergeant who had been detached to the Defense Intelligence Agency because he had learned German as a child in his native Leipzig. He was engaged in the primeval contest of man against man. It is doubtful if he had even a casual knowledge of the machines of intelligence or of the scholars who used them. Although only twenty-two, Gottfried was of the Old Breed—the human spy.

His mission was routine, as was the discomfort of the black and rain-splashed night among the trees only a few miles northwest of the finger of land where East Germany, Poland and Czechoslovakia meet. Two years before, he had come to the town of Radeberg as a farm worker with forged papers. Many times since then he had gone into the border area to see what he could see, hear what he could hear, and to check the drop used by the Polish border guard who supplemented his soldierly earnings by keeping his own eyes and ears open for American intelligence.

Gottfried's swift glance at the map told him he was within five hundred yards of the drop. He had been there many times, and by now he felt he could have located in his sleep the flat stone in the bed of the meager, two-foot-wide brook. It was in the middle of the trickling, gutter-like stream, just where the water poked a wet finger into a cranny left in the bank by some unknown eccentricity of the flow.

But Gottfried did not know by whose hand the material he picked up was placed in the drop, nor was the Polish border guard acquainted with Gottfried. As a matter of fact, the Pole for the most part filled the role of courier for a third agent, a former soldier in the Wehrmacht of Adolf Hitler's Third Reich who had been captured in Poland and who had stayed on as a machinist in Wroclaw, once known by the German name of Breslau. And in turn, the machinist was a courier for the DIA agent in Poznan who obtained the microfilm copies of Communist Poland's secrets.

On this night in May, 1968, Gottfried had neither seen nor heard anything of significance. Indeed, it was too dark to see more than a few feet in any direction, and thus he had no idea of whether there was any unusual activity in the border area. There was no sound of aircraft engines, nor the rumble of military vehicles along the narrow roads on any side of the squared-U-shaped border. The hour allotted him for reconnaissance had elapsed; it was time to check the drop.

Gottfried stowed his flashlight in the pocket of his shabby Peoples Cooperative jacket and cautiously moved forward between the trees. His feet were soaking wet in their thin, perforated Peoples Cooperative "summer shoes," and he thought wistfully of the heavy waterproof American military shoes he used to take for granted when he was on garrison duty in Frankfurt. Gottfried liked his present job; he enjoyed its sometimes spine-chilling excitement, and the extra pay was of a munificence heretofore beyond his wildest dreams. But he hated the shoddy clothing he was forced to wear even more than he hated the dawn-to-dusk drudgery in the fields of the collective farm outside of Radeberg. He suffered from almost constant constipation, too, because the filthy communal latrine inhibited his bowels.

Nevertheless, he admitted to himself that his lot was a better one than that of the other farm workers. No one had ever told him so, but it was obvious the farm director was working for the Americans, too, for he had assigned Gottfried to the regular duty of running various necessary, and unnecessary, errands to villages in the border area in the farm's decrepit Volkswagen pickup truck. Gottfried himself had invented a girl friend in one of the villages to explain his nighttime lingerings, but the director had never questioned his tardiness in returning to the farm.

Now he stepped forward in a half-crouch. He could scarcely hear the sound his footsteps made in the dead leaves and twigs above the steady hissing of the rain. Then suddenly, he heard louder footsteps, and it took him a second or two to realize that the reason they were louder was that they were made by more than two feet, somewhere just ahead.

Gottfried slipped as noiselessly as possible to the ground, his body pressed hard against the trunk of a tree. He heard brusque, guttural voices speaking German. Obviously East German border guards. He risked a split-second peek around the trunk of the tree and made out three figures standing in a semicircle in a little clearing less than fifteen feet away. In the gloom, all he could pick out was the peaks on the uniform caps, but that was enough. They were border guards, all right. But why three? Glued to the tree trunk, Gottfried fought off a trembling that started in his legs and threatened to spread throughout his body. He clamped his mouth shut to lock his chattering teeth together. Why three?

He felt in his pocket for the cyanide pill. It was his decision and his alone. They had made that clear. He could take it— or take his chances with his interrogators. There was still time —a little time—to think about it, to postpone a decision.

This was unusual activity, too unusual. Something must have happened. There must have been an alert, an alarm, Gottfried told himself. They must be looking for somebody, that was the only explanation for three of them working together.

He could hear their voices, but he couldn't catch their words, except for one phrase of growled complaint about the rain. They stood there as if waiting for someone. Then Gottfried heard the crunching of footsteps nearer and something cold clutched at his insides, as he froze against the tree. One of the men apparently was walking about, aimlessly kicking at stumps and clumps of underbrush. Gottfried felt and heard the man's boot against the tree to which he was fastened and found himself closing his eyes. With a silent curse, he opened them again. The man's footsteps receded just as Gottfried was set to spring up and make a wild run for it. He could hear the man rejoining his comrades, and a short, low, burst of laughter.

Now there was the sound of footsteps again, but off to the right, and Gottfried dared another look. A fourth man emerged from the trees into the clearing. Apparently he was an officer or at least a sergeant, because he barked an order at the other men. There was some conversation, dominated by the new arrival, and the the four men stepped off into the trees on Gottfried's left. He could hear their receding footsteps, and then nothing.

They had gone in a northeasterly direction. The drop was off to Gottfried's right, almost directly southwest. Since the officer, or sergeant, had come from the southwest, the way should be clear to the brook and the drop. Apparently, the guards already had covered that area, and almost certainly they would not retrace their steps. At least not in the next five or ten minutes. Gottfried estimated he could still make it to the drop and away again before there was any more "unusual activity." The thought pleased and excited him. He never felt nervous when he was moving, when he was doing something.

Still pressed against the tree, he counted to sixty, slowly. Then he straightened up and started for the brook, putting one foot before the other cautiously but with a measured cadence. There wasn't much time; perhaps less than he had estimated; he had to take the chance of making a little noise.

Yet, hours seemed to pass before he reached the bank of the miserable little rivulet, and more hours before he located the cranny, the crevice, which was his landmark. Stepping into the gurgling water, Gottfried lifted the stone and plucked two spools of microfilm from the bed. Swiftly, he dropped the spools in his jacket pocket, then replaced the stone exactly as it had lain, his fingers searching out its outlines in the bed.

An hour and thirty-five minutes later, Gottfried slipped into bed in the men's quarters of the communal farm in Radeberg. It had taken him forty-five minutes of that time to reach the Volkswagen, hidden in the barn of a farmer on a rutty cow path only three miles from the brook. He had waited another ten minutes in the farmer's cellar for the man in the dark, food-spotted business suit to whom he had turned over the rolls of microfilm. The rolls of microfilm and his semimonthly letter to his parents in Toledo, Ohio,* which would be mailed from Frankfurt.

The two rolls of microfilm Gottfried plucked from the drop

---

* Gottfried is a pseudonym. He worked on a collective farm, but not in Radeberg, and his parents lived more than one thousand miles from Toledo.

under the flat stone in the woodsy brook contained one of the most spectacular pieces of information ever picked up by any intelligence agency of any country during the Cold War. There, in amazing detail, was the Soviet Union's plan to invade and occupy Czechoslovakia in mid-July in order to "turn back the clock" on the liberal reform movement of Alexander Dubcek, leader of the Czechoslovakian Communist Party.

By still another courier, the rolls of film were delivered the next evening to the "personal representative" of Lieutenant General Joseph F. Carroll, director of the DIA, in the Börsenstuben Restaurant on the tree-lined Hardenbergstrasse in downtown West Berlin. The courier, actually a top aide to General Gerhard Wessel, head of the West German Intelligence Service, had been briefed on the film's contents by General Wessel himself, to whose Bonn headquarters they had been dispatched by the man in the food-spotted black suit.

As they sat in the Börsenstuben, a converted mansion where meals are served in a series of small sitting rooms with overstuffed velvet and velour chairs, Wessel's aide attempted in turn to brief General Carroll's "representative." Carroll's man was horrified. They would "talk business," he told his companion, the next morning at American military headquarters. Hadn't German intelligence ever heard about security?

A few days later, there was a top-level meeting at the American Embassy in Bonn attended by General Wessel of West German Intelligence, Carroll's man and United States Ambassador to West Germany Henry Cabot Lodge. At that session, the information in the microfilm was dissected and discussed. It was most explicit:

The invasion was to be made by Soviet and East German troops after maneuvers along the Czech border. Its aim was to restore to power the conservative wing of the Czech Communist Party, which had ruled the country until the ouster in January of that same year of President Antonin Novotny. Apparently, there was no thought of reinstating Novotny; the film spoke instead of installing a man close to Novotny's views as a successor to Dubcek. Between fifteen and twenty thousand troops were to be involved in the initial stages of the invasion.

A high-level Czech diplomat also figured in the plans. He

was the Czech Ambassador to Moscow, Vladimir Koucky, a hard-line, pro-Soviet holdover from the Novotny regime. Official Soviet documents reproduced on the microfilm noted that Koucky had informed a General Yebichev, described as "senior political commissar" of the Red Army, that Dubcek was determined to move ahead with his liberalization program, that he had "sold out" to "agents of American imperialism," and was prepared to proceed on an anti-Soviet course even if it meant the eventual rupture of relations with Moscow.

Koucky, as both American and West German intelligence had learned earlier, was to be recalled by Prague and shunted to an unimportant post in the Foreign Office. This circumstance might have suggested to the Russians that he had a rather important axe to grind and therefore was not to be absolutely trusted, but it did not.

Although Premier Aleksei Kosygin was hesitant to move against the Czechs, the Red Army ran a power play. General Yebichev sought and was granted a meeting with Soviet Defense Minister Marshal Ivan Grechko, and later the two military men consulted with the Soviet party chief, Leonid I. Brezhnev. The result was that the invasion plan was adopted as a "last resort" to eliminate the "stinking head of the rotten Czechoslovak fish"—Dubcek.

Two devices were adopted to give the invasion an air of legitimacy. The Soviet and East German press were to report the discovery of a large cache of Western arms in western Bohemia and describe the cache as weapons and materiel for the use of anti-Communist guerrilla forces. And just before the invasion troops crossed the Czech border, Novotny—"or someone of equal importance"—was to ask for Soviet intervention "to save the Socialist state of Czechoslovakia."

General Carroll's "representative" had waited impatiently for the discussion of the intelligence at hand to run its course. As soon as he could, he offered a plan of action he said would force the Russians to cancel the invasion.

It was a plan, he admitted, that went contrary to all intelligence doctrine. It involved "leaking" the information that had been obtained to the world press, a course which could have led the Soviets to the Allied sources of information. Carroll's man said this course had the approval of General Carroll, who had agreed it was a chance the Allies profitably could take. By such an early "leak," he argued, the West could mobilize world opinion to such an extent that the Russians would be forced to draw back at the last minute.

General Wessel agreed. This was somewhat surprising, since Wessel had a reputation as an intelligence conservative who believed intelligence should not be squandered on tactical situations but "put in the bank" for strategic use. This was a special case, the general said; any move by the Soviet Union in Czechoslovakia could set off World War III, and thus every means should be used to frustrate it.

But Ambassador Lodge had orders from Washington, and he turned thumbs down on the proposal. The war in Vietnam, said Lodge, had so complicated the international situation that the United States could not afford to engage in a brinksmanship contest with the Soviet Union. Should such information be leaked, he said, the United States would be forced to issue a strong statement, warning Russia to desist. Washington just did not want to get into such a situation at this time, Lodge said.

Wessel was furious. He pointed out that the intelligence had come from one of the United States' own espionage agents, and that the microfilm of the official Soviet documents met every test of authenticity. He noted also that his own German intelligence had collected bits and pieces of information supporting the microfilm information, and that American spy satellites had intercepted radio messages indicating that the Soviets planned to take a hard-line position against the Czechs.

Lodge's response was cool. He acknowledged that "by some accident," the intelligence had gone to Wessel instead of directly to the DIA. He knew that Wessel had intercepted it, and Wessel knew Lodge knew.

Wessel replied stiffly that he had had no intention of receiving information meant for the Americans. It had come to him by error, he explained. But that was irrelevant, he added. The point was that intelligence, hard intelligence, on the Soviet plans existed.

The general was right, Lodge replied. He was not denying that there was intelligence or saying that it was open to question. He was saying instead that the United States was not prepared to risk an armed confrontation with the Soviet Union over an internal matter within the Soviet bloc. It was prepared to pass the intelligence on to the Czech government and to do anything else, in utmost privacy, that could be done to persuade the Soviets to stay their hand.

And there it stood. The last word was Washington's, and Washington had given it. Wessel knew that his own government would not think of bucking the President of the United States and thereby endangering its special relationship with the U.S. Besides, without the United States, the West German government was helpless.

Helpless, perhaps, but not entirely without a kind of devious initiative. West German Chancellor Kurt George Kiesinger dutifully passed along to his top aides the Washington orders to play down the warning of Soviet intentions, but on May 24, the official West German spokesman, Guenther Diehl, let the cat out of the bag. No one knows whether Diehl got a secret go-ahead from on high, or encouragement from General Wessel, but he went ahead anyway.

Diehl told a press conference: "The Bonn Cabinet has received reliable reports that ten thousand to twelve thousand non-Czech troops of Warsaw Pact countries will shortly enter and be stationed inside Czechoslovakia."

Bonn denied this statement even before the first furious American protests began coming in. Diehl was reprimanded for "irresponsible and panic-creating talk." Perhaps someone had hoped the statement would set world opinion aflame, despite the reprimand to Diehl, but it curiously had no impact despite the fact it was prominently reproduced in all major cities around the globe.

That is to say, there was no worldwide demand that the Soviets cease and desist. Indeed, the invasion plan seemed to be proceeding as scheduled in early June when Western intelligence learned that a partial mobilization of the 650,000-man reserve of the East German People's Army had been ordered, that controls had been tightened on the East German border with Czechoslovakia, and that hundreds of East German tourists had been told to come home.

Meanwhile, the strategists of the Defense Intelligence Agency took another tack. They agreed that an attempt should be made to influence the Kremlin to think again about the invasion, but by covert means.

At a Pentagon meeting chaired by Defense Secretary Clark Clifford, two approaches were discussed. One was to plant intelligence, via an American agent, with the Soviet Foreign

Office bureaucracy to the effect that France and Great Britain would join the United States in intervening if Czechoslovakia were invaded. (There was some substance to this. The three Allies had conferred on the intelligence Gottfried took from under the rock in an East German forest, and while no one favored intervention, the subject was left open.) The other approach was to stir Russian fears that Communist China might take advantage of the situation to make trouble. After some debate, the second approach was adopted.

A few days later, the scene shifted to the Thong Nhat Hotel in downtown Hanoi, where a Vietnamese and a Soviet diplomat were sharing a bottle of vodka among the rubber plants in the bar. The Vietnamese was a Soviet agent of unimpeachable credentials. His information had always proved accurate and, indeed, on at least two occasions the Russians had evidence that he had risked his safety and perhaps his life in getting information.

The two men sat there, sipping their vodka and chatting with apparent casualness for more than an hour. During that time, the Vietnamese told the Russian he expected to have some material for him the next day and they arranged a meeting in front of a rice warehouse under one of the causeway sections of the two-mile-long Long Bien Bridge over the Red River.

Both men arrived promptly at the rendezvous. The Vietnamese, who apparently had come on foot, joined the Russian in the latter's battered Volga (Russian) sedan. He immediately handed over to the Russian an envelope which the Russian opened and found to contain a sheaf of Xerox copies of documents in Chinese.

The Russian asked the Vietnamese what was the gist of the documents. They contained, he was told, details of a partial mobilization of Chinese troops along the Soviet border, across from the Soviet-Kazakh city of Alma Ata, and they had been obtained from an official Chinese source. The Chinese, the Vietnamese said, apparently were preparing for a possible series of border clashes or even a probing invasion of Soviet territory in case the Czech situation got out of hand. The Russian wanted to know what the agent meant by the Czech situation. The Vietnamese said he didn't know, but he assumed the Russian did. All he knew, the Vietnamese added, was what he read in the papers.

He was telling the Russian the truth as he was aware of it. He had obtained the material from a French businessman, whose relationships with the bureaucracy of the Red Chinese embassy were most cordial. The Frenchman had fed the Vietnamese agent information for more than two years and it had always proved satisfactory. What the Vietnamese did not know was that the Frenchman worked for the U.S. Defense Intelligence Agency, and that the Xerox copies—undated—which he had just handed over to the Russian were three years old. They came from documents in the files of the State Department's Bureau of Intelligence and Research (INR) which had been squirreled away for just such an occasion as this.

The Vietnamese also was unaware that he had been under more or less regular surveillance by various agents of Western Allied governments for more than five years. It is likely he had proved as valuable to the Allies as he had to the Russians.

American knowledge of the Russians' reaction to these documents is based mostly on informed speculation, but there was evidence of considerable apprehension within the walls of the Kremlin. It is known, too, that Soviet military patrols and intelligence teams did some poking about along the Kazakh border in the days following the meeting under the Long Bien Bridge. There was, indeed, some Red Chinese activity along the border, but this had been true on various occasions during the past ten years. The question the Soviet Politburo had to answer was whether the present activity had a particular significance in the light of the Soviet plan for a strike at Czechoslovakia.

Apparently, the Russians couldn't immediately make up their minds. On July 19, the Soviet press agency Tass put out the previously agreed-upon story that an arms cache had been uncovered in western Bohemia. The dispatch stated flatly that the cache contained arms sent to "anti-Communist guerrilla bands" by Western governments.

This was supposed to be the signal for the invasion operation to begin, although American intelligence didn't know it. But nothing happened. Prague heatedly denied the Tass charges, and insisted the cache had been planted by East Germans, and there was no rebuttal from Moscow. It was later learned that moderate elements in the Soviet leadership, led by Premier Kosygin, were demanding that the invasion be canceled, or at least postponed, because of that "suspicious" Red Chinese activity on the Kazakh border.

The moderates won out. The invasion was postponed. Plans for the invasion were not abandoned, but the date was left up in the air pending a Soviet-Czech summit meeting to thrash out the differences between the two governments. Two meetings subsequently were held, at Cierna and Bratislava during the last days of July and first days of August, after which it was announced that the air had been cleared. At the meetings, Dubcek was reported to have made certain concessions which caused the Soviets to stay their hand.

Curiously, Walter Ulbricht, the East German Communist party chief, now made a switch. He had been one of the most vociferous of the hawks, arguing that an occupation of Czechoslovakia was necessary both to stem the liberal tide in that country and to force the Czech regime to reconsider its friendly approach to West Germany. Above all, Ulbricht wanted protection from West German troops. But East German sources reported that Ulbricht suddenly joined the moderates in arguing that an invasion was too perilous at that time. Ulbricht, it was said, was hopeful of making a deal with the Dubcek government in exchange for economic concessions by East Germany that would dull Dubcek's eagerness to do business with the Bonn regime.

At any rate, the meetings at Cierna and Bratislava proceeded, and every intelligence source reported that Ulbricht had got much of what he wanted. Notably, this included a pledge by both Czechoslovakia and the Soviet Union to protect East Germany and its upholding of the anti-West German line. A kind of "peace in our time" apparently had been achieved.

But ten days after the Cierna-Bratislava sessions, Ulbricht went to Prague for consultations and was handed what U.S. agents described as a setback. That is to say, he failed in the main reason for his visit: to persuade the Czech reformists to accept his conditions for establishing diplomatic ties with Bonn. Publicly, Ulbricht announced he had adopted a policy of "conciliation" with Prague; privately, he angrily informed Moscow that Dubcek was reneging on the Cierna-Bratislava agreements.

There were other, more ominous signs. A Central Intelligence Agency memo, prepared from material provided by agents of the CIA, the DIA and State's INR, informed President Johnson that despite postponement of the invasion, the buildup was continuing and, indeed, had been expanded. Polish troops now had joined the Soviet-East German mobilization. Intelligence sources in Yugoslavia reported that President Tito had told other Yugoslav leaders there were indications the Russians might invade that country. Moreover, the intelligence memo declared that the mobilization had now progressed to the point where it was "adequate" for the Czech invasion. Excerpts from a report of a Soviet Central Committee meeting indicated the troop exercises were designed as a rehearsal for military intervention.

At about this time, too, the DIA was offered another contribution by the American Army sergeant turned spy, Gottfried. It was his last.

Gottfried made one of his periodic checks of the drop under the flat stone and picked up a roll of microfilm. He had no difficulty getting to the drop, nor in returning through the forest to the barn where his Volkswagen pickup had been hidden. But on the drive back to Radeberg, the little truck was sideswiped by an aged but highly polished Mercedes Benz sedan. Gottfried was uninjured, and so were the three occupants of the Mercedes. Unfortunately, however, two of the Mercedes occupants were high East German party officials en route from Leipzig to a reception at one of those country homes scattered about East Germany which are used for official merrymaking. Although the accident was the fault of the officials' chauffeur, Gottfried, as an obscure farm worker, naturally got the blame.

He was placed under arrest and taken to the jail at Radeberg, where he was thrown into a cell. He had been forced to surrender his identity papers, but he was not searched, the police obviously deciding that such a faceless individual was not worth the effort. This was sheer luck, since Gottfried still had the microfilm in his jacket pocket. His contact, the man in the gravy-spotted black suit, had failed to appear at their rendezvous, and Gottfried had been en route to another, secondary location to deposit the microfilm at an emergency drop.

Two hours later, by means not disclosed, Gottfried had broken out of the jail and was being shuffled by various agents through an underground route to West Germany. The microfilm, duly delivered to the DIA at Frankfurt, revealed among other things that detailed maps of Czechoslovakia had been issued, down to the battalion level, to the Russian, Polish and East German invasion troops.

In Washington, this accumulation of intelligence reportedly set off a bitter debate among U.S. spy chiefs. CIA Director Richard Helms, whose agency had prepared the most recent intelligence memo, nevertheless was unwilling to agree that all signs pointed to the invasion being on again. As the story goes, he noted that Soviet leaders expressed themselves privately to friendly neutrals and to Bulgarian and Rumanian diplomats as being delighted with the commitments made at Cierna and Bratislava. Helms also pointed out that Communist China had launched an attack on Russia for its attempts to manipulate the Czech regime by force, and that there were new—and this time authentic—reports of Chinese troop movements on the Soviet border.

General Carroll of the DIA and FBI Chief J. Edgar Hoover argued vigorously that an invasion was imminent, that the evidence was there for anyone to see. At one point, Hoover reportedly declared he had "certain information" which backed up the DIA position. According to various sources, Helms didn't even ask what the information was, but asked Hoover coldly how he obtained such information, since the FBI's espionage duties are limited to within the borders of the United States. What answer Hoover offered is not known, but it is a fact that FBI agents also are stationed in various cities abroad and besides performing their assigned roles as coordinators with foreign law enforcement agencies often do a little extracurricular spying on the side.

Predictably, the earlier policy decision prevailed in the end. The United States had too much on its hands with the war in Vietnam to risk a showdown with the Soviet Union on an "internal Communist matter." The "play-down" remained in effect.

Troops from the Soviet Union, Poland and East Germany invaded Czechoslovakia a few days later—on August 21, 1968. It was learned later that Soviet intelligence reports convinced the Kremlin leadership that it had been led down the garden path by the reports planted with its Hanoi agent by U.S. intelligence. With the risk of a confrontation with Red China thus apparently dispelled, the Russians decided it was safe to let Alexander Dubcek know in the most brutal terms that he could not get away with hedging on the concessions forced on him at Cierna and Bratislava.

7

Rendezvous in Copenhagen

In the Czech crisis, American military intelligence was amazingly well informed about what was going to happen, but it suited American foreign policy—and the national security interest—to take no overt, military action against the Russian invasion. In the Greek crisis of 1967, Washington tried to act on excellent intelligence, but was frustrated by the clock and by the temperament of a young monarch.

Shortly after King Constantine of Greece visited Washington and President Johnson in September, 1967, a National Security Agency listening post somewhere in Europe intercepted a radio message from Colonel George Papadopoulos, leader of the ruling Greek military junta, to one of his commanders in the field. NSA cryptanalysts, who had cracked the Greek army's code a month earlier, routinely dispatched copies of its text, in English, to the State Department's Bureau of Intelligence and Research and the Central Intelligence Agency.

The message said that Papadopoulos' agents had picked up reports that King Constantine was contemplating a move to overthrow the junta, with the help of "certain monarchist officers of the armed forces," and warned the commander to be on the alert.

This was startling news to both the CIA and Foggy Bottom. During the king's conversations with President Johnson he had seemed cool to Johnson's suggestion that he use his royal influence to try to persuade the junta to soften its police-state methods which had resulted in the detention of six thousand political prisoners. Johnson also had made it plain to the king that the United States favored all possible pressure on the junta to restore constitutional rule. But Constantine seemed sunk in depression; he indicated the junta was so firmly established in power that there was little he could do.

Now efforts were made to determine if there was any substance to Papadopoulos' message. Ambassador Phillips Talbot arranged an audience with the king, and various American "contacts" in Greece were ordered to dredge up every piece of information. Constantine told Talbot the report was false, that he was powerless. Other informants could find out nothing.

Talbot did get from Constantine a promise that if he should decide to act he would keep the United States informed of his plans. Had Constantine kept his promise, he might have been spared his flight into Roman exile. But when he made his move he caught Talbot by surprise, and thus when the NSA code-readers cracked another message—this one from Copenhagen to junta headquarters in Athens—the ambassador couldn't find Constantine to warn him that his planned coup didn't have a chance.

Although reports of a royal plot had reached Washington from various sources for several weeks prior to the king's abortive attempt to seize power on December 13, there was little reason to attach much credence to them. Constantine had been informed of Papadopoulos' message to the field commander revealing the colonel's acquaintance with rumors of a coup. And, of course, the king had steadfastly denied he had any such plans. Besides, Constantine's background and preoccupations and his earlier futile attempts to influence the junta hardly stamped him as a strong-man type.

In December, 1967, Constantine was twenty-seven years old, boyishly handsome and with a certain jet set style that helped earn him a reputation as a playboy monarch. He devoted most of his time to graceful yachts, purebred horses and fast cars, and so far as the business of reigning was concerned he seemed much under the influence of his mother, Queen Frederika, who had become notorious as a palace intriguer. He had a beautiful wife, Queen Anne-Marie, daughter of the king and queen of Denmark, and an infant son, Prince Paul. One irreverent State Department memo had described him as a young man "with the approximate intelligence of a society band leader."

Since the colonels' coup of April, 1967, there had been some in the State Department who had advocated United States support of Constantine as a lever to topple the junta. Similar pressure had come from Greek politicians. Thus, when Constantine visited Washington in September, both President Johnson and various influential members of Congress were favorably inclined toward the youthful monarch. But in his talks with Johnson and in his appearance on Capitol Hill, Constantine dissipated this feeling. Everybody liked him, but wrote him off as a lightweight who could not understand either the political complexities of his country or the responsibility of a monarch to exert influence on public opinion in favor of the democratic processes. Johnson in particular couldn't understand a king who seemed unwilling to exert himself for his subjects.

Perhaps at that point Constantine was haunted by the harsh fortune that had dogged Greece's monarchy during its 134-year history, and was determined merely to survive. Of Greece's kings, only two had not been exiled or removed from the throne by more violent means, and Constantine's father and one of his uncles had been driven twice into exile. Perhaps Constantine felt a stranger in the land over which he reigned. Greece had never had a Greek king. Its first monarch, when the country won its independence from Turkey after four centuries of subjugation, was the Bavarian prince Otto in 1833. Since then all Greece's kings had been members of the Glucksburg branch of the Danish royal family.

At any rate, State's Intelligence and Research Bureau emphasized in "alternative" memos as early as the summer of 1967 that there was no widespread support among the plain Greek citizens for their young king that could be translated into an uprising behind him against the ruling junta. Constantine, said the INR memos, was tolerated rather than loved or even respected; the Greek people took it for granted that he would spend a lot of money on needless luxuries, because their kings always had. Besides, intelligence reports indicated that the repressive measures of the junta regime, after the first fearful weeks, had reduced the people to a state of apathy. There seemed little likelihood that any large numbers of Greeks would be willing to risk their necks by supporting a monarchist putsch, and the INR memos carefully pointed out that there had been no public pledges to the king from any key military leaders.

To be sure, reports from American military sources in Greece indicated that some military units would be loyal to Constantine in the event of a confrontation with the junta. The units were listed as the 28th Tactical Air Force, the commander and chief of staff of the Third Army Corps and the commander of Greece's lone armored division. This intelligence sounded impressive, but INR memos to Secretary Dean Rusk pointed out that it was based solely on rumors, that there was no hard evidence such as private statements of support for the king.

Constantine had assumed the throne at an auspicious time for a Greek king, since his father, King Paul, had died in March, 1964, without spending a day in exile as a monarch. The Greek people had accepted Paul in a cool and casual way; there was little anti-royalist feeling. But there was some resentment coupled with sly ridicule when the young Danish monarch called himself Constantine XIII, as representing the latest in the line extending from the emperors of Constantinople, who had no blood ties with Western Europe.

At any rate, Constantine seemed to get along well with his premier, the center-left leader, George Papandreou, until a dispute over a move to purge the army caused Papandreou's resignation in July, 1965. INR memos told of Constantine's "bewilderment" during the political crisis which lasted almost two years before the military coup of April, 1967. The king, said the INR, seemed uncertain of his role.

Then, suddenly, Constantine seemed to change. State's intelligence reports noted that his palace guard, including the highly capable Lieutenant Colonel Michael Arnaoutis—later exiled as military attaché to the London embassy—were saying that the king was determined to "fight the junta to the end." There were other reports of a monarchist plot to discredit Colonel Papadopoulos by exposing his involvement in a financial scandal. How much of this was wishful thinking by royal household hangers-on was not known, but for a few months at least Constantine acted like a king who was determined to take a hand in the ruling of his country.

Shortly after Constantine legitimized the junta, INR memos were reporting he was prepared to take the position as having done so merely to spare Greece a bloody civil war. Shortly, the king issued a statement saying just that. INR reports subsequently reported Constantine would attempt to exert a moderating influence on the junta and to bring pressure on it for a return to constitutional government.

Constantine did make the try, but earlier appraisals of his personal weakness were borne out by his failure to make a dent in either the junta or in public opinion. He was unable or unwilling to lift a hand as the ruling colonels purged his sympathizers in the armed forces and arrested six thousand leftists branded by the junta as Communists, although many of them had been members of the center-left coalition under Papandreou. He did nothing when the junta banned Greece's major left-wing party, dissolved various youth movements within all parties, clamped down on free speech and imposed heavy censorship on the press.

His only victory was a small one, an INR memo reported. He refused to swear in the junta until it accepted Constantine V. Kollias, a civilian, as the figurehead premier. The INR noted dryly that Kollias could hardly serve as an operational constitutional premier in a nation that was under virtual martial law.

This was the situation in the late fall of 1967 when intelligence reports reached the State Department of Constantine's purported plans to attempt a counter-coup. Although his background and record agitated against the credibility of these reports, INR Director Thomas L. Hughes dutifully prepared a series of memos which presented reasons why a monarchist coup could be regarded as logical.

These memos noted that the junta had lost face when it was forced to accept Turkish demands for the withdrawal of Greek troops from the island of Cyprus as part of the settlement of that crisis worked out by Cyrus Vance, special envoy from President Johnson. The junta was unpopular in the rest of the world—not a single nation had recognized its legitimacy—and Constantine might be able to force reforms on the colonels in exchange for respectability. There had been stirrings in Greece among both the military and the people as a result of the blast at the junta "putschists" by former Greek Premier Constantine Karamanlis in Parisian exile. It was possible the king had found some stiffening for his spine from a perusal of the draft of the new constitution, which he was said to have found "impossible."

But on the whole, advice from the State Department's intelligence people was pessimistic. Or, as Hughes remarked at a high-level White House conference, Constantine seemed to lack the "muscle" to overthrow or even to force concessions from the junta.

Nevertheless, it was clear in Washington that Constantine was persisting in miscalculating his strength. Reports of an impending attempt at a coup continued to flow across State Department desks. Even those in intelligence who accepted them at face value, however, concluded that any move by the king would end in disaster.

It was now Tuesday, December 12. In its gray early-morning hours an agent of the Greek junta rendezvoused with a Danish contact in a quiet side street of Copenhagen. As prearranged, the Dane passed on to the Greek spy certain confidential information he said he had obtained from Danish government sources. Shortly before noon that same day, the Greek transmitted in code by commercial wireless the gist of this information, including a long list of Greek names, to junta headquarters in Athens.

A National Security Agency listening post, probably in Turkey, intercepted the message and dispatched it forthwith to NSA headquarters in Fort Meade, Maryland, where it was turned over to one of the cryptanalysis sections which dealt with Middle Eastern codes. The code used by the Greek agent was a variant of the Greek Army code the agency had solved several months before, and it took longer than usual to read it. It was late that night when the cryptanalysts finished decoding the message and dispatched English copies to the CIA and the INR.

The message contained two vital pieces of information:

1. A plot by King Constantine to overthrow the junta was "imminent."

2. The names of certain monarchist military commanders whom Constantine had lined up to support his move.

It was early in the morning of December 13 when CIA and State Department officials finished dissecting and evaluating the message and the decision was made to dispatch a warning to Constantine. A verbatim copy of the message was transmitted in code to Ambassador Talbot in Athens. But by that time, night had fallen in Greece and it took more time than usual to decode the message. It didn't matter. By that time, Constantine had cast the die.

Without informing Talbot, as he had promised to do, Constantine had flown off that morning to Larissa, 140 miles northwest of Athens, where he proclaimed his counter-coup from a weak and rarely used radio station. He appealed to the armed forces to turn against the "totalitarian regime" of the junta, and asked the Greek people "to assist me in reestablishing in this country the moral values which were born in this land and from which all civilized people take their moral, social, economic and cultural development."

Meanwhile, Colonel Papadopoulos took full advantage of his knowledge of the king's plans. Between 4 A.M. and 7 A.M. on December 13, he placed under arrest every one of the monarchists on the list received from Copenhagen—and he did so in total secrecy, a tribute to the brutal efficiency of the police state.

Constantine was left with no military support. The junta went over the heads of the commanders of the Third Army Corps and the armored division who reportedly had pledged loyalty to the king. The 28th Tactical Air Force made no attempt to follow Constantine's orders. Constantine flew off to exile in Rome with his queen and his infant son.

Given the impossible circumstances, Constantine's move probably was doomed to failure anyway. No blame could be attached to American intelligence; it collected plenty of information and reported and evaluated it promptly. (A month after the abortive coup, United States agents abroad identified the Greek spy and the Danish contact and even located their meeting place in Copenhagen.) But aside from Constantine's inadequacies, the monarchist plot was the victim of a leak from high Danish government sources. Constantine obviously had informed his wife's parents, the king and queen of Denmark, of his plans. Somewhere along the government line some official who had been made privy to this information blabbed it—probably unwittingly—to someone who did odd jobs of espionage for the junta. It was a classic example of the breakdown of one of intelligence's cardinal rules—that information of this sort should be limited exclusively to those with a "need to know." It proved again, as Allen Dulles was fond of deposing, that the greatest danger to the protection of secrecy lies in "letting one person too many know something he shouldn't."

What the State Department called the "Constantine Crisis" also raised again the question in some Capitol Hill circles of whether the United States should eavesdrop on the communications of nations with which we are not at war. In the context of the world situation since 1945, intelligence leaders tended to couch their replies in terms of a national necessity. The United States, they said, must try to learn what other nations are saying to each other because the United States has so many vital interests in so many parts of the world. Besides, they added, everybody else is doing it—notably the Soviet Union and France, whose electronic snooping devices probably are just as sophisticated as ours.

This was the pragmatic rationale behind the United States' successful "meddling" in the Cyprus crisis of November, 1967, which, as has been seen, was one of the contributing factors to Constantine's decision to challenge the junta. For better or for worse, U.S. welfare and security is affected by any unrest in the Middle East, especially when it concerns two of its allies, such as Turkey and Greece. Indeed, INR "production" for the June-July period of 1967 reflected the high degree of interest in that neighborhood. The State Department's intelligence unit issued fifty-nine Intelligence Notes and seventeen Research Memos on the Middle East during June and July, compared with only five Intelligence Notes and no Research Memos on South Vietnam and eleven Intelligence Notes and two Research Memos on North Vietnam. Yet we were at war in Vietnam, while managing to keep out of the Israeli-Arab conflict.

In the "Constantine Crisis," it was in the interest of the United States to encourage any move toward a restoration of constitutional government in Greece, since Greece is one of our NATO partners. In the Cyprus crisis, two NATO partners were involved—Greece and Turkey. They constituted the eastern end of the American-built defense organization, which was already under heavy strain as a result of France's withdrawal from its military force. This is not necessarily to say that the United States should be so involved in so many places around the globe, but only to point out that such involvement is one of the bases of American foreign policy.

At any rate, when the Cyprus crisis erupted over a Cypriot

government attack on two Turkish Cypriot villages in reprisal for the firing on two policemen, war between Greece and Turkey was near enough to cause considerable anguish in Washington. Turkish jets roared over Cyprus and Greek forces on the island were put on alert to protect the 80 per-cent-Greek population. In this situation, the INR was forced to tackle the unhappy task of telling Lyndon Johnson he had been wrong.

Stepping into a previous Cyprus crisis in 1964, Johnson had warned the Turkish government that it might have to go it alone against a Soviet threat if it opened hostilities with Greece. The warning became a political issue, stirred up anti-American sentiment in Turkey and caused the Turkish gov-ernment to look more kindly on Soviet efforts to drive a wedge between Turkish-U.S. relations.

In its Intelligence Notes, the INR noted the danger that the United States and Russia would be trapped into a physical confrontation over the Cyprus issue. This would be particu-larly disadvantageous to the U.S., with half a million troops tied up in Vietnam. And, in any event, even if a Greek-Turkish conflict did not involve the U.S. and Soviet Union, there would be painful strategic embarrassment for Washing-ton in the spectacle of a war between two nations which together had received more than 4.5 billion dollars in Ameri-can arms since 1946.

Fortunately, reported the INR, there would also be risks for the Soviets. With the Israeli-Arab issue unresolved, no one yet could predict the future state of the balance of power in the Mediterranean, where Soviet naval and air power re-cently had intruded. Soviet communications intercepted by American listening posts had indicated the Russians were concerned over the fate of their supply line to the Mediter-ranean, from the Black Sea through the Dardanelles strait, in the event of a Greek-Turkish war. The Russians also were nervous about the possibility of fighting so near to their bor-der with Turkey and the Turkish-Bulgarian frontier.

The Soviet Union had supplied the Greek-dominated Cy-prus government with weapons during and after the 1964 crisis. But since then Soviet policy had shifted to a denuncia-tion of the military regime in Greece. A careful reading of the intercepts revealed that the Soviets were inclined to call down a plague on both Turkish and Greek houses because of the danger their war cries posed to the Russian presence in the Mediterranean. Thus, the INR notes concluded, Russia probably would go along with a prudent and careful attempt by the United States to mediate the current crisis.

More important, an American military intelligence operative had discovered by unrevealed means—probably by discreet electronic bugging—what President-Archbishop Makarios of Cyprus would be likely to accept in the way of a peace formula. The information came from conversations between a Makarios envoy and a Turkish official in a hotel room in Athens. Briefly, Makarios' terms included withdrawal of both Greek and Turkish troops in excess of the numbers permitted by the 1960 Zurich and London agreements on independence for Cyprus, and renewed pledges by both governments to respect Cyprus's independence.

At this juncture, the Defense Intelligence Agency submitted estimates of the respective military postures of Greece and Turkey. Turkey, it pointed out, had nearly 500,000 men in her armed forces and another 500,000 trained reservists, and 450 combat aircraft. Greece had 160,000 men in uniform and another 175,000 in the reserves, and 250 combat aircraft. The DIA gave Greece an edge in naval strength, but concluded that if there were war Turkey would win.

It was in this atmosphere, a mixture of hope based on what Makarios probably would accept and fear that Turkey and Greece both felt committed to armed conflict, that President Johnson dispatched Cyrus Vance to both Ankara and Athens. Vance, a former Deputy Secretary of Defense, had helped damp down the summer rioting in Detroit, and had a well-earned reputation as a brilliant mediator. Vance carried with him a peace package patterned after the formula Makarios' envoy in Turkey had told the Turkish official the Cypriot president would accept.

Less than a week later, Vance had wrapped up a settlement which contained pretty much what Makarios wanted. Both Turkey and Greece would withdraw troops illegally stationed on Cyprus, Turkey would dismantle her invasion force and both Greece and Turkey would give new pledges to respect Cyprus's sovereignty. In addition, there was no mention of the Turkish demand that Makarios disband the Cypriot police force, a paramilitary organization consisting mainly of Greek Cypriots. Instead, it was agreed there would be a "controlled" reorganization of the force under United Nations supervision.

Vance had done yeoman, and speedy, work. It detracts nothing from his performance, however, to take note that his task was eased by advance knowledge, furnished by an American military intelligence operative, of what merchandise he would be able to sell. In this case, intelligence had successfully performed its prime function—collecting those facts necessary to the explicit guidance of policy.

More important, Cyrus Vance refused to permit any opinions held by either his superiors in Washington or himself to blunt his appreciation of the intelligence made available to him. He didn't argue with it, he acted on it. His acceptance of the product obtained by covert means was in sharp contrast to the reaction of the American military command in Vietnam, whose own ideas were so fixed it refused to give proper credence to the information provided by a lively lady and others during the several weeks preceding the tragic Communist Tet offensive of January, 1968.

8

Prophets Without Honor

In a little cafe outside the major city of Kontum, in the bicep of the bent arm which is South Vietnam, an American Army intelligence officer attached to II Corps kept a rendezvous one night in November, 1967, with a prostitute who peddled her uncertain charms among the Viet Cong forces in the nearby highlands.

From the American viewpoint, the lady was not a complete tramp. For thirty American dollars a month she fed bits and pieces of information to II Corps which over a period of almost a year had proved unusually reliable. Several times the information she provided had enabled small Allied forces to avoid ambushes, and she had correctly identified Viet Cong units in the area and their commanding officers. "Miss Nguyen," as her intelligence contacts called her, was no Elizabeth Taylor, but she obviously got around.

On this particular night, Miss Nguyen offered no information on Viet Cong activity in the area. She mentioned almost diffidently, however, that there had been an escalation in the accustomed boastfulness which was her clients' chief conversational stock in trade. "They say the war will be over next year," she told the American officer. "They say they will soon take over the cities and seize the government and Vietnam will be one nation again. They are always talking about January 30, just as if it were a holiday. January 30, January 30, they keep saying. That is the day, they say."

At II Corps headquarters, the officer typed out what Miss Nguyen had told him. It became part of the mixed bag of intelligence reports which daily flowed into the headquarters.

So far as is known, no one found her conversation particularly significant.

At just about that time, as it happened, General William Childs Westmoreland, American commander in Vietnam, and Ambassador Ellsworth Bunker were in Washington radiating optimism for the edification of Congress and the stateside press. Neither of them mentioned January 30 or Miss Nguyen.

What they told Congress and the Washington journalists, in effect, was that the United States was winning the war, that it was steadily wearing down the enemy. They noted the decrease in the rate of infiltration of troops from Hanoi from a peak of 14,000 men in June, 1966, to the current 5,000-6,000 a month. They reported that supplies to the Viet Cong by sea had been seriously interrupted. They said soldiers were defecting in increasing numbers from the Viet Cong and that as a result the Communists were forced to draft very young and middle-aged recruits. They submitted statistics which showed that the Viet Cong controlled only 2,500,000 people out of a total South Vietnam population of 17,200,000, whereas in 1965 they had controlled 4,000,000.

The only part of their testimony that might have given their listeners pause was their admission that although Hanoi had large reserves of trained troops in the North, it was not committing them to the battlefield and thus had been unable to win a major engagement. Something was holding them back, Westmoreland and Bunker said, but they didn't know what it was.

As November wore on into December and then January, American intelligence collected the kind of information that might have given the general and the ambassador a clue to this mystery.

A captured enemy document dated October 3 stated that a "general offensive early in 1968" would "emphasize attacks on enemy key units, cities and towns and lines of communication." It went on to predict that "the revolution will succeed by mid-1968 and therefore civilians [in North Vietnam] should be advised to expect their troops home around August 5, 1968." In the ancient imperial capital of Hué, an itinerant Vietnamese peddler of Buddhist tracts turned over to United States intelligence officers a circular which proclaimed that "the time is ripe for implementation of a general uprising to take over power in South Vietnam. The masses are ready for action."

At about the same time, reports reaching the State Department's Bureau of Intelligence and Research from Eastern Europe told how representatives of the Viet Cong's political arm, the National Liberation Front, had boasted to an international conference in Bratislava, Czechoslovakia, of widespread subversion inside the Saigon regime. The conference, attended by New Left delegates from the United States, was told that one third of the South Vietnamese government had been penetrated and that a major offensive would be directed at South Vietnamese cities early in 1968. With its men "in positions of influence," said the NLF, the assaults were assured of success.

In mid-November, American spies like Miss Nguyen provided a flood of information about Viet Cong agents moving through villages with the message that the war would be over in February and that a coalition government would be set up that would be dominated by Communists. Captured enemy documents and prisoners of war told the same story.

Throughout December and the first weeks of January, Communist military and propaganda documents were captured in bales by American reconnaissance patrols. They verified reports of native spies that Viet Cong agents and even soldiers in North Vietnamese uniforms were circulating openly in several cities, spreading the promise of "liberation." In some instances, the enemy agents made street-by-street canvasses, knocking on doors to tell the occupants: "We are from the National Liberation Front. We have come to liberate you. Cooperate with us and you will be safe." Others warned passersby that they no longer could expect to be protected by the Americans "because President G-xon [Johnson] has been disowned by his own people, and he is fighting against the Saigon usurpers."

Again and again, these agents predicted that "the end" would come on January 30, when the "democratic peoples" of the National Liberation Front would liberate the cities of South Vietnam. One captured document boasted that "On February 1, the seat of government in Saigon will be occupied by the National Liberation Front and our soldiers will be able to go home."

Almost all the documents specified that at first the "ruling power" would be in the hands of a coalition government containing representatives of "the American-dominated, corrupt Saigon regime." But they added that the "key role" would go to the National Liberation Front. "It is unquestionable that our immediate objective is not to obtain any type of coalition government," the documents said, "but a coalition government with the NFL in power after the withdrawal of the U.S. aggressors."

Other captured documents and reports from U.S. agents were filled with Viet Cong boasts that the last months of 1967 and the year 1968 would be a "historical period" for Vietnam. The aim of the general offensive to be launched January 30 was described as "the obtaining of an extraordinary victory in a relatively short period of time."

Unfortunately, the stratosphere in which intelligence operates was muddied, as it had been so often in the past, by the jungle-like competition of the two agencies with operatives on the scene—the Central Intelligence Agency and the Defense Intelligence Agency, with its satellites from the armed services. Apparently, nobody from the CIA told the DIA anything—and vice versa.

The DIA had access to captured documents and reports of prisoner interrogations; the CIA did not. Thus the CIA's pickings were limited almost entirely to purely political intelligence, that is to say, reports from operatives in North Vietnam and, presumably, behind the enemy lines in the South, whose mission was to obtain information on the enemy's diplomatic strategy.

As a result, although the CIA did pick up some information on the purported plan to hit at the cities, its soundings in the politico-diplomatic field gave no support to the DIA's proposition that Hanoi would go for broke in a nationwide assault. CIA memos to the White House continued to maintain that Hanoi was committed to a long drawn-out war designed to sap the American will to fight. Its conclusion was that some attacks could be expected on the cities, but that these would be diversionary moves to try to draw American reinforcements from the northern sector.

The problem here was familiar, and exasperating. It was that the DIA and the CIA—and, indeed, some of the service intelligence units—were working independently of one another. They competed for information, and for the most part reported only to their own tribal chieftains. Thus much of the CIA's information went direct to CIA headquarters in Washington for transmission to the White House. While the DIA and the service intelligence mostly brought their information bag to Westmoreland's headquarters, some of the material dredged up by the DIA went first to Defense Secretary McNamara. The reason for such practices is that Washington is the center of power and the agencies both wanted to be the first in getting their information to the capital. The comparison with competition between two newspapers in the same city is relevant. Whenever the CIA reported a piece of information the DIA didn't have, it reflected unfavorably upon the DIA, and vice versa. They sought what used to be called "scoops," in order to impress the White House.

Moreover, the DIA and its former boss, McNamara, had been suspicious of the CIA ever since the Bay of Pigs fiasco. At the Pentagon, there was a feeling that the CIA had got into the bad habit of coloring its intelligence to support various mysterious foreign policy projects of its own. Since the abortive invasion of Cuba, McNamara and the Joint Chiefs had fumed over their "betrayal" by the CIA, which had sold them on the adventure. In plain English, they were not sure the CIA could be trusted, and DIA reports to President Johnson on the developing situation in Vietnam implied as much.

The gold brick McNamara believed he had been sold on the Cuban invasion was one of the main reasons why he created the DIA in August, 1961. In the briefest of terms, he wanted military intelligence to have a direct line to the center of power in the White House. He made this possible by specifying that the DIA, although serving the Joint Chiefs, would not be directly under JCS control and would report directly to the office of the Secretary of Defense. This put the DIA on equal political terms with the CIA, which had always had a direct and constituted pipeline to the President.

In Saigon, General Westmoreland and his staff were preoccupied with the situation at the Marine strongpoint of Khesanh, just below the Demilitarized Zone along the border between North and South Vietnam. Everything pointed to the development of a major battle there, with intelligence reporting up to forty thousand enemy troops massing in the neighborhood. As a result, the American military leadership gave only passing attention to the tales told by captured documents and prisoner interrogations of a coming assault on the cities.

Neither Westmoreland nor his advisers, including Brig. Gen. Philip Davidson, his intelligence chief, believed that the enemy's open threats could be anything but a diversionary move to lure the Allies into weakening their position in the North and, specifically, at Khesanh. General Davidson pointed out the fact that the date of January 30 kept recurring in captured documents and prisoner interrogations, but he did not press the point with any considerable vigor.

Westmoreland reported to Washington that the enemy probably would use the coming truce during the Tet holidays to build up and re-supply his forces. He also predicted there would be diversionary attacks in various areas in an attempt to prevent reinforcement of the DMZ sector. He admitted that Saigon, as an open city without fortifications, was almost indefensible against a concerted enemy attack, but he saw no indication that such an attack would be made.

The general's appraisal of the strategic situation was supported by certain developments. Since early November the North Vietnamese had been moving troops into the area near the border, within and south of the DMZ. There was a feeling in the American command that General Vo Nguyen Giap, the North Vietnamese Minister of Defense, hoped to repeat at Khesanh his climactic victory over the French at Dienbienphu in 1954. In line with this thinking, considerable numbers of American troops had been moved north from I and II Corps to confront the new North Vietnamese force.

In the lower echelons of intelligence, there were those who warned that the Americans were playing into the Communists' hands. It had always been the enemy's publicly stated objective to draw American forces away from populated areas in order to give his guerrillas and cadres freer access to the people, and to fight the Americans in the more difficult terrain such as that around Khesanh and Dakto. But Westmoreland paid slight heed to such warnings. He felt he could not, in any case, ignore the massing of such a large enemy force in the north. Moreover, he saw at Khesanh an opportunity to deliver a knockout blow.

In Washington in November, Westmoreland had talked about the low state of the enemy's morale. He had told his governmental audiences that the Communists were suffering from the fact that "American troops have won every major battle in which they have been engaged." Perusing intelligence reports predicting an enemy onslaught on the cities and noting the promises of the Communist leadership that the war would be won early in 1968, he tended to dismiss them as internal propaganda intended to stiffen the spine of the common soldier.

Unfortunately, Westmoreland's insistence upon sticking to his master strategic plan had passed the initiative back to Hanoi. His plan had three parts:

Frontier defense, consisting of the establishment of a series of border outposts between South and North Vietnam and South Vietnam, Cambodia and Laos. Escalation of search-and-destroy operations to wipe out enemy bases. Pacification of the countryside.

But the establishment of the strongpoint at Khesanh had immobilized more than 30,000 troops. More than 5,000 Marines were cooped up in Khesanh and another 25,000 were in reserve in the DMZ area. So long as the enemy posed its threat to Khesanh, these American and Allied troops could not be used elsewhere. Hanoi had forced Westmoreland to weaken his defenses in the south in order to strengthen them in the north.

In another captured document, General Giap was quoted as describing this situation as just his strategic cup of tea. In a message to his troops, Giap declared that "if the United States concentrate their forces to stop reinforcements from North Vietnam, they cannot stand firm in the cities. If they oppose our people's movement in the south, they will be unable to stop reinforcements from North Vietnam." In short, Hanoi expected to benefit heavily whether Westmoreland chose to concentrate on the defense of Khesanh or to pull troops back into the populated areas.

In mid-January, with almost every intelligence source continuing to warn of a general offensive against the cities, General Davidson recommended to South Vietnam President Nguyen Van Thieu that he declare martial law, with a 10 P.M. curfew, in every major city in the country. Thieu refused to do so. He said such a drastic step was not necessary, that it would interfere with the celebration of Tet and that his opponents would seize on it to accuse him of adopting dictatorial methods.

Shortly thereafter, General Westmoreland acted—after a fashion. He called off the Tet truce in South Vietnam's northern provinces, but not around Saigon or the other major cities.

With all eyes on Khesanh and what everybody expected would be the biggest battle of the war, no one of any considerable authority was worried either about the cities or about the one billion dollars' worth of United States bases scattered around the country. The bases had officers' clubs and television and 10,000-foot runways, but no substantial fortifications or bunkers for the troops. Had it occurred to anyone that the 2.6 million-dollar American embassy in Saigon was in danger, there was comfort in the assurance of its architect, Frank J. Martin, that the new building was safe "from just about any type of minor attack. Security is our primary consideration in this building."

When the enemy launched its attack on the first night of Tet, the embassy was one of its first targets. Guerrillas blasted a hole through the 10-foot high concrete wall of the complex with an antitank gun and swarmed through it. Then they ran wild in the grounds for six and a half hours before they were all killed and the embassy once again was secure—except for five dead Americans and two dead Vietnamese chauffeurs. The Communists struck at more than 100 points from the DMZ to the islands of Phu Quoc off the Delta coast 500 miles to the south. They attacked 28 of South Vietnam's 44 provincial capitals, destroyed or damaged more than 1,000 Allied planes and helicopters. For two long weeks, they brought the war into the cities and towns of South Vietnam, and left the old capital of Hué in almost total ruins—and 1.2 million American and South Vietnamese troops on the defensive. It was no "diversionary" attack, but the major offensive all those captured documents and spies had predicted. President Thieu proclaimed martial law throughout South Vietnam on January 31, after two days of attacks.

In Washington, White House Press Secretary George Christian told reporters the American military command had had "intelligence evidence beforehand" as to the day the Viet Cong attacks would occur. Under questioning, he refused to name the day.

In Saigon, a Catholic leader named Nguyen Gian Hien, a member of the upper house of the South Vietnam legislature, said, "Our generals knew that the Viet Cong were planning to attack Saigon. The public knew it. I knew it. And still, the generals did nothing. They were playing cards or dancing. This country still badly needs some real leadership."

The Saigon newspapers reminded their readers that they had predicted the attacks in their columns.

Curiously, General Westmoreland now seemed to find comfort in the reports of his intelligence corps. He talked about a captured Viet Cong document that had called for an "uprising," and admitted, "I felt that there would be fireworks during Tet and therefore had my command throughout South Vietnam on full alert." Yet when the attacks came there were less than 300 men instantly available for battle among U.S. forces in Saigon, and the Marine guard at the embassy had been increased from only two to only three.

Both American and South Vietnamese intelligence were grossly overly optimistic in their earlier claims that the Saigon regime had wide control of the country. They had claimed, and were echoed by Deputy Ambassador Robert Komer, the United States pacification chief, that 67 percent of South Vietnam's population lived in secure areas. But almost all the cities judged secure were attacked during the general offensive.

Indeed, even after more than two weeks of fighting, U.S. military intelligence sometimes couldn't seem to grasp what was happening. It first underestimated the strength of the enemy occupying Hué, with the result that South Vietnamese troops were left to try to recapture the city unassisted, and American firepower was used piecemeal instead of massively. Then, on February 21, Lieutenant General Robert Cushman Jr., commander of the U.S. Marines in Vietnam, used intelligence reports as the basis for a prediction that the battle for Hué probably would continue for another several weeks. The city was taken three days later.

Insofar as the whole picture was concerned, it was obvious that although the American command had plenty of warning, documented and verified in numerous ways, it failed to anticipate the scope and power of the Viet Cong attacks. The assault was so widespread it must have involved long planning and careful coordination, as, indeed, the intelligence reports beforehand indicated. Yet it apparently never occurred to either General Westmoreland or his staff that the blow would be a major one. Like General Bradley in the days before the Battle of the Bulge, they were too intent on their own plans—the battle they believed to be developing at Khesanh—to pay proper attention to the enemy's plans.

What columnist Marquis Childs called America's wartime "propaganda curtain" tended to both obscure and protect from scrutiny the reasons why the U.S. and South Vietnamese forces were caught by surprise. But there were leaks from within the intelligence community. Added up, they told a story of the perils of unbridled optimism when a war is being waged.

This optimism pervaded the entire governmental establishment, from President Johnson down but not including the cautious Defense Secretary McNamara. It was an optimism that kept repeating the wishful thought that the United States was winning the war, that the corner had been turned. Confronted with intelligence that the enemy was up to something that had all the earmarks of a major offensive, this optimism refused to be dimmed. The United States leadership had the intelligence it required to act, but it neglected to evaluate it realistically. Most tragically, President Johnson, Secretary of State Dean Rusk, the Joint Chiefs of Staff and General Westmoreland apparently were unable to face up to the fact that the North Vietnamese had infiltrated deeply into every level of life in South Vietnam. The attacks would not have been possible without this subversion from within.

Even after the Communist offensive had been launched, the Johnson Administration refused to permit any of its members publicly to express concern over the Saigon regime's weaknesses. Almost as soon as the fighting began, the official line was to stress that the attacks had been a total failure and that the Thieu government continued to enjoy Washington's full support. And, indeed, at the outset there was a surprising unity and stick-togetherness on the part of the Thieu regime and various groupings of opposition politicians.

But again, the Administration seemed to be turning a deaf ear to what its intelligence insisted was the prime objective of the attacks, to wit, to demonstrate the inability of the Saigon government to provide security for its citizens. As the fighting raged, new intelligence reports were received showing that businessmen in Saigon, Hué, Danang and other cities had given secret support to the Viet Cong attackers in return for immunity. Implicit in these reports was the warning that other businessmen, having seen the Viet Cong wreak millions of dollars' worth of damage, would be more amenable to Communist overtures the next time.

The organization through which this support would come, said intelligence, was the Alliance of National and Peace Forces, whose formation had been announced only a few days before the offensive. The Alliance claimed that its goal was to unify various sectors of the urban population to present a strong front of opposition to the Thieu regime, and eventually to form a coalition government whose first move would be to demand the withdrawal of American forces.

In the meantime, because he had ignored intelligence warnings against dispersing his troops, General Westmoreland found himself with no reserve forces to go out and pursue the enemy. His men were tied down throughout South Vietnam. Washington rushed 10,500 new troops to Vietnam to provide the general with a "reaction force" that would be available to meet whatever crisis might develop in any given area. The rest of Westmoreland's troops were holding defensive positions, waiting outside the cities for new attacks, and stretched thin over areas which earlier had been stamped "secure."

Moreover, it was now plain to any objective observer that the grand strategy of the American military leadership, devised during the early months of 1965 when the first substantial numbers of U.S. troops were committed, had been proved an utter failure.

By sending more and more men to Vietnam, President Johnson and his generals had aimed to crush the enemy's main forces, secure the countryside, and destroy or disperse the guerrillas. In March, 1968, the Communist forces had retaken the intiative, pillaged the cities at will and inflicted record casualties on the American forces.

The bombing of North Vietnam had failed to sufficiently punish the enemy, halt the infiltration of North Vietnamese troops into the South and force the Communists to the peace table. With more than 400,000 fighting men in South Vietnam, the enemy had matched the American escalation almost step-by-step. There were some 5,000 North Vietnamese troops in the South when the bombing of the North began; there were now at least 125,000 despite American air attacks which had dropped more bombs than U.S. planes unloaded during all of

World War II. The Communists may have been willing to talk peace, but not because their will or military capacity had been crushed; the Tet offensive proved they were capable of mounting brilliantly planned and savagely executed attacks more powerful than any they had launched there before.

Washington had hoped to give added strength and stability to the Saigon regime and to enlist the assistance of other nations in the Free World. About all that could be said about the Thieu government in March, 1968, was that it had survived. As for the rest of the Free World, only a few smaller nations such as Australia and Korea had come to our aid, and of the major powers only a diminished Britain officially offered moral support.

Now, the American intelligence network which had reported so accurately on the enemy's plan for a coordinated attack on the cities seemed plunged into confusion. Privately, some high officials at the Pentagon admitted they had no idea where the Viet Cong would strike next, because of contradictory intelligence estimates. One of these, on February 10, reported that attacks by North Vietnamese air power were "imminent." By mid-March, not an enemy plane had been sighted over the battlefields. Another insisted that Hué would be the next major enemy objective, with the assault on that ancient imperial city "firmly scheduled" for March 2. A year later, no such attack had been launched.

There was still talk at United States military headquarters in Saigon that the wave of attacks on population centers was an attempt to divert American attention from Khesanh and other strongholds. Most of the captured enemy documents and prisoner interrogation reports disagreed. They said the enemy's intention remained to draw the main American forces away from the cities in order to give the guerrillas a free hand to harass and subvert the cities' people. Taken at face value, this meant that the diversionary effort was at Khesanh.

General Giap's own words after his defeat of the French at Dienbienphu supported this premise. "The enemy was confronted with a contradiction," said Giap. "If he did not disperse his troops, it was impossible to occupy the invaded territory. But in dispersing them he got himself into difficulties."

Possibly, no one in the American high command had ever read Giap. More likely, its determined resistance to intelligence reports from the field reflected the traditional suspicion on the part of the operations officer of any information gathered by "odd types" in the employ of the intelligence sections. In this era, with its emphasis on machines, the military brass tends to be much more receptive to electronic intelligence—that is to say, intelligence stolen by gadget. Fortunately, the American taxpayer has provided its military with a profusion of intelligence machines, such as the ill-fated U.S.S. *Pueblo* and other spy ships.

9

The Spy Ships

As a symbol of America's naval might, the U.S.S. *Pueblo* would have looked fine unloading cases of Coke and shaving cream. She lumbered along in the icy January waters off the coast of North Korea at flank speed of 12.2 knots, a 906-ton, 179-foot converted Army freighter no wet-eared ensign would favor with a second look. But the *Pueblo* was more important than she appeared to non-technical eyes. Her superstructure bristled with antennae, and below deck she was loaded down with electronic eavesdropping gear. The *Pueblo* was a spy ship, a "ferret" whose mission was the interception of radio signals whose esoteric matter was transmitted to Fort Meade, Maryland, for decoding by the intelligence cryptanalysts at the National Security Agency.

On its first intelligence mission hard by the headquarters of the Soviet Pacific fleet in Vladivostok, the *Pueblo* had already struck pay dirt by January 23, 1968. During its two weeks of snooping, it had passed on to Washington intercepted North Korean governmental and military messages whose texts indicated a new development in the Cold War.

Specifically, the messages made it plain that the recently initiated campaign of harassment against American and South Korean troops below the 1953 cease-fire line would continue, as a device intended to throw off balance the massive United States effort in Vietnam. There also were hints in the messages that the Communist North Korean regime—probably with the encouragement and support of Communist China—hoped to lure the United States into an undeclared "non-war" in that area and thereby divert some U.S. military power from Vietnam.

(In Washington, both military and civilian intelligence sources snickered up their sleeves at a summary released by the *Pueblo* Court of Inquiry in March 1969. The summary quoted *Pueblo* officers as declaring that the vessel's spy mission was "unproductive." In fact, the *Pueblo* relayed all sorts of vital intelligence to Washington, including—as will be seen —information on North Korean military equipment.)

The *Pueblo* was commanded by Commander Lloyd M. Bucher, thirty-eight, and carried a crew of eighty-two, including two civilian oceanographers, whose job was to sample the water for salinity tests and to collect militarily valuable data on currents, depths and bottom topography. Besides its electronic interception equipment, the *Pueblo* was equipped to lay networks of sophisticated sonar cables, known as Caesar and Sosus, to detect the presence of Soviet submarines.

Later there would be disagreement over the *Pueblo's* position as she waddled along somewhere off the port of Wonsan. At noon (Korean time) on January 23, however, this was a matter of only academic interest to the *Pueblo's* crew. A North Korean subchaser appeared from the seaward and asked that the *Pueblo* identify herself. She did so. Whereupon the subchaser sent up two more signal flags whose flutterings carried the blunt message: "Heave to or I will open fire." Four hours later, the *Pueblo* was a captive of the Cold War, herded into Wonsan by four heavily armed North Korean vessels. She was the first U.S. naval ship to surrender to the enemy without a fight since the Union gunboat *Harriet Lane* was captured by the Confederates during the Civil War.

(The *Chesapeake* was intercepted at sea by the British frigate *Leopard* during the press-gang nastiness in 1807 and was forced to surrender after firing only one shot. That one shot was ignited by a red-hot coal carried in the fingers of a young lieutenant after it was discovered the *Chesapeake* lacked matches, gunlocks, powder horns and wadding for charges. The *Chesapeake* again surrendered to a British ship, the frigate *Shannon,* off Boston, but only after a hand-to-hand battle directed by Captain James Lawrence who died with the famous words, "Don't give up the ship!")

Crammed as she was with esoteric eavesdropping equipment, the *Pueblo* was a prize catch, both from an intelligence and political viewpoint. In Washington, the Navy's first reaction was to change several of its codes. In point of fact, however, the Communists did not capture the *Pueblo*'s espionage gear intact. From the moment it appeared that boarding was imminent, Commander Bucher and his men worked furiously to destroy secret documents and sensitive equipment.

As the North Korean sailors prepared to board the vessel, the *Pueblo* sent a radio message that her crew was taking action to prevent papers and equipment from falling into unfriendly hands. This was in line with rigid standing orders given all intelligence ships. Unfortunately, the *Pueblo* had not been fully equipped with built-in destructive mechanisms, and so Commander Bucher and his men could only do their manual, ingenious best. As a result, the North Koreans were able to seize a number of secret documents, including a mattress cover filled with classified material, as well as some of the secret equipment.

Bucher and some of his crew took the ship's code books, other documents and some smaller pieces of electronic equipment into an armored deckhouse just before the boarding. There, they ripped up the code books and other documents and tossed the pieces out of portholes. They also employed makeshift explosives, including hand grenades, to destroy some of the gear. Several days later, military intelligence reports from South Korea would indicate that the North Koreans were "furious" over this destruction and that Navy officials had called an inquiry into the failure of their gunboats' command to prevent it.

Nevertheless, there was consternation in Washington over the seizure. At the White House, President Johnson summoned a meeting of military and civilian officials and bombarded them with questions. He was assured that the *Pueblo* was outside territorial waters. He was told the *Pueblo* was virtually defenseless, with only three .50-caliber machine guns, against the North Korean subchasers. Secretary of State Dean Rusk and Secretary of Defense Robert McNamara noted that intercepted North Korean messages had spoken of "diversionary tactics" against American forces in the neighborhood, and concluded that the seizure of the *Pueblo* was a part of the harassment campaign. The President rejected a Pentagon proposal that U.S. planes bomb the *Pueblo* as it lay in Wonsan harbor. His primary objective, he said, was to effect the return of the ship and its crew, and he would take no action that might endanger the lives of crew members who might still be quartered on the vessel.

Intelligence also brought the President up to date on the number of Soviet spy ships operating off American coasts, and he decided to drop a subtle hint to Moscow. American Ambassador Llewellyn Thompson called the next day on Soviet Deputy Foreign Minister Vasili Kuznetzov and urged that the Soviet government intervene. He reminded Kuznetzov that governments friendly to the United States might seize one of the Russians' eavesdropping vessels, an act which would further upset the "gentlemen's agreement" by which Washington and Moscow refrained from interfering with each other's ferrets. Kuznetzov was cordial, but non-committal; he told Thompson the Soviet government was not inclined to "dictate" to its allies. Johnson called up 14,787 Air Force reservists.

Meanwhile, the North Koreans claimed that the *Pueblo* was within the North Korean twelve-mile territorial limit and thus in violation of "international agreements." What they meant was that the *Pueblo* had violated the North Korean regime's unilateral pronouncement that any drop of water within twelve miles of its coast was "territorial." Most nations, including the United States, are parties to agreements setting three miles as the territorial limit. At any rate, both the Navy and the State Department insisted the *Pueblo* was "about" twenty-six miles off the North Korean coast at the time of its seizure.

Since the *Pueblo*'s seizure was a *fait accompli,* the argument over territorial jurisdiction was academic, although it brought demands in Congress that the United States impose a twelve-mile limit on Communist vessels. "We ought to operate on a tit-for-tat basis," said Senate Majority Leader Mike Mansfield of Montana. Such sound and fury on Capitol Hill, however, was of only cursory interest to the average American, to whom the *Pueblo* incident offered a few hard and fascinating facts on the extent of U.S. electronic espionage around the world.

Almost a year later, the American public was given an insight into the extent its government will go to recover the crew of a spy ship, while still maintaining the myth of its innocence. The *Pueblo*'s crew was released by the North

Korean government in December, 1968, after U.S. Army Major General Gilbert H. Woodward signed a document prepared by the North Koreans which stated that:

The *Pueblo* had illegally intruded into the territorial waters of North Korea "on many occasions."

The United States "solemnly apologizes for grave acts of espionage."

The *Pueblo*'s crew members "have confessed honestly to their crimes."

But before he signed the document, General Woodward issued a formal statement in which he declared: "The position of the United States has been that the ship was not engaged in illegal activities, that there is no convincing evidence that the ship at any time intruded into territorial waters claimed by North Korea, and that we could not apologize for actions we did not believe took place. My signature [to the document] will not and cannot alter the facts. I will sign the document to free the crew and only to free the crew."

General Woodward's ploy was in the classic tradition of espionage everywhere, which blithely allows that a nation may even resort to looking particularly silly in order to preserve its official position that it never stoops to spying.

L'affaire Pueblo was another example of how the unromantic advances in espionage have replaced man with a gadget. NSA's electronic spies provide more intelligence in a single day than Kim Philby stole in a month during his untidy career as a Soviet agent preying on his native Britain. Even under conditions of the most sophisticated security, no nation can be entirely safe against the prying of such spies.

The *Pueblo* was one of fifteen ships of the United States' ELINT (for electronic intelligence) fleet prowling the world's seas. Since it takes time to eavesdrop on an unfriendly nation's radio and radar systems, a ship is a natural listening post. It can cruise almost indefinitely in a limited area or remain on station for months, and can operate effectively even beyond the artificial twelve-mile limit because of the listening power of its expensive gear. Also, of course, ships can carry a much bigger load of equipment and more technicians than a plane or submarine.

Ships of the ELINT fleet carry devices for the carrying-out of an assortment of intelligence missions. Their complicated antenna systems intercept radio signals and, often, telegraph and telephone conversations. Radar domes serve as direction-finders and triangulators for locating the precise positions of the radio transmission sets. Below deck, the ship's various receivers are connected to banks of tape recorders and computers, and data from these machines are transmitted to the NSA in Washington for decoding and analysis. From this information, NSA analysts often can determine a nation's "order of battle"—the location of its military units, their state of readiness, their strength and even the line of command.

In simplistic terms, radar is a system whereby radio signals are bounced off an object to determine its location. In wartime, it is used to locate enemy ships, planes, and missiles. U.S. ferret ships make tape recordings of radar transmissions to determine the frequencies on which they are operating, the speed of their pulses and other characteristics of their radio waves. With this information at hand, U.S. warships and bombers in wartime theoretically can "confuse" the radar system, either by transmitting powerful static signals to jam the system or by emitting fake signals that "look" like those transmitted by the enemy. The fake signals are timed to make it appear the ships and bombers are, say, one hundred miles away, when actually they are nearing their targets. Ships like the *Pueblo* also intercept so-called "plain language" communications between enemy naval commanders and aircraft pilots which often provide information on the nation's armed strength and the condition of its war-making equipment.

The *Pueblo* picked up at least two pieces of information on the state of North Korean armaments. Eavesdropping on conversations between fighter pilots, the ship's electronic listeners learned from the pilots' gripes that they were having problems with a certain type of rocket launcher. From another message, intelligence in Washington got its first news of the delivery of a new type of Russian tank to the North Korean Army.

Around the world, the ferret ships spy on both surface ships and submarines of the Soviet Union's expanding Navy. They can listen to surface ships passing by for fifty miles around through the "ears" of a long line of hydrophones they trail behind them as they move through the water. And since each ship makes a distinctive sound underwater, surface ships can be identified by feeding those "signatures" picked up by the ferrets into a computer for comparison with signatures

recorded by other ferrets or land stations. Submarines are
tracked and identified in the same fashion, but with more
sophisticated gadgets. These infrared devices pick up "scars"
—heat and turbulence signatures caused by a submarine's
passage through the water. Their sonar systems, a far cry
from the underwater detectives that were a World War II
marvel of science, sort out the various sounds of the sea and
record only those made by the sub. By the spring of 1968,
U.S. Naval Intelligence and the NSA had identified the heat
and sound signatures of every one of Russia's 450-plus submarines.

The ferret ships also are used to help keep track of Soviet
missile and space launches; they are stationed regularly in the
Pacific to observe the reentry and splashdown of Soviet intercontinental ballistic missiles fired into the ocean. Their oceanographers and hydrographers help track down submarines by
recording the water's temperature levels, salt content and
algae growth—all factors that affect sonar waves. U.S. destroyers on "routine" maneuvers slip close to hostile shores and
intercept radio talk and coded telegraphic and cabled messages by means of "black boxes" which have become standard
equipment on most of the Navy's fighting vessels. The Pentagon now admits that the two destroyers involved in the Tonkin
Gulf attack by North Vietnamese patrol boats were on such
an intelligence-gathering mission.

Understandably, both the Defense and State Departments
are reluctant to discuss the operations of these spy ships—or
spy planes or spy satellites. After all, intelligence is at its most
effective when it is carried on under conditions of the utmost
secrecy. But the *Pueblo* incident showed that the American
government, wisely or not, had decided to accede to the
public's demand for a fuller explanation when one of its ferrets is discovered in a situation that endangers the lives of
American servicemen. Washington's speedy release of information on the plight of the *Pueblo* was in marked contrast to
its bumbling doubletalk when the U.S.S. *Liberty* was fired
upon by Israeli planes and gunboats during the Arab-Israeli
war of June, 1967.

The *Liberty,* a larger edition of the *Pueblo,* was carrying
much more snooping equipment when it got too close to the
fighting off the coast of Egypt and lost thirty-four American
dead and seventy-five wounded to the over-eager, or simply

reckless, Israeli attackers. Neither a U.S. Navy Court of Inquiry nor an Israeli government investigation managed to explain the gross mistakes made by the Israeli jet fighters and motor torpedo boats in failing to identify a vessel flying the American flag, distinctively marked, and hoisting radio and radar antennae that clearly marked it as a noncombatant vessel.

"Did the attackers in fact know that the *Liberty* was an American ship?" asked the Washington *Star* editorially. "It seems to us they must have known. If so, why was the attack made and who ordered it? . . . The only official word from Tel Aviv has been that the attack was a 'mistake.' "

But both the *Star* and the *New York Times* heaped blame of another kind on the Pentagon for its inchoate attempts to explain the incident.

Ever since President Eisenhower admitted that Francis Gary Powers' U-2 plane was on an intelligence-gathering mission over the Soviet Union, Washington had been sensitive about giving any hint of America's espionage activities. Eisenhower's admission, it was generally agreed, had been a mistake; the United States should have retreated into an "investigation" which, as Winston Churchill suggested at the time, "could have lasted forever." But when the *Liberty* was attacked, the Pentagon promptly rushed into print with two ridiculous cover stories that left large segments of the American public in a state of righteous indignation and caused the rest of the world to come down with a case of the giggles.

At first, a Pentagon "spokesman" explained that the reason the *Liberty* was so close to El Arish and other battle zones was that the ship was using the moon as a passive reflector in its communications. But no one came forward to explain how hitting the moon—238,000 miles away—could have anything to do with moving the *Liberty* a few miles closer to shore. In order to keep up with the changing position of the moon, quipped one navigation expert, the *Liberty* would have had to "sail right across the sands of Sinai."

Shortly, the Pentagon offered another explanation. In a press release, it said the *Liberty,* when attacked, was "approximately fifteen miles north of the Sinai Peninsula . . . to assure communications between U.S. government posts in the Middle East and to assist in relaying information concerning the evacuation of American dependents and other American citizens. . . ."

This story sounded a little better, if only because it didn't mention the moon. But the *Liberty* carried specialized spying equipment. Any destroyer would have been more helpful in "assuring" American communications. Besides, every embassy in the Middle East was equipped with long-distance radio communications with which it could transmit messages to Washington instantaneously.

The fact was that the *Liberty* was exclusively a spy ship, although this was never officially admitted. Its electronic eavesdropping chores were performed by NSA specialists in the ship's bowels who had no connection with normal Naval communications. And its assignment was to see how much it could learn, with the aid of some brand new interception equipment, about what was really happening on the battle-fronts.

Actually, the *Liberty*'s ears picked up only what American intelligence already knew—that the Egyptian camp was in a state of military and political disarray. Ground communications, decoded and analyzed by the NSA in Washington, were littered with contradictory orders, inchoate conversations between President Nasser and his commanders in the field and implicit admissions that the Egyptian war effort had collapsed.

But the *Liberty* also managed to complete a routine intelligence chore before the Israeli attack fell. This was a testing of Egypt's radar defenses, designed to learn the configuration of the installations, the intensity and duration of their signals and the degree of their arcs. There was at the time the grim chance the United States might become involved in the hostilities, and it was essential to know at exactly what point ships approaching the Egyptian coast would be discovered by shore radar. American spy ships had done and were doing the same thing in various parts of the world in order to store up information against the day when it might be militarily useful.

Such radar testing was a part of the mission of the destroyers *Maddox* and *Turner Joy*, which were attacked by North Vietnamese patrol boats in August, 1964, an incident that caused Congress to approve the so-called Tonkin Gulf resolution endorsing "all necessary measures" against North Vietnam to "prevent further aggression." In reprisal for the two attacks—one on August 2 and the second on August 4—the

Johnson Administration ordered the first air strikes against North Vietnam and subsequently poured more than 500,000 American troops into South Vietnam.

In typically convoluted Navy language, the *Maddox* and *Turner Joy* were ordered to "stimulate ChiCom/North Vietnamese electronic reaction." That is to say, by their mere presence in the neighborhood, the destroyers presumably would be able to check on the efficiency and reliability of shore-based radar. After years of evasive tactics with Senator J. William Fulbright's Senate Foreign Relations Committee, former Defense Secretary Robert S. McNamara finally admitted this during hearings in February, 1968.

But because the Tonkin Gulf incident led to massive American intervention in the Vietnam war, the matter developed into a question of whether such spying forays constitute a provocation of the country spied upon. Fulbright, Oregon's Senator Wayne Morse and others insisted it did. In their view, the United States had engaged in practices almost sure to result in a military confrontation and thus was guilty, intentionally or not, of seeking to widen the hostilities.

McNamara vigorously denied this, and from the standpoint of international practice he was on solid ground. The *Maddox* and *Turner Joy*, he said, were on "routine patrols in international waters. They were open patrols and no hostile actions were ever taken by the United States forces involved . . . The purpose was to learn what we could of military activity and environmental conditions in these parts of the world, operating in waters where we had every right to be."

But in the era of the Cold War, the operative word was "routine." Fulbright, Morse and others were mounting a valid argument when they insisted that in times of world tension, and especially in an area in which a war was being fought, it was neither wise nor prudent to make such "routine patrols." In their view, the United States was asking for trouble, and found it. McNamara denied this, too, and described as "monstrous" thinly veiled charges that the Johnson Administration had sought and found an excuse to justify American intervention. Privately he would admit that making such patrols did constitute a risk. However, both he and his military team pointed out that the information picked up by electronic surveillance is of particular importance in times of international stress. Or, put another way, if there were no such thing as a Cold War, spying would be unnecessary.

Although the issue probably will be debated for years, it was the American political system more than any other factor which should get the blame—or the credit—for the Tonkin Gulf resolution. In August, 1964, President Johnson and members of Congress were still on their honeymoon; Johnson could get practically anything he wanted on Capitol Hill. Besides, an election was coming up three months hence, and the Democratic majority was not about to sabotage its candidate by refusing his request for action "in defense of American servicemen."

Parenthetically, the Tonkin Gulf resolution had ironic overtones. President Johnson was running as the candidate who opposed sending "American boys" to fight in Asia, while the Democrats were attacking Senator Goldwater as a warmonger. Yet the resolution paved the way for the first United States air strike against North Vietnam, an act of war in any language.

At any rate, it was a trifle absurd for some members of Congress to put all the onus on Johnson. No American was so much as scratched and neither the *Maddox* nor the *Turner Joy* was damaged during the two attacks. In passing the resolution, therefore, Congress was guilty of one of the most flagrant examples of over-reaction in the nation's history. The Senate especially was derelict. Its role in foreign policy is to advise as well as consent, but clearly its members were unusually stingy with their advice. Apparently its members had grown to accept the premise that espionage is one of the necessary evils of the Cold War.

Although they are, to put it mildly, much less candid about their activity in this field, the Russians would go along. Ever since the end of World War II, they have had their own *Pueblos* and *Libertys* and *Maddoxes* and *Turner Joys*.

Many of the Soviet Union's four thousand trawlers—the largest ocean-going fishing fleet in the world—double in electronics as spy ships, and its ELINT fleet is composed of about forty vessels whose sole mission is intelligence gathering. The Russians also have the world's largest oceanographic fleet, an armada of two hundred vessels which collect underwater data for use by their submarine-tracking ships.

When, after the seizure of the *Pueblo*, the Navy ordered

the 85,000-ton, nuclear-powered carrier *Enterprise* into the Sea of Japan, the Russians went along. They assigned the trawler-spy ship *Gidrolog* to shadow the *Enterprise*. Other Russian spy ships operate regularly within a 45,000-square-mile area of the Tonkin Gulf known as "Yankee Station" from which American air strikes over North Vietnam originate. They shadow the Sixth Fleet in the Mediterranean, keep watch off Cape Kennedy to monitor U.S. space shots, and prowl the waters off American Polaris submarine bases at Holy Loch in Scotland, Rota in Spain and Charleston, South Carolina. Pentagon officials are fond of remarking that they could pick up fifteen to twenty Soviet reconnaissance trawlers a night if they wanted to.

They do not, because that is not the way the Cold War is run. As first-class maritime powers, the United States and the Soviet Union comply with their gentlemen's agreement not to interfere with each other's espionage activities except in case of flagrant violation of territory which leaves them no choice. In seizing the *Pueblo*, North Korea thus was breaking an unwritten rule, a surly practice not uncommon among the steerage nations.

North Korea and other deprived nations could argue that there can be no such thing as a gentlemen's agreement in a business whose survival depends upon the exclusion of gentlemen, but the *Pueblo* affair showed that the alternative to operating under some kind of rules is dangerous. This was the position Moscow and Washington perforce adopted. It was espionage's own curious *modus vivendi*.

Besides, it has been accepted as one of the Cold War's sordid facts of life that no nation of any considerable consequence can be without a far-flung, expensive and active espionage system. Country A's security may depend on how much it knows about Country B, and vice versa. Thus, although Russia and the United States get all the spy-story headlines, such nations as Great Britain, France, East and West Germany, Israel and Egypt also spend vast amounts of money on intelligence operations.

The *Pueblo* incident was another reminder that spying poses serious diplomatic risks, especially when it involves a country, such as North Korea, which acknowledges none of the international conventions, written or implicit. Yet, although Washington was well aware that North Korea was an outlaw state

—a state that only recently had dispatched a band of assassins to murder the President of South Korea—U.S. military intelligence felt the risk of spying on North Korea was worth taking. The Pyongyang regime's resort to a series of armed attacks and other violent provocations against South Korea made it important to try to find out what new aggressive moves, if any, were being pondered by the belligerent Premier Kim Il Sung.

This decision was prompted in part by study papers produced by the State Department's Bureau of Intelligence and Research on the state of American power around the world. With a major war being fought in Vietnam and the country still unconverted to a wartime economy, the INR suggested that this power was stretched too thin and that the situation was most tempting to some of the world's troublemakers, especially Kim Il Sung and Fidel Castro.

Those INR experts charged with submitting highly educated guesses on the intentions of assorted international strong men had the record of Kim Il Sung's own utterances and Cold War maneuverings to guide them. Kim had long held that the military defeat of the United States was necessary before he could weld North and South Korea into a united, Communist-ruled paradise. He admitted that North Korea alone could not be expected to deliver such a defeat, but he saw the day coming when, as he put it, "It will be comparatively easy for us to defeat the United States under conditions where they must disperse their forces on a global scale."

In January, 1968, therefore, it behooved the INR to wonder whether Kim Il Sung might decide those conditions had been fulfilled. The U.S. had more than a half a million men in Vietnam, and it was harassed by explosive situations in other parts of the world, notably in the Middle East, where it had treaty commitments to intervene in case of conflict. At the time of the *Pueblo* incident, the United States was pledged to help defend forty-two nations on every continent except Africa under eight post-World War II treaties. And in Africa, it was committed to ponder what action it would take should Liberia be the victim of aggression. Saudi Arabia had a Presidential promise that its integrity would be protected.

Some heretics in the INR further suggested that while all these commitments might have been considered both wise and prudent in a day when the United States had numerous allies able and willing to help out, they had been outmoded by events. Great Britain was a military has-been, and the other European nations were firmly embarked on a policy of non-intervention. Other countries, such as South Korea, the Philippines, Australia, New Zealand and Formosa, perhaps could be counted on for assistance, but they were discounted as lacking in muscle.

In short, said the INR, the United States was attempting the impossible task of policing the world all by itself. At any moment, Communist guerrillas could stir up trouble anywhere in the world, posing the question of whether the United States could fight so-called "little" wars in say, Iran, Cambodia, Pakistan, Brazil and the Caribbean, all at the same time. Since it was obvious Premier Kim was aware of the crunch in which Uncle Sam found himself, the INR urged that every intelligence effort be made to learn his intentions.

As it happened, the INR's gloomy viewpoint was shortly verified. Not only did Kim Il Sung seize the *Pueblo*, but the United States' thinly-spread defenses were exposed as incapable of dealing with the incident by force, had such an action been approved. There were only four American planes in South Korea the day the *Pueblo* was captured. Of these, three were equipped with small tactical nuclear weapons and thus could not be used. The other was under repair. Yet for weeks Kim Il Sung had been hinting that the time had come to divert American attention from Vietnam.

This is not necessarily to say that an attempt would have been made to rescue the *Pueblo* and its crew by force even if planes had been available. Unfortunately, dealings with outlaw nations such as North Korea are too complicated for simplistic solutions. Premier Kim undoubtedly knew that the United States would tread cautiously in the affair from a sensible and prudent consideration of the greater risks involved. Those risks touched on the role of the Soviet Union, which publicly at least is bound to support even the lawless provocations of its more irresponsible comrades in the community of "fellow people's democratic republics." The U.S. could risk war with North Korea; it would not risk war with Russia over something North Korea had done.

In April, 1969, a little more than a year after the *Pueblo* incident, a new President, Richard Nixon, underlined the problem in discussing at a news conference America's response to the shooting down by North Korea of a Navy EC-121 spy plane over the Sea of Japan a few days earlier. While announcing such reconnaissance flights would continue and that protection would be provided for them, Nixon reminded his audience of a fact of life.

Without mentioning the Soviet Union by name, the President declared that there was always "the question as to what reaction we could expect not only from the party against whom we respond, but other parties that might be involved." That reaction, he noted, "might affect a major interest of the United States in another area—an area like Vietnam."

Nixon's decision to continue the flights was based on evidence that they produced results. For example, in February, 1969, an electronic spy plane similar to the ill-fated EC-121 intercepted radio messages that confirmed earlier reports that Communist China had begun delivery of a squadron of jet fighter-bombers to North Korea. Other flights had picked up intelligence that the North Korean armed forces had stepped up the processing of fish for field use, had stockpiled new supplies of medical drugs and had placed a big order for uniforms. And, after the seizure of the *Pueblo* fifteen months earlier, a reconnaissance flight had contributed to the information that the Soviet Union had boosted the number of surface-to-air (SAM) missile sites in North Korea from sixteen to thirty-eight.

Yet Nixon was careful to let the Russians know publicly that Washington was aware of their interests. Or, as he put it, he had tried "to pose the problem that great powers confront when they take actions involving powers that are not involved in that league. We must always measure our actions by that base."

In short, in the era of the Cold War, right does not necessarily make might, because any vigorous assertion of that principle could lead to nuclear war and self-destruction. The *Pueblo* incident was a lesson to the United States in the limitations of power, just as the Middle East war of June, 1967, was a lesson to the Russians, who had to sit back and watch their Arab friends take a clobbering from Israel, knowing well that if they intervened militarily so would the United States. It also emphasized that even in an age of espionage by gadget there is still personal hazard to be found in the black art.

10

Stokely Carmichael's Travels

Admittedly, it is a far cry from the furtive maneuverings of a spy ship in North Korean waters to a conference of leftist revolutionaries in Havana. But grist for the intelligence mill is harvested wherever it is found, and it was an exercise in practical, string-saving espionage when the State Department's own personal spook shop turned its attention—and the electronic marvels of the National Security Agency—to the Cuban conclave. It was important to learn what Fidel Castro might be cooking up in Latin America. Besides, the entire intelligence community was interested in the attendance at that meeting of an American Negro militant, whose status as a bona fide revolutionary was still uncertain, despite the inflammatory content of his oratory. In street-corner jargon, the mission might have been described as an attempt to answer the question: What kind of a guy *is* Stokely Carmichael?

Stokely Carmichael, in the late fall of 1967, was not a young man easily impressed by the interest of others in his activities, but his cool might have been measurably thawed had he known he was the subject of an exchange of admiring if somewhat perplexed messages between the Communist regimes of Cuba and North Vietnam.

The messages, which related to Carmichael's visits that year to Havana and Hanoi, were intercepted by American military intelligence, over Cuba. They included both radio and radiotelephone transmissions, and undoubtedly were picked up by either spy satellites or ferret planes equipped with National Security Agency eavesdropping devices.

Carmichael would have been intrigued if not pleased to

113

learn that while he impressed both Fidel Castro and the Hanoi Establishment with his ideological sentiments and his revolutionary enthusiasm, neither had been moved to take him for granted. The messages revealed that both Havana and Hanoi were concerned over whether he was as serious a dogmatic Marxist as desired. From both ends of the conversations came suggestions that there were traces of the dilettante in the young Black Power activist and that he tended to be "too independent"—in Hanoi's words. In short, although both parties found Carmichael an agreeable and probably valuable ally—as a troublemaker if in no greater role—they wondered whether he was The McCoy. It would seem that Havana and Hanoi were indulging themselves in the suspicious prudence of the Old Guard in thus placing the Trinidad Terror on probation. At any rate, it is always pleasant for an agitator to know that he is taken seriously enough to be noticed and discussed, especially by the big wheels.

A lean twenty-six-year-old at the time, Carmichael had been in the thick of first the civil rights movement and then the Black Power campaign almost since the day his parents brought him to the United States at the age of eleven. He had been arrested twenty-seven times in Mississippi and Alabama as a result of assorted civil rights ruckuses. It was during a Mississippi civil rights march in 1966 that he popularized the slogan, "Black Power," which he explained in a book, *Black Power: The Politics of Liberation in America,* published at about the time Havana and Hanoi were discussing his revolutionary qualities.

In New York City's Harlem in August, 1966, Carmichael noted that "they're building stores with no windows in Cleveland," scene of race riots earlier that year. He added, "It just means we'll have to move from Molotov cocktails to dynamite . . . if we had any sense we'd have bombed those ghettos long ago."

On various occasions, Carmichael had publicly advised youths to "say hell no" to the draft, and when he took a pre-induction physical examination in New York City on October 28, 1966, he told newsmen, "I'll go to Leavenworth first," before being drafted. Subsequently, Carmichael was classified 1-Y, indicating a registrant whose physical or mental condition makes him subject to induction only in a time of national emergency. At the time Carmichael was chairman of the militant Student Nonviolent Coordinating Committee (SNICK); he stepped down in May, 1967, in favor of H. Rap Brown.

Carmichael was arrested in Atlanta in 1966 after a grand jury charged him with inciting to riot in connection with two outbreaks which caused injuries to thirty-five persons and resulted in 128 arrests. Later in the same year he told a meeting of Negroes in Washington: "You ought to get together and tell The Man that if you don't get the vote you're gonna burn down this city. Tell him, 'If we don't get the vote you're not gonna have a Washington, D. C.'"

After defying a State Department ban on travel to Cuba to attend the conference of the Latin-American Solidarity Organization, sponsored by Fidel Castro, Carmichael continued his travels to several European countries, to Africa and to Hanoi. In Havana, he declared, "We are going to start with guns to get our liberation. Our only answer is to destroy the government or to be destroyed." He was refused permission to remain in Great Britain after he told a meeting of Negroes in London they should resort to violence to get what they wanted.

Predictably, there was a hue and cry that Carmichael be prosecuted both for violating the Selective Service law and for treason. It was argued that Carmichael was liable for prosecution because he had defied that section of the Selective Service act which forbids any person to "knowingly counsel, aid or abet another to refuse or evade registration or service in the armed forces." Other critics charged Carmichael was guilty of treason for violating Article III of the Constitution which defines the crime as "adhering to" the enemies of the United States or giving them "aid and comfort." However, the Justice Department took no action against him.

In any event, Carmichael hardly could be considered unfriendly to the joint cause of the Havana-Hanoi axis when he arrived in the Cuban capital to join the Communist-oriented delegates in lambasting American imperialism. Indeed, he was singled out by Fidel Castro for special, affectionate attention during his stay in Havana, given VIP treatment by the delegates, and interviewed every hour on the hour by Cuba's kept news media.

One of the delegates to the conference, however, was

merely going about the duties of his calling in keeping the proceedings under close scrutiny. He was a citizen of a South American country who will be called Jorge for the purposes of this narrative. Jorge was known to, and respected by, the Cuban secret police as an agent of the East German Communist regime. What Castro's Gestapo didn't know was that Jorge was a double agent, who also earned a fat day's pay as a "confidential informant" for the State Department's Bureau of Intelligence and Research.

There is nothing unusual about an American intelligence outfit hiring a spy who also works for a Communist government. Jorge was, and probably still is, a professional. He was a highly competent operator who hired out his competence for money and served his various bosses with what, in another business, would be called honesty. That is to say, Jorge ordinarily did not sell intelligence bought by the United States to East Germany, or vice versa. Some people from the State Department checked this angle unceasingly, and so, undoubtedly, did Jorge's employers in Pankow.

For the INR, moreover, there was a special advantage in availing itself of Jorge's services at this particular conference. Mere delegates did not attend the private, unannounced sessions of a select little group presided over by Fidel Castro to discuss the more delicate matters of revolutionary policy. But as an agent of the East German regime, Jorge was an invited guest. So, he reported, was Stokely Carmichael. And from Jorge the State Department received a complete briefing on what was talked about at the sessions. In this case it was not important that Jorge transmitted some of this same information to East Germany; it would have been suspicious if he had not, since Pankow had assigned him to the conference and thus nothing could be done about it. All the INR cared about was getting the information too. And after all, without his East German credentials Jorge would have been barred from the sessions.

At any rate, Jorge picked up a mass of information at the after-hours conferences, and he was able to check his notes with those of a journalist from a Communist bloc country who owed him some favors. It was, as Jorge noted, a "nice, friendly family party." Each time he left the party, he organized his findings under proper headings and transcribed them on a typewriter in his hotel room. In substance, his report to his American employers emerged from his typewriter like this:

POPULAR FRONTS. Speakers urged the necessity of organizing popular revolutionary fronts in both Latin America and in the United States to take advantage of "discontent." Various delegates, including Carmichael, rejected any partnership of Negroes with poor whites in the U.S. on the grounds the whites would be a divisive force, or at least undependable. Castro urged that the fronts acquire and store weapons, but warned against any massive use of firearms until the "right moment" arrived. It was generally agreed that the black militants in the United States should use civil rights demonstrations and demonstrations against "political injustice" to build up their status as leaders with the Negro population. There also was a discussion of a proposal that black militants take over various forms of vice in their communities to build up their treasuries.

PANAMA CANAL. It was agreed that every pressure should be applied in favor of the pending treaty by which the U.S. would return sovereignty of the Panama Canal Zone to Panama. Speakers described the treaty as one which eventually would lead to the deterioration of U.S. defenses south of Mexico and thus strengthen revolutionary forces throughout Latin America. Some suggested that the Canal would become a political plaything under Panamanian management because of the well-known corruption of Panama's politicians and this would in the "proper" chaotic conditions be conducive to a coup by the Left. The conferees hoped that articulate Negro leaders such as Carmichael and others who control blocs of votes would do everything possible to influence the Senate to ratify the proposed treaty.

DOMINICAN REPUBLIC. Fidel Castro admitted he had not expected President Lyndon Johnson to act so swiftly in dispatching troops to that island when it was torn by civil strife in 1965. The arrival of American troops, he said, "complicated the situation" and prevented "liberation forces" under Castro's direction from organizing the "necessary coalitions" which would have resulted in a revolutionary government. However, Castro said the

Communist underground was still strong and was receiving regular shipments of arms, presumably from Cuba. The conferees agreed that the Organization of American States (OAS), which installed a caretaker government pending an election, had done so only under pressure from Washington, and remained divided over its responsibilities and authority in Latin America. As such, it was said, the OAS probably could be influenced by anti-intervention propaganda within its member countries.

HAITI. Inevitably, it was agreed, President François Duvalier would be overthrown; thus every effort must be made to prepare for that eventuality. As outlined by Castro, the Communist strategy called for remaining neutral at the time of the coup, which undoubtedly would be staged by Duvalier's palace guard, and then moving in "in the name of the people." Castro and others declared there was little or no chance of a mass uprising, and that would make the Left's job easier, since its forces would be opposed only by the remnants of Duvalier's unpopular regime.

Some of this intelligence, especially that concerning the strategy of black militants in the United States, undoubtedly sent shivers down assorted State Department spines. It is almost certain that State's top policy planners found little comfort in the conferees' plans for the Panama Canal, since State had been plugging the new treaty as being in the highest interests of the United States, as well as a security blanket for the Panamanian politicians. But Jorge must have realized he was also telling his employers some things they enjoyed hearing.

For example, several months after the 1965 American intervention in the Dominican Republic, Under Secretary of State Mann had told the Senate Foreign Relations Committee that Juan Bosch, a contender for the Dominican presidency, had made a secret alliance with three Communist splinter groups to bolster his candidacy. Jorge's report quoted Castro as stating he had done "my best" to advance Bosch's unsuccessful candidacy in the June, 1966, elections because he felt he could do business with Bosch.

Bosch, who served as president of the Dominican Republic for seven months in 1963, was not one of State's pets. In

Foggy Bottom's view, he had always made the Communists welcome in his house. Indeed, the INR had been most undiplomatic in discussing Bosch in its 1965 annual report.

The Bosch administration, deposed the report, "pursued an open-door policy which permitted all those Communists who wished to return to do so . . . Laws against Communist activity were not enforced during the Bosch regime . . . Pro-Communist influence increased among university and secondary school students and in organized labor."

By the time Castro convened his tame delegates in July, 1967, Bosch was firmly in State's doghouse. He had returned to Santo Domingo from the safety of Puerto Rico after the American intervention to immediately demand that someone levy a one-billion-dollar fine against the United States for interfering in the internal affairs of his country.

Presumably, State also licked its elegant chops over Jorge's revelation that there was unanimous agreement among the conferees that Castro's Cuba pursue its policy of trade with America's Western allies as a divisive tactic. It was a tactic that worked. Only a few months earlier there had been a king-sized flap in Washington when it was announced that Great Britain had agreed to grant Castro a five-year credit for construction of a 39 million-dollar fertilizer plant by a British firm, and State had made unremitting and unsuccessful attempts to persuade other allies, notably France and Spain, to reduce their business dealings with the Caribbean Napoleon.

What effect Stokely Carmichael's privileged presence at these revolutionary sessions had on his later activities is speculative, of course. But it is a matter of record that he stepped up his militant activities upon his return to the United States. Or, as one State Department official put it, "The experience did not persuade Stokely to make application for membership in the American Legion and the United States Chamber of Commerce."

However, before returning to "hell," as he described his adopted country, Carmichael continued on to Europe, Africa and, finally, North Vietnam. His activities in Hanoi were more or less scrupulously reported by another agent of the State Department's intelligence unit, a European businessman holding what were described as "excellent credentials" with Hanoi's leadership. Carmichael's reception in Hanoi, according to this agent, was most cordial if somewhat less emotional than the welcome he had enjoyed in Havana. Although he enjoyed his stay and held what the agent called "enthusiastic discussions" with various top-level officials—including the venerable Ho Chi Minh—Carmichael was reported to have been miffed that his hosts regarded him more as a likable and potentially valuable curiosity than as a serious revolutionary.

By other means, through the interception of messages between Hanoi and Havana, it was learned that Ho found Carmichael a most agreeable guest, "but quite young, and therefore not too practical." Ho also reportedly was inclined to regard Stokely as being "too individualistic, and having too many unrealistic ideas." But Ho was said to be pleased that Carmichael showed so much interest in Ho's efforts and plans to "unite" his country, with or without the compliance of South Vietnam. Ho also considered Carmichael a "patriotic American," who was dutifully and properly disturbed by his country's involvement in an unjust war.

The European businessman also reported that whenever Carmichael had time on his hands he dropped in at the Museum of the Revolution, which the agent described as "a real chamber of horrors." The museum is dedicated to a portrayal of Vietnamese history, but many of its exhibits show the horrors suffered by the Vietnamese in their struggles with the Chinese, French and Americans. Most of the exhibits consist of photographs of hangings, torturings and other atrocities. "These seemed to inspire the young man," said the agent.

Presumably, Carmichael's interest in Vietnamese suffering under "imperialist" tyrants was pleasing to his Hanoi hosts. Yet Ho Chi Minh continued to have reservations concerning Carmichael's dedication to the global revolutionary cause.

In one radio message from Ho to Castro after Carmichael's departure from North Vietnam, Hanoi's chief commented in what seemed to be a wry manner that "The United States black leader at this stage takes a narrow provincial view of events. He does not relate his role to international problems, instead regarding the black revolution in the United States of America as a chauvinistic movement." There followed what seemed a curious *non sequitur*. "He enjoys parties."

At any rate, upon his return to the United States Carmichael seemed newly inspired by his attendance at the "international" strategy planning conclave in Havana and his visit to North Vietnam. He landed in New York on December 11, 1967, and the authorities forthwith relieved him of his passport. "To hell with the State Department," said Carmichael —and went back to work.

Within a few weeks, Carmichael had taken up residence in Washington, issued a call for the formation of a "Black United Front," and summoned the capital's Negro leadership to a "unity" meeting. At that meeting, held in early January, 1968, some Negro moderates said they were impressed by the discovery that "Stokely is a human being," and by his "amazingly moderate views." Such impressions raised more than one eyebrow at the State Department, whose intelligence reports, supported by newspaper accounts of Carmichael's global wanderings, noted that Stokely had called for nationwide guerrilla warfare against the American white population, and that he had made common cause with Fidel Castro and Ho Chi Minh. Press dispatches had quoted Carmichael as telling a cheering crowd in Paris, "We don't want peace in Vietnam, we want the United States to be defeated."

Nevertheless, one of those named to the Black United Front's steering committee was the Reverend Walter E. Fauntroy, vice-chairman of the Washington City Council, the capital's governing body. Another was Marion Barry, head of a youth organization named Pride, Inc., whose salary also was paid by the taxpayers. Later, it was announced that steering committee membership had been granted to the Reverend Channing Phillips, president of the Housing Development Corp. and Democratic National Committeeman for the District of Columbia.

By July of 1968, Carmichael was able to report that the BUF's "unity" was complete, with representatives of both moderate and militant Negro leaders included in its membership. That same month, the BUF took official cognizance of the death of a white policeman, shot down while trying to arrest a robbery suspect. Three Negroes—a man, his wife and their son—were charged with murder.

BUF's contribution to the brouhaha that ensued was to issue a resolution deposing that "The methods of self-defense used by the family charged with the alleged slaying of the honky [white] cop is justifiable homicide in the same sense that police are allowed to kill black people and call it justifiable homicide." Newsmen asked the Reverend Phillips whether he approved the resolution. "Well, I was there," he replied, "and the vote was unanimous." The Reverend Fauntroy, who did not attend the meeting at which the resolution was adopted, declared that "no homicide is justifiable," but urged the community to "read the text of the resolution . . . and look beyond the rhetoric." He described the BUF resolution as an effort to provoke "a constructive dialogue on the system which invites such violence. We must change a system that forces a decent officer . . . to go into a hostile community and get killed."

One BUF member said that "all" those who approved the resolution were "very, very responsible people." Since Stokely Carmichael was one of them, this statement could be expected to bring sardonic comfort to Fidel Castro and Carmichael's other associates at the Havana conclave.

Whether or not Carmichael was putting into practice the doctrine preached at those Havana sessions, his continued activities could not have been displeasing to Castro. At least, Stokely's preachings *sounded* like revolutionary doctrine.

In March, 1968, for example, Carmichael told an audience of Negroes in Washington's Presbyterian Church of the Redeemer that every black man in the country should "get a gun"—startling words to hear in an edifice theoretically erected to spread the doctrine of brotherly love. Carmichael argued—as Fidel used to argue in the days of Fulgencio Batista's Cuban dictatorship—that only people who are armed can achieve power. He quoted Mao Tse-tung as declaring that "Political power comes out of the barrel of a gun," and argued that "the only reason the honky is able to rule is because he has a gun. That's why the brothers call a gun an equalizer."

A few hours before the worst riots broke out in Washington following the assassination of Dr. Martin Luther King in April, 1968, Carmichael called a press conference at which he declared that the minor vandalism and looting of the night before was "just light stuff" compared to "what will happen." He urged Negroes to "get guns" and "retaliate against white America," and said "black people have to survive, and the only way they will survive is by getting guns. . . ." That night, the real rioting erupted and before the mobs were brought under control three days later whole sections of Washington had been razed by fire at a loss of more than 25 million dollars. At least ten persons were killed as a direct result of the rioting, and four other deaths were believed attributable to this civil war. More than one thousand persons were injured.

Both Ho Chi Minh and Fidel Castro, according to State Department intelligence, had expressed concern over whether Stokely Carmichael was capable of taking orders and submerging his individualism in the cause. It may be, of course, that Carmichael was acting on his own in those wild months after his return from abroad. But American intelligence insisted there was at least minor significance in that section of the report of the agent, Jorge, which said the Havana conferees urged black militants in the United States to "use civil rights demonstrations and demonstrations against political injustice to build up their status as leaders with the Negro population."

By coincidence or not, Stokely Carmichael had won new status as a "leader" by his activities in the demonstrations and riots of 1968, and by his acceptance as a "responsible" organizer of a Black United Front to which many Negro moderates had repaired.

11

Eavesdropping on the Kremlin

As should be expected, *The Super Spies* looked upon their surveillance of Stokely Carmichael and the Latin-American revolutionaries as not much more than a *divertissement*. Such exercises necessarily must be performed more or less left-handedly, as a corollary to the top-priority chore of U.S. intelligence. This is to discover, as far in advance as possible, what the Soviet Union is up to. As the other major nuclear power, the Soviet state, its activities and moods, is examined and appraised by more American espionage agents of varying classifications than any other nation.

Nevertheless, it will come as a pleasant surprise to most Americans that that part of the U.S. espionage community known as the military-diplomatic complex knew almost as much as the Russian experts did about Zond 5, the Soviet unmanned spacecraft which circled the moon in September, 1968, and was brought back for a successful recovery in the Indian Ocean.

This is not based on hindsight claims. A joint memorandum from the Defense Intelligence Agency and the State Department's Bureau of Intelligence and Research detailing what was known about Zond 5 was placed on President Johnson's desk in late July, nearly two months before the moon flight. The information in that memo, gathered by both electronic devices and human spies inside Russia, has not been fully disclosed, but some of the details are known.

Zond 5, for example, was the first Soviet spacecraft which was not brought down on land, although American craft for several years had regularly plumped down on water. The

Soviet water landing, however, came as no surprise to high American officials, since the DIA-INR memo had reported the Russians had solved this problem on an unpublicized shot in June. Moreover, the memo offered both electronic evidence and a report from an operative in Moscow that the Soviets had suffered four failures in attempts to circle the moon before Zond 5 made it. (Later published reports said there had been only two failures.)

Although some of this intelligence was the product of electronic eavesdropping on official Soviet messages by National Security Agency interception stations, most of it came from human agents, one of them installed in the super-secret bureaucracy of the Russian space program. The latter, a highly-rated technician, "disappeared" late in the summer of 1968, undoubtedly to take refuge in a new identity and new life provided by his American employers within the DIA and State Department.

The events leading up to the man's "disappearance" had all the elements of a spy thriller on the Late Late Show. To his contact, a diplomat from a neutral country also on the American payroll, he suddenly announced that he was "under suspicion." The diplomat arranged an emergency meeting with the Russian in a subway train the next evening.

As the train rattled its way under Moscow's streets, the spy filled in the diplomat on the chilling details. He had left his office a few nights earlier with two microfilm spools bearing texts of official and secret government papers on the space program. As he walked to the parking space adjoining his office building to get his car, he was accosted by a lower-echelon member of the space program's security force, a man with whom he had a nodding acquaintance.

The security officer wasted no time. He told the secret U.S. agent he had obtained "certain information" about his espionage activities, and ordered the agent to accompany him in his (the security officer's) car so that they could "talk it over." When the security officer—or "X," as the agent referred to him—mentioned two items of information the agent had stolen from official records, the agent decided he had no choice but to go along with him.

They drove out into a Moscow suburb, and there on a quiet, tree-lined street high on a hill, "X" made his proposition. He would "cooperate" with the agent if the United

States paid him $50,000, deposited in a numbered account in a Swiss bank. The agent said he made a split-second decision. He said he knew "X" could not be trusted, that to give in to him was to agree to be blackmailed the rest of his life, and perhaps in the end, to be denounced to the secret police. Because of his status, the agent carried a revolver with a silencer attached.

"I shot him dead," the agent told the startled diplomat.

He dragged the man's body out of the front seat and crammed it into the tiny luggage compartment of the car. Then he drove the car to an unused rock quarry several miles away and pushed it over the side. He walked three miles to a bus station, picked up his car at the parking lot adjacent to his office building, and drove home to his bachelor apartment.

The agent figured he had a little time. "X's" car, he said, probably would not be discovered for several days, and even then there almost certainly would be a delay in tracing "X's" movements, since it was most unlikely he had told anyone of his plan to confront the agent. "But I can't stay in the Soviet Union too much longer," the agent told the diplomat.

Thirty-six hours later, the agent was safe in a neutral country.

*   *   *

The loss of this "defector-in-place" undoubtedly was a severe blow to U.S. intelligence in the Soviet Union. Although there is every indication that both the DIA and the INR— as well as the CIA—still had agents operating in the country, none was as well placed as the man they lost. (It is probable this particular operative already has resumed his profession in some other part of the world.) In the meantime, Washington's military-diplomatic spy shops could take comfort from the bales of information produced before he fled.

For example, he had produced facts and figures *before* the Zond 5 shot which supported the contention of many U.S. scientists that the Russians would be most unlikely to land a man on the moon before the Americans. Whether this information supported such a conclusion actually was irrelevent; the U.S. was primarily interested in the flood of technical material contained therein. Earlier in 1968, he had confirmed American estimates of Soviet space capability. The Soviets, he reported, had developed boosters with an estimated thrust of only two million to three million pounds—inadequate for a manned moon mission, and much less powerful than America's 7.5 million-pound-thrust Saturn 5.

From this information, U.S. experts were able to conclude in the fall of 1968 that the Russians still lacked vital flight experience, particularly in docking and rendezvous techniques, and that they would be forced first to attempt to land an automatic station on the moon and bring it back before risking astronauts on such a mission.

As can be seen, therefore, the "defector-in-place" usually is the source of the most critical intelligence—as the Russians showed the world during the years after World War II, when a succession of defectors fed them juicy morsels ranging from the secret of the atomic bomb to details of a projected American guerrilla operation in Communist Albania. For the rest, the U.S., like every other nation seriously engaged in the art of espionage, depends to a great extent on both the hard intelligence and the gossip of neutral diplomats who are either on the American payroll or friendly to American purposes.

It was secret reports from such Moscow-based diplomats that—when pieced together by U.S. intelligence experts—revealed in the fall of 1968 that Western Communist leaders were "blackmailing" the Kremlin in the wake of the invasion of Czechoslovakia. The object was to force the Russian leadership in the future to "share its world responsibilities" more fully with its allies, as one diplomat put it. In plain language, the blackmailers were telling the Russians they would not tolerate any more Czechoslovakias.

A neutral diplomat with excellent contacts in the Italian Communist Party offered the information, at the height of the Czech occupation, that Luigi Longo, leader of the Italian party, had called for a Western European conference to "protest" the Soviet coup. Both Rumania and Yugoslavia, he said, wanted to attend such a meeting. Two weeks later, Longo confirmed this in a story leaked to a few European reporters. It was a calculated leak. By then, Longo and others had withdrawn the proposal for a conference as a result of private Russian pressure. But the neutral diplomat produced written evidence that the Longo bloc decided to make the aborted proposal public in order to put Moscow on notice before the world that its high-handed tactics in Czechoslovakia would not be tolerated on future occasions.

In any event, the blackmailing job achieved some success. Warsaw Pact troops were withdrawn from the Czech cities. And in October, 1968, a communiqué issued by an international Communist committee announced that a world Communist summit meeting scheduled for November in Moscow had been postponed. This was a bitter blow to the Kremlin, whose leadership had called the conference as a demonstration of loyalty to Moscow as the center of the world Communist movement. U.S. intelligence sources within European Communist parties furnished verbatim notes of the meeting at which the summit conference was postponed. These notes showed that various Western European Communist leaders had used bitter language to denounce the Czech occupation, and—without using the word—declared that the summit meeting should be put off to punish the Kremlin for its Czech adventure.

At about this time, too, a neutral diplomat stationed in Prague created a minor sensation at DIA headquarters in Washington when he dispatched "incontrovertible" evidence that Czech Party Leader Alexander Dubcek had been physically mistreated during his mission to Moscow just before the invasion. The evidence consisted of front-and-back photographs in color of Dubcek's torso, snapped by a Czech Foreign Office official, which showed ugly red welts and open wounds on both chest and back.

Results such as recorded here provide a certain balm, usually only temporary, for the intelligence professional. He enjoys his successes while he can, knowing that his masters will always demand to know what he has done for them recently, and that in the secret, nervous world of high officialdom his is the position most exposed to criticism.

When he was director of the Central Intelligence Agency, Allen Dulles was fond of remarking dryly to visitors that there was really only one thing a spymaster could be sure of, in any century. "He knows," said Dulles, "that in any catastrophe everybody involved will try to make intelligence the scapegoat."

History supports Dulles's viewpoint. Apparently there is something about intelligence's esoteric activities, its freewheeling and freedom from conventional restraint that sets it up among its governmental colleagues as the obvious fall guy when things go wrong. For a long time after the event, intelligence took the rap for the German successes during the Battle of the Bulge and was initially blamed for the tragedy of Pearl Harbor. In both cases, intelligence provided enough information to cause serious concern among those charged with acting upon it. Viewed in the context of the Cold War, it made an even more important contribution during the waning days of World War II. Through the United States Navy's monitoring of Japanese dispatches and the reports of agents in the Soviet Union, it offered solid evidence that Russia's official policy of perfidy had not been softened by the comradeship of the war.

Had President Truman and others listened more attentively to intelligence, it is almost certain there would have been no Hiroshima and no North Korea. The Soviet Union probably would not have secured a foothold in the Far East, and China might not have been lost to the Communists.

In short, American intelligence made it clear in July, 1945, that Japan was willing to surrender if some provision was made for the survival of the Emperor. Such a surrender would have made the Soviet Union's entrance into the Pacific War unnecessary and invalidated the Allies' pledges of Far Eastern concessions to Moscow, which were dependent on Russia going to war against Japan.

Looking back, Harry Truman said that the Cold War "started before the hot war ended," that is, during the summer months of 1945. In any event, the realization that the Soviet Union was uninterested in any permanent alliance with the capitalist nations was strengthened only a year after the Japanese surrender when the United Nations had to force the Soviets to withdraw their troops from Iran and to stop giving aid and comfort to the rebels seeking to overthrow the royal regime. The Berlin blockade came in 1948, followed two years later by the Korean "police action." Meanwhile, the Soviets through their tame "liberation forces" had completed their takeover of Eastern Europe. Clearly, it was imperative that American intelligence agencies turn most of their efforts to learning as much as possible about the attitudes, plans and plots of its erstwhile ally, lest miscalculations by both sides result in World War III.

Besides the necessity, dictated by considerations of national security, of seeking information on the state of the Soviet missile and bomber programs and nuclear testing, espionage is deemed essential in trying to determine Russian attitudes. Faced with a closed Soviet society, American policy makers have no other means of discovering how the Soviet leaders feel about a given international problem—how they will react to a contemplated American foreign policy action. The Russians seldom tip their hand, and even when they do they frequently say one thing—for the benefit of domestic consumption or to soothe the feelings of their allies—and mean another. Even on such trivial matters as the location of a new American embassy in Moscow, it is often impossible for Washington to get a clear idea of Soviet policy without stooping to cloak-and-dagger methods. Where the problem is more serious, spying is indispensable.

Thus, when John F. Kennedy moved into the White House in January, 1961, one of his first demands was for some hard information on the danger of Nikita Khrushschev intervening militarily in the crisis of Laos, where the Communist Pathet Lao, backed by Moscow, and the forces of General Phoumi Nosavan, backed by the United States, were locked in civil war. It was this intelligence, augmented by political guidance provided by the State Department's Bureau of Intelligence and Research, which enabled Kennedy to resolve the crisis, at least temporarily.

At that time, Laos technically was existing under the protection of the 1954 Geneva Accords which pledged its neutrality. But in the years since 1954, rival factions had used American and Soviet money to serve their own political ends. The neutral coalition government envisioned in Geneva was first violated by the Soviet Union and then, in retaliation, by Washington. The result was chaos, with the Pathet Lao plundering the northern provinces, General Nosavan wandering about the country in search of support, and the neutralist Premier Souvanna Phouma reduced to seeking an accommodation with the Soviets.

Finally, Souvanna Phouma was forced to flee to Cambodia, having found that his credit with the British and French was no protection from either the Communist Pathet Lao or the ambitions of General Nosavan, Uncle Sam's newly adopted son. The Pathet Lao, newly strengthened by the defection of the popular Captain Kong Le and his personal, neutralist army, was consolidating its position in northeast Laos and on the strategic Plaine des Jarres, thus threatening a Communist conquest of the entire kingdom. The United States was airlifting supplies to General Nosavan in the Mekong Valley, the Soviets to the Pathet Lao and Kong Le forces.

In this situation, Kennedy decided, as he put it, that the time had come for the United States "to stop horsing around —to get out of this king-making competition." He made it clear to his advisers that he couldn't care less about General Nosavan's ambitions; all he wanted to do was avoid a physical confrontation with the Soviet Union.

Since the CIA was committed to Nosavan, in one of those sad arrangements by which Allen Dulles sought to install rigid anti-Communists in power everywhere, regardless of their competence, Kennedy privately decided to have none of the CIA's arguments at this stage. Instead, he depended on the INR and the Pentagon's various spy shops to furnish him with alternatives, together with advice backed by hard intelligence on what results could be expected from whichever course he chose.

The Pentagon had agents operating in Laos, Vietnam, Cambodia and Thailand. The INR was collecting intelligence from its sources in Europe, with particular emphasis on probable Soviet reactions to American moves. Neither Defense nor the INR might come up with any comforting information, but Kennedy felt they could at least offer a fresh viewpoint.

As digested and evaluated by the INR, the new intelligence look-see gave Kennedy four alternative choices and their possible consequences. None of these choices was ideal, but they emphasized that an ideal choice did not exist.

First, Kennedy could stand by and let the Pathet Lao take over Laos. But the INR told him what he already knew, that is, that it would destroy the faith of other small nations in American protection. It could mean that the United States would have to move against the Communists later, at heavier cost. It was this consideration which in another year would persuade Kennedy to dispatch the first troops to Vietnam.

The President also rejected the second choice. This called for providing whatever military muscle was necessary to enable the pro-Western forces to prevail. INR memos stressed that the Laotians were not interested in becoming an American base in Southeast Asia, but wished only to be left alone.

Moreover, it would mean the deployment of American troops to the unfavorable jungle-and-rain-forest terrain of Laos for an indefinite period in the defense of an unpopular government. Laos was landlocked and had few good roads, which meant supply would be difficult. Communist China and Russia might match American troops with their own.

The INR's warnings about the third choice were almost as strong. This was to accept a division of Laos into Communist north and democratic south. INR memos warned that this might require the commitment of U.S. ground forces to defend the southern nation, and pointed out that the division of Korea and Vietnam had solved no problems.

Although the INR is not supposed to advise, but merely to state alternatives, its presentation of the fourth choice left no doubt that this had to be it. The only way out, the INR seemed to be saying, was to negotiate for the restoration of a neutral coalition government. Intelligence reports from Europe and the Soviet Union indicated that the Russians would buy this one, for the simple, pragmatic reason that it would not impair their vital interests. Other reports minimized the danger of either Red China or North Vietnam opposing a coalition regime militarily. Kennedy was warned that a coalition government posed dangers; he was reminded of the postwar Communist coup in Czechoslovakia. It was also pointed out that it would not be a popular solution, since it meant negotiating with Red China and giving American backing to the same Souvanna Phouma the CIA denounced as a fellow traveler.

In the end, one consideration was paramount to Kennedy. It was that this was the choice that Nikita Khrushchev could live with.

Kennedy insisted that a cease-fire precede the new conference. If not, he said, the United States would have to intervene in order to prevent the conquest of Laos by force. This was in March, 1961. Khrushchev huffed and puffed; he warned Washington that the Soviet Union could not indefinitely ignore American efforts to "sabotage" a peace conference. INR operatives abroad insisted Khrushchev was bluffing.

Convinced that Khrushchev eventually would agree to a cease-fire, Kennedy stayed his hand. He did land one unit of guerrilla experts and helicopters in Thailand and ordered Marines in Japan and Okinawa alerted for a possible airlift to the Laotian neighbor. Meanwhile the Communist Pathet Lao continued to consolidate and strengthen its positions. INR memos stated bluntly that if the United States intervened in Laos it would get no help from its allies and, indeed, probably would be denounced for making the move.

On March 23, Kennedy held a news conference at which he voiced a determination to stand firm, a statement based on INR assurances that Khrushchev would come around if the United States made it clear it would not negotiate without a cease-fire. "No one should doubt our resolution" [to intervene if necessary]—Kennedy told the world. Our policy, he said, was to support "a truly neutral government in Laos, not a Cold War pawn, a settlement concluded at the conference table, not on the battlefield." He set no deadline for a cease-fire, but he said that "every day is important."

American military advisers in Laos were donning their uniforms, more troops were alerted to fly to Thailand, the Seventh Fleet was standing by for action. Then, in the late spring of 1961, Khrushchev decided it was not in the interest of the Soviet Union to overplay his hand. He came out in favor of a cease-fire. It took more than a year of haggling at Geneva before a shaky coalition government for Laos was stuck together, but the result—as American intelligence had insisted—was what all the major powers really wanted. In the years that followed, the Pathet Lao broke out of the neutralist regime and resumed its guerrilla warfare, but Russia showed a distinct lack of interest in developments and refused to send aid to the rebels, while Peking refrained from any attempt to force another showdown.

Thus intelligence had served one of its more attractive purposes. The information it collected and the evaluation of this information by its experts helped avert a possible military confrontation between the United States on the one side and the Soviet Union and perhaps Red China on the other. The 1962 Geneva agreements were imperfect, but they were agreements; they were better than nothing. And as Kennedy remarked, the situation remained "uncertain and full of hazard—but so is life in much of the world."

Because it involved a military crisis, the development of the Laos accord was an example of the more spectacular, if unheralded, accomplishments of Cold War intelligence. On a day-to-day basis, however, the collection of information

surreptitiously serves more mundane, if often vitally important, purposes. It is also important to American foreign policy
to know about a crop failure in a Chinese province, an embezzlement scandal in a Soviet factory, a row between North
Vietnamese military leaders in Hanoi. The President must be
kept informed, through expert guesswork based on both information and careful evaluation, about what Soviet leaders
are thinking.

For example, Lyndon Johnson was most interested to learn
about the private reaction of Russian leaders to American
bombings near Hanoi in August, 1967. Reports of the reaction
were transmitted from neutral diplomats to American agents
in Moscow and then to Washington, where INR experts
evaluated them for the President's perusal.

According to these reports, neither Premier Kosygin nor
Party Boss Brezhnev was particularly disturbed by the heavy
bombings within ten miles of the Communist Chinese border.
On different occasions, they both told neutral diplomats they
could not believe either increased bombing or commitment
of more U.S. troops could achieve a military victory, and thus
there was nothing for the rest of the world to do but wait for
the United States to stop the escalation of a "senseless and
dirty war."

This confirmed the long-held belief in Washington that the
Soviets would never intervene in Vietnam because they saw
it as Communist China's problem. But, of course, it is always
nice to find new verification for an official point of view, and
the report undoubtedly was cordially received in the White
House.

Another portion of the INR memo was of more interest.
It passed on the intelligence report that in the opinion of
Russian leaders Red China was powerless to intervene because Mao Tse-tung's "Cultural Revolution" had reduced
China to chaos. Again, this had been an official State Department opinion, and so again it conveyed the special warmth
of reassurance.

That same memo offered an insight into Russian understanding of American politics. Both Kosygin and Brezhnev
had been telling diplomats that the increasing disenchant-
ment of the American people with the war would compel a
change of course either before or right after the 1968 Presidential election. They took the position that either President

Johnson would have to end the war to insure his reelection or the Republicans would come to power and stop the conflict as they did in Korea. Of more significance, the Russian leaders indicated that although they were helping to supply Hanoi and would continue to do so they would support "any kind of a settlement" that would end the war.

At about this time, too, there was a sharp disagreement between INR on the one side and the DIA and CIA on the other concerning the effect of the Vietnam war on the nations of the European Communist bloc. The CIA and DIA mounted the familiar argument that the Communists could only understand firmness in the application of power and thus were impressed, if reluctantly, by the American stand in Asia. The war, President Johnson was told, had served notice on the Communists that wars of liberation could not succeed. INR Director Thomas L. Hughes painted a far less glowing if more scholarly picture.

In an Intelligence Note to Secretary of State Rusk, Hughes quoted intelligence sources in Europe as reporting that the war was damaging the United States' image among the satellite nations as a country with which they could live in peaceful coexistence. As a result, said the note, the war was strengthening the hands of the conservatives, who were arguing that it showed the worldwide struggle for power was continuing, with the U.S. determined to achieve a permanent foothold in Asia. The war was said to have become a weapon in the hands of those orthodox leaders who resisted any attempts at reform or the relaxation of party discipline.

Such intelligence studies revealed a proper INR interest in what is going to happen in the Soviet Union and in the satellite nations next year, and the year following that, and the year following that. Because its field is the intelligence of diplomacy, the INR more than any other espionage agency must look into the future and try to predict the order of Communist succession in the event the current leaders fall from power.

When Khrushchev got the sack in Russia the INR batted .500 percent. Its experts had correctly predicted that the hard-boiled party functionary, Brezhnev, would move up, but didn't give Kosygin the prophet's time of day. In 1969, the INR was predicting that when and if Brezhnev and Kosygin were ousted, the new strong man probably would be Shelepin, the trade union autocrat. The prediction was based on the theory that the Brezhnev-Kosygin team would depart only if the hardliners sold their argument that the pair had been too "soft on capitalism," and thus their replacements would be from the hardliners' camp.

Some of INR's "research" on such matters is done by outside consultants, experts in various fields who sell their expertise and advice to the State Department on a contract basis. INR Director Hughes found this practice difficult to explain to New York's Representative John Rooney, a veteran State Department baiter, during House hearings in 1965. Hughes was explaining that his bureau was unable to contract for certain "studies" of the political situation in several countries because of budgetary limitations. He noted that "One of those which went by the board would have been a study of the political dynamics of Tanzania. Tanzania at the moment is in a real crisis. It would have been of great use to our policy makers . . ."

"You could not do that out of an appropriation of $4,068,000?" put in Rooney. "You couldn't spend three or four thousand dollars? Stop kidding."

"We did not give it priority over some of the other contracts," replied Hughes. "The Soviet succession problem had higher priority."

ROONEY: Who made that study?

HUGHES: I must explain, too, that when we are talking in a general way here about external research, we are talking not only about contracts but about consultants who are brought from time to time to Washington . . . for discussion with departmental figures on problems like the Soviet succession. Just a couple of months ago we had a conference here bringing experts on the Soviet Union and the Communist movement from Indiana University, Columbia University, and the Rand Corporation . . . We benefited enormously after Khrushchev's fall by bringing to Washington on a crash basis some of the leading Sovietologists around the country . . .

ROONEY: The question is, who made the study?

HUGHES: We now have in process for completion next year a study on Soviet leadership . . .

ROONEY: I thought the study was completed.

HUGHES: No, I tried to suggest, Mr. Chairman, that we have—

ROONEY: Who made the study? Has it been finished?

HUGHES: There is a continuing consultation with Professor Dallin of Columbia University; with Professor Morris of Indiana University, and Professor Rush of the Rand Corporation.

In this instance, Hughes reported, the consultants received seventy-two dollars a day and sixteen dollars per diem for expenses, plus travel costs. Under questioning, he also disclosed that there had been a conference—Rooney called it a "clambake"—at Airlie House, a resort in Warrenton, Va., of consultants on Africa and State Department officials. The two-day cost, he said, was $986.

Rooney was displeased that the cost of the conference had been listed under "contracts," but Hughes did his best to assure the Congressman that it was "a unique operation. It seemed to us by far the best method of bringing African experts from outside the government into touch with African experts inside the State Department . . . All of these things are somewhat intangible . . . but there are real benefits to be derived from a very occasional mingling of the best experts in the United States on African problems with African experts inside the government. Africa is in enormous turmoil at the moment. . . ."

As a Government official involved in strategic intelligence, Hughes had done his best to explain the complications and problems that beset the United States in its role as the leading Western power. But John Rooney's irritable perplexity was understandable. In a sense, he was speaking for the plain, Main Street American who in the sixties was wondering aloud why his country tried to do so much. To this citizen, and John Rooney, it sometimes seemed that big-hearted and big-spending Uncle Sam was employing altogether too many people suffering from an obsessive desire to poke Sam's nose into every troublesome nook and cranny on the globe.

12

The Yellow Peril Papers

In relative terms, describing the Soviet Union as a "closed society" is to be unfairly critical of a ruling government that in recent decades has permitted its people some superficial association with the outside world. Compared with Communist China, Russia under its collective dictatorship is a wide open country, doing normal business with its global neighbors.

Red China is, in effect, a gigantic prison camp. Its leadership will not voluntarily tell anyone the time of day, let alone the latest crop figures for Yünnan province. As has been seen, the United States has resorted to the eavesdropping-in-space of spy satellites in its attempts to penetrate this continental fortress. But it is a tribute to the ingenuity of human beings, in many cases admittedly motivated by a liking for money, that America's super spies also have done some successful prying into Peking's secrets by employing old-fashioned cloak-and-dagger methods carried out by ordinary people.

In short, the Defense Intelligence Agency and its armed service helpers, and the Intelligence and Research Bureau of the State Department have managed to plant spies even in Red China. This achievement is not bruited about in Georgetown drawing rooms, but occasionally an inkling is let drop in official governmental circles. Such was indicated by INR Director Thomas L. Hughes in an off-the-record statement before Representative John Rooney's House subcommittee on appropriations on February 3, 1964.

Rooney had been questioning Hughes sharply about payments for special studies made by academicians on Communist China. In his role as watchdog over Foggy Bottom's multifarious and complex activities, Rooney made it clear he didn't think the taxpayers were getting their money's worth.

"Just a moment, Mr. Chairman," said Hughes. "May I go off the record for a minute?"

Rooney sighed. "Very well. If it's really necessary."

Hughes thereupon explained that the studies were necessary in order properly to appraise some particularly interesting "raw material" on Communist China which had come into the State Department's hands during the previous year. Some of this material had come from "reliable sources," and some was obtained from a contact in a Chinese Communist bank in Hong Kong.

The material obtained from "reliable sources" gave the State Department its first hard evidence of dissension within the Mao Tse-tung regime which would erupt two years later in the violence of Mao's "Cultural Revolution." From the bank contact came copies of official Peking documents stating as a decision of highest policy that Red China must face the eventuality of a military confrontation with the Soviet Union over their common frontier.

But Hughes naturally did not give the subcommittee a fill-in on the details of how the INR acquired this information. It is a fascinating story which reveals among other things how the impossible can be achieved by trying harder and taking a little more time, and the profit that accrues to the American community when spy shops work together. In Red China, considerable information was obtained as a result of close cooperation among the DIA, the INR and the intelligence branches of the Army, Navy and Air Force.

The story opens one afternoon in November, 1962, in Peking, when a Chinese bundled in a heavy overcoat with a fur collar against the rainy cold emerged from a big but nondescript building at No. 15 Bow String Alley, headquarters of the "Social Affairs Department" of the Red Chinese Government. The "Social Affairs Department" has nothing to do with pensions or child day care centers or widows' assistance. It is the polite front name for the Chinese Communist Party's central office for security and intelligence—the secret police and espionage apparatus. The Chinese, who shall here be given the cover name of Chen, was a career official in the Ministry of Public Affairs, the Gestapo unit responsible for domestic security. (Foreign intelligence is assigned to the

United Front Workers Department and the International Liaison Department.)

Chen held up an arm to beckon in the direction of the official car stand across the street, then crossed the street and got into the car assigned to him. He opened the door of the car himself; in Communist officialdom only the highest-ranking are pampered by their chauffeurs. The car drove off, and several minutes later Chen was deposited at a restaurant specializing in Burmese food. There, at one of the better tables, he joined an Indian commercial traveler who may as well be known as Singh, since his actual identity is a secret. Chen and Singh had worked together frequently over a period of several months on matters concerning Chen's department. There is no indication Singh was on the secret police payroll; the likelihood is that he was consulted from time to time on applications from assorted foreigners to do business in Red China, for Singh had been peddling his wares in the country since 1950 and his information on other foreign businessmen was encyclopedic.

An American military attaché at an embassy in the Far East—not India—also had been working with Singh. It had taken the attaché two years of careful work to cultivate Singh to the point where he could tell Singh what he wanted of him, for pay. In turn, Singh had winnowed through his acquaintances among the Peking bureaucracy for another eighteen months before deciding that Chen was his man. Now Chen was about to make his first delivery.

In the convoluted, furtive language of spies everywhere, Chen informed Singh that he had put his hands on certain material of an interesting nature. He briefed Singh on its contents and significance, and named some names. He also agreed to a price for the material. Singh, attacking his food heartily, told Chen where the material could be delivered and to whom, and Chen gave his approval to the procedure. No more was said.

A few days later, Chen turned three large envelopes over to a minor functionary in a neutral embassy in Peking as they brushed past each other on a crowded bus. The envelopes contained copies of secret police memoranda on certain investigations conducted by the Ministry of Public Affairs. Within a week, the envelopes had been carried out of Red China in a diplomatic pouch to a foreign mission in Singapore. There, they were duly handed over to an American on assignment from the INR, for whom the embassy functionary in Peking had been working for more than five years.

Many months before Chairman Mao's purge of his leadership therefore, the State Department was in possession of a kind of scorecard identifying the players. It showed Mao, his wife, Chiang Ching, a former actress, and Mao's Defense Minister Lin Piao drawn up in line of battle against such powerful political leaders as Chief of State Liu Shao-chi; the mayor of Peking, Peng Chen, one of the most influential members of the Politburo; Party Secretary General Teng Hisao-ping; and Teng To, editor-in-chief of the prestigious Peking *People's Daily*, the Chinese Communist Party's principal mouthpiece.

All these ranking members of the hierarchy and many others were described in the official documents acquired in Peking as "right opportunist anti-party renegades," who sought to undermine Mao's authority. Apparently they had challenged Mao's leadership "in many adroit and cunning ways" and sought to slow down the "continuing revolution and class struggle" laid down in the Mao dogma.

Moreover, these same papers revealed that the internal dispute in Peking had been raging since 1959, when Mao purged his Defense Minister, Marshal Peng Teh-huai, for allegedly heading an "anti-party clique."

A copy of a 1959 Central Committee resolution detailed charges against Peng which indicated the marshal had considerable support in defying Mao. He was charged with "trying to restore capitalism and advocating improved relations with the imperialistic, politically corrupt United States." He engaged in "illicit relations with foreign countries, including the Soviet regime of Khrushchev." He "summoned about him a mob of revisionists who had tried in vain to sabotage the Great Leap Forward."

This was the first verification of reports of massive opposition within the Party structure to the Great Leap, Mao's "socialistically pure" campaign to modernize China rapidly with vast labor projects and backyard steel furnaces. Its failure disrupted the country's economy, caused widespread famine and tarnished Mao's image in the rest of the Communist world.

According to the Central Committee resolution, Marshal

Peng challenged Mao at a Politburo meeting and Central Committee plenum in July and August, 1959, when he denounced the Great Leap as "a rush of blood to the brain." He also warned Mao that his "excesses" would lead to a people's revolt, and added that "only the inert state of the masses" had saved him "from the kind of uprising staged by the people of Budapest" in 1956.

Peng, said the resolution, was dangerous "because he feigned candor and thus attracted many supporters who were deceived by his cunning." His dismissal and that of his Army chief of staff, Huang Ke-cheng, was described as "essential to defeat a wild attempt to pull China into the orbit of revisionism." Although Peng was dismissed, he kept his Politburo seat and later became manager of a state farm.

In his drive to discredit Chief of State Liu, Mao later ordered portions of the charges against Marshal Peng published in the Chinese press—in August, 1967. At that time, the authoritative Maoist publication, *Red Flag,* declared that Liu had collaborated with Peng "to usurp the leadership of the party." It also charged that Liu had been a "renegade" as early as 1923. This was a curious revelation, inasmuch as Liu was one of Mao's closest associates until the purges of the mid-sixties.

In any event, the policy makers at the State Department did not have to wait for Mao's belated revelations of trouble in his official household. Thanks to INR's operatives in the Far East, they had inside information two years before the trouble erupted into headlines around the world, and presumably made their plans accordingly. Having material like this at hand provided as good an explanation as any of Secretary of State Dean Rusk's patient persistence in following a policy of containment of the Mao regime. It is easier to contain a government whose leaders are fighting among themselves.

The means by which State's INR arranged to smuggle out of Red China the documents revealing Peking's "decision" accepting the inevitability of armed conflict with the Soviet Union was a different package of intelligence goods. It was an illustration of how unceasingly espionage networks labor at sweeping up bits and pieces of information which may not mean anything at the time but which sometimes can lead to pay dirt.

Mining the rich lode of Hong Kong, which probably harbors more spies than any city in the world, INR people over a period of months picked up scraps of information which indicated that a fairly highly-placed employee of the Bank of Communist China could be bought. From his perch in the bank, which occupies a skyscraper virtually cheek by jowl with the new Hong Kong Hilton Hotel on Victoria Island, Ling apparently had been running some errands for intelligence straw bosses of various countries. The jobs he did were considered of little importance, but he was kept in mind.

Then, a few months later, information from Peking dealing with assorted personalities in the Foreign Office mentioned Ling's name. Over the years, it appeared, he had played host at his Hong Kong apartment to an old friend from the mainland who was a member of what in State Department language would be called the policy planning staff of the Red Chinese Foreign Office. The friend, here called Yuan, was a high liver who looked kindly upon wine, women, fast automobiles and good horseflesh.

Naturally, this information suggested an opportunity. Since Ling was not averse to earning an occasional fast buck by peddling intelligence, perhaps he would listen to a proposition from the INR. It would suggest that Ling get together with Yuan and arrange matters so that the United States could lay its intelligence hands on some juicy material from the Red Chinese Foreign Office.

An Air Force attaché in another Far Eastern city had done some business with another friend of Ling's. The attaché arranged to have the friend put the proposition to Ling the next time he visited Hong Kong, for the usual fee, of course. The friend did so, and reported that Ling was interested, although wary. Whereupon, Ling was proffered, and accepted, a five-thousand-dollar good-faith retainer. Ling warned the intermediary, however, that it might be months before he came up with anything worthwhile.

It was. Nothing was heard from the banker for over eleven months. Then, when it seemed that the project was a flop, Ling came through. A large package was delivered to a tailoring establishment in Kowloon used as a drop by Ling's INR employers. It was crammed with copies of documents bearing the Chinese Foreign Office seal and stamped TOP SECRET. Ling and his pal in the Foreign Office split a payment of forty thousand dollars.

In due course, the INR was able to present Secretary Rusk with an Intelligence Note on the subject dealt with in these copies. Its gist was that the situation could not be stated in quite the simplistic terms of the pieces of paper from Peking, but the Note did not reject the idea of a Sino-Soviet clash at a time convenient for the Red Chinese.

As brought up to date in the spring of 1968, the INR analysis saw little likelihood of any major military encounter between the two Communist giants before 1970. The border situation was seen as becoming crucial to the Soviet Union only when China had built up its military strength, including nuclear power, to a level at which it could threaten the destruction of Russian centers of population. China could then use this threat as blackmail to try to wring concessions from Moscow.

The appraisal went on to paint a broad picture of the sticky Sino-Soviet relationship:

Common borders would be a likely major source of friction and conflict between the two countries, not only because China claimed certain lands under Soviet control but because Moscow and Peking each had reason to fear incursions by the other as part of the propaganda gambit of flexing national muscles for the benefit of other Communist states. As China grew in military power, this game could become explosive.

In the next few years, both countries would seek to colonize certain areas of Central Asia with their own people in an effort to give more substance to their territorial claims.

The split probably was irreparable, because of the deep ideological cleavage between Moscow and Peking. Only a complete reversal by the Chinese Communist leadership in adopting Russia's policy of mutual coexistence would repair the split, and even then there would be a residue of hostility.

Eventually, as with other great powers, the Sino-Soviet relationship probably no longer would be determined by ideological divergence but by various and changing factors of national interest. That is to say, the relationship would depend on the answer to the question on both sides: Is this or that policy good business?

The United States should consider adopting a "carrot and stick" policy toward China as well as the Soviet Union in order more effectively to exploit the division. While remain-

ing firm against Chinese aggression, the U.S. should explore
the possibilities of developing cultural interchanges, exchanges
of journalists, and face-to-face discussions of problems with
Peking. But it was pointless to approve Red China's admission to the United Nations under any conditions, since Peking's present course of fomenting world revolution demanded
that it have an enemy, to wit, the United States, and thus it
undoubtedly would reject UN membership.

Complementing this analysis was an official outline of the
Soviet view of Communist China's aims acquired by a State
Department operative in Eastern Europe. The outline pur-
portedly was a secret document intended for the perusal of
Soviet satellite leaders, and it was picked up in late 1966,
when the Russians and Chinese were rowing over which side
was the Biggest Brother to North Vietnam.

In terms that might have been used by Lyndon Johnson or
Dean Rusk, the outline accused the Peking regime of expansionist and imperialistic aims which even a change of leadership would not alter. These aims were said to have taken
shape as far back as the 1950's, shortly after China's intervention in the Korean War, and the Russians declared they had
been given the official label of "The Great Strategic Plan of
Mao Tse-tung." It was a plan calculated to make Russian
leaders toss fitfully on their beds at night:

Peking would set up an Asian empire, similar to the pre-
World War II "Greater Asian Co-Prosperity Sphere." The
empire would include Vietnam, Cambodia, Burma, Laos, In-
donesia, Korea and the Mongolian Republic in its first phase.
The second phase would bring in part of India, the Soviet Far
East and Soviet Central Asia.

Such an ambitious project could not be accomplished without a global nuclear war, which Mao saw as the first step
necessary to decimate the decadent democracies and, of
course, the Soviet Union.

The answer was to do whatever was necessary to prevent
China from exporting revolutions among her neighbors or
gaining any kind of major influence over them. China must
be isolated "at all costs," including "the use of military per-
suasion," else the Soviet motherland "will become a battlefield."

This document became one of the working papers of the
State Department's policy makers. Its gist has been used,

without attribution, to help round up support among the smaller Asian nations for the American policy in Vietnam. Again without attribution, it was used as the basis of a number of private consultations between American and Soviet diplomats, including President Johnson and Russian Premier Aleksei Kosygin. As a result of those talks all doubts about the authenticity of the document were dispelled. Among other things, it helped explain why the Russians privately sought to mediate the Vietnam war; to the Kremlin, a protracted struggle could leave North Vietnam so enervated, both economically and politically, that Communist China could take over the nation lock, stock and barrel, without any argument.

Inside information on conditions within a country and its long-range foreign policy and military plans come under the heading of strategic intelligence, which can be described in street-corner terms as the thinking man's spookery. Its aim is to assemble all the information collected by spies, both human and electronic, mix it with an appraisal of the political and diplomatic situation in a given neighborhood of the world, and then predict what will happen a year, or three years, hence. Sometimes it works. When it does, it is a tribute to the professional competence and patience of the American intelligence community in plucking information even out of padlocked countries such as Communist China.

Looming ever larger in this difficult process is the role of the sophisticated machines which have become the servants of espionage. They range from the eavesdropping devices worn in the inside pocket of a neutral diplomat or commercial traveler earning some pin money from Uncle Sam to the space satellites whose ears intercept both voice messages and signals set off by the movement of ships, airplanes and ground troops. Satellites and spy planes photograph a continent in less time than it used to take to get from New York to Le Havre by ship. The pictures they take can pinpoint the location of a missile base or a wheat region hit by unpublicized drouth.

Space satellites, spy ships and submarines, and secret ground stations pick up coded governmental messages from Radio Peking and transmit them to the experts at the National Security Agency in Fort Meade, Maryland, for cracking. These eavesdroppers intercept instructions to espionage agents throughout Asia broadcast by Radio Pyongyang in North Korea. They "read" the flow of intelligence to Peking from overseas Chinese earning their living in Thailand, Burma, Vietnam, Laos and Indonesia. They tune in on orders to North Vietnamese troop commanders in South Vietnam transmitted by Radio Hanoi.

A Chinese agent employed by the DIA once recorded garbled portions of a discussion among members of the Chinese Communist Central Committee merely by standing in an outside courtyard fifty feet from the building in which the meeting was taking place with a highly sensitive microphone and tape recorder in his inside jacket pocket.

Another U.S. agent, a Chinese nuclear scientist, was able to transcribe the minutes of a conference on the H-bomb from a recording device concealed in his hearing aid. The man actually was deaf, and had been so certified by a board of medical examiners on duty with the Chinese Army.

False information has been planted by double agents in a Peking Post Office box maintained as a drop by one of Red China's intelligence organizations, the *Guozi Shudian,* or International Bookstore. The number of this box is changed at irregular intervals; in the fall of 1968 it bore Number 101.

Chinese are trained in special spy schools at military bases throughout the United States and Southeast Asia, where they are taught as many Chinese tongues as they can manage. Both officers and enlisted men fighting in the Vietnam war were offered special courses in espionage, with bonuses and special pay for those who passed. The war also offered an opportunity to pass special agents into Red China through North Vietnam, Cambodia and Laos. In the fall of 1968, a number of American spies were successfully posing as representatives of various European and Asian firms in Red China, North Vietnam and several Southeast Asian countries where Communist Chinese agents were active.

A Chinese-American graduate of Annapolis, who specialized in southern Chinese dialects, was landed on the Chinese coast from a submarine in a rubber boat. He used forged credentials to get a job in the headquarters of the Red Chinese secret police in Peking and within two years was a special assistant to K'ang Sheng, director of the internal security-foreign intelligence complex known as the Social Affairs Department. He has since returned to the United States to take an assignment with the Central Intelligence Agency. Meanwhile, K'ang Sheng moved up to the No. 5 position in the Communist hierarchy, despite criticism from Mao for permitting "leakages" in his department. Most American experts believe K'ang has relinquished his spy job for the more politically important assignment of promoting the Mao brand of Communism abroad.

At any rate, the flow of intelligence from Red China, although never a flood and more often than not a trickle, continued. Among other information wrested from Mao's police state were expert periodic appraisals on Peking's status as a sophisticated maker of war.

In the spring of 1968, some Pentagon intelligence analysts suggested that new information on Peking's nuclear capacity cast at least a small shadow of doubt on the theory that Red China was preparing itself for war with the Soviet Union. This was the discovery that the Chinese had not yet begun the deployment of a medium-range ballistic missile system aimed at such neighboring nations as Russia, Japan and India.

The Chinese had tested a missile-borne atomic bomb more than a year before, and there was then every indication that they planned to build a medium-range delivery system. But American spy satellites, reconnaissance planes and old-fashioned human spies had failed to come up with any evidence of construction of missile silos and related equipment. Therefore, the argument was raised that Peking might have decided to skip the development of a medium-range system and concentrate on building an intercontinental system whose missiles could reach the United States and, incidentally, provide Red China with credentials as one of the world's super powers.

However, the counter-argument prevailed. This was that there had been a slippage in the Chinese nuclear program—that it was not progressing as fast as previous intelligence reports had indicated. Those reports had predicted that the Chinese would be capable of launching an ICBM before the end of 1967, and they had failed to do so. A majority in both the Pentagon and the State Department agreed that this failure was a result of the chaos produced by Mao's Cultural Revolution which at one point had threatened the security of the nuclear testing areas in Sinkiang Province. Besides, Pentagon and State analysts kept pointing to that Soviet document on China's imperialistic aims, the Chinese papers on the inevitability of an armed clash with Russia, and border incidents involving the two countries.

Before and since the acquisition of these documents, verified armed clashes between Soviet and Red Chinese border units reflected the mutual fear and hostility behind the Peking-Moscow split. Verifications came from Defense Intelligence Agency operatives in Asia and from both American and neutral diplomats reporting to State's INR. The role of the DIA in this "politically strategic" area predictably was questioned sharply by the CIA as a usurpation of CIA's own "traditional" role, but McNamara's powerful intelligence band sloughed off this criticism on the grounds it was interesting itself in a situation that had definite military overtones. President Johnson, with his obsession for getting "consensus" intelligence, was loath to intervene in this squabble.

In any event, the DIA and INR were able to offer more or less detailed reports on most of these border clashes long before they reached the public prints, and in many cases their reports were exclusive.

For example, only a few weeks after the event, the DIA-INR network reported the "massacre" in May, 1962, of nearly five hundred non-Chinese in the province of Sinkiang who had sought permission to emigrate to the Soviet Union. Wild and arid, Sinkiang had for a hundred years been a sphere of Russian influence, with the Czars and later the Soviet Politburo seeking to assimilate its mixture of disparate races— Uighurs, Kazakas and other Moslems. For a time, the Russians and Chinese Communists made of Sinkiang a cooperative venture in what might be called state-controlled capitalism; in 1950 they signed an accord setting up joint Sino-Soviet companies to develop the area's oil and metal resources.

But when Peking made Sinkiang its principal nuclear test area, the Russians apparently decided that cooperation was dangerous. At any rate, Moscow embarked on a campaign to play the minorities against the Chinese by issuing Soviet passports to thousands of tribesmen and urging them to cross over into Russia.

About 70,000 had fled into Soviet territory before the Chinese took steps to halt the flow. They sent fresh troops into the area and closed the frontier, thus precipitating a series of Moslem riots. The riots were put down at first without bloodshed, but in May, 1962, the Chinese turned tough. According to DIA-INR reports, about 40 residents of the Ili-Kazakh-sakya District waited upon the local party committee for permission to emigrate to the Soviet Union. The committee refused to hear out the delegation, and a crowd of some 500 persons gathered in front of party headquarters. Whereupon, the Chinese turned machine guns on the crowd and mowed them down. Agents in Sinkiang reported "several tons of corpses" left on the ground.

Other Sino-Soviet armed clashes were reported, in the mid-sixties, in Sinkiang, on the border between Kansu and Soviet Mongolia, and on the border between Chinese Inner Mongolia and Soviet Mongolia. In 1966, large-scale redeployments of Chinese troops were reported from the quiet Ladakh front facing India to the Sino-Soviet border in Sinkiang. Other reports in the same year told of the arrival of Soviet rocket troops and jet fighter squadrons in the Mongolia and Sinkiang areas and in the Trans-Baikal sector. Peking countered with the transfer of several armored units to the borderlands, and boasted that its rockets "commanded" Soviet Mongolia.

Intercepted Soviet and Communist Chinese messages, decoded by National Security Agency cryptanalysts, constantly spoke of the Soviet fear of Chinese expansionism and of Peking's determination to "protect" the outer provinces in order to maintain a buffer for the Chinese heartland. From Moscow there issued dispatches to Russian agents in the border provinces to set up subversion among the ethnic minorities and to take advantage of Mao's "Cultural Revolution" to encourage rebellion by Moslem youths.

Indeed, Mao's revolution backfired in Sinkiang and Inner Mongolia, where in late 1967 and early 1968 American intelligence sources reported Red Guard factions still battling the army and fighting among themselves. Mao had told youth to fight the "out-worn institutions of government," and he found he could not call them off at his whim.

Meanwhile, various insurgent groups, including the "Ghengis Khan Combat Corps," were receiving shipments of Soviet arms, radio equipment and propaganda materials to be employed in "asserting nationality issues." Commander of the Ghengis Khan unit was reported to be the Mongol Prince Ulanfu, who had been dismissed by Peking as Communist boss of Inner Mongolia in May, 1967. Ulanfu was described as "owned and operated" by Moscow.

Red Guards wrecked Moslem mosques and Communist headquarters alike in Sinkiang and Inner Mongolia. Soviet-based guerrillas under the command of Sunun Taibov, a Sinkiang Kazakh who formerly had been a Chinese general, raided Chinese frontier posts. Both the Red Guards and the Russian-oriented guerrillas were fighting regular army units under General Wang En-mao, the semiautonomous military commander and Communist chieftain of Sinkiang, who ran the province as a personal police state. Mao's Cultural Revolutionists, meanwhile, were denouncing Wang as a "counter-revolutionary bandit" and demanding his removal, even as Premier Chou En-lai sought to assure Wang that he had Peking's support and that Mao was just letting his rebels blow off steam. As dictator of the province where Peking conducted its nuclear tests, Wang's cooperation with the central government was vital, and by early 1968, Chou apparently had convinced Wang that his position was secure. At least, Wang appeared in Peking in January to pledge anew his allegiance to the Mao regime and to receive VIP treatment.

Communist China struck back at Moscow by various diplomatic intrigues in Eastern Europe, most of them centered on urging Soviet satellites to demand the return of territories acquired from them by Russia in World War II. Neutral diplomats in various satellite capitals have reported to the INR that emissaries from Peking were mainly responsible for Rumania's campaign to force the Soviet Union to relinquish jurisdiction over Bessarabia. These emissaries also were said to be making progress in their campaign to persuade Poland to demand the return of its eastern provinces and Czechoslovakia to press for settlement of the dispute over Ruthenia.

Beginning in 1963, Red China also publicly has attempted to split off the Soviet Union from the rest of the Communist world by charging "collusion" between Moscow and Washington to dominate the world. This charge, first published in the official Chinese newspapers, *People's Daily* and *Red Flag,* came as no surprise to the State Department, whose proper —and not so proper—diplomats abroad had predicted such a development as early as 1956.

At that time, neutral diplomats in the ideological if not the financial thrall of the INR reported that Nikita Khrushchev's speech at the 20th Congress of the Soviet Communist Party in which he denounced Stalin was viewed in Peking as an attempt to curry favor with Washington. Further, an INR man back from a duty tour of the Far East brought with him copies of official Red Chinese documents which indicated that the Mao regime secretly had adopted a policy of denunciation of Khrushchev's attempts to seek what later would be called "peaceful coexistence" with the capitalist powers.

There followed, that same year, two events that supported this evidence of a Moscow-Peking split. When the Polish Communist leadership demanded greater autonomy, the Soviets moved up troops in what the Chinese called a demonstration of "great-power chauvinism." But when the Hungarians rose in mass revolt, Peking chided Moscow for being slow to intervene against a "counterrevolutionary" action.

Since that time, INR experts have urged that the United States intensify its perfectly sincere attempts to arrange a *modus vivendi* with Moscow in order to take advantage of the Sino-Soviet falling out. Moscow made this difficult by its need for seeming to seek unity with its Chinese comrades and for reassuring the rest of the Communist world that it was not about to leap into bed with decadent America. But both John Kennedy and Lyndon Johnson made some progress in moving toward an accommodation with Russia, notably with the nuclear test ban and nuclear non-proliferation treaties, and—perhaps just as important—kept the lines of communication with Moscow open. Predictably, Peking viewed these developments with great suspicion.

Apparently, it was the war in Vietnam that prompted Mao's regime to proclaim that it had perceived a Russian-American plot to run the world through what Lyndon Johnson saw as a "partnership for peace." At any rate, Peking assumed the role of North Vietnam's principal cheer leader, urging Hanoi to pursue the war vigorously, to ultimate victory, while Moscow secretly and most cautiously attempted to use its influence to arrange a negotiated settlement. At the same time, State Department intelligence people abroad relentlessly peddled the line that Washington would be delighted to sit down with Moscow and work out a formula for real "peaceful coexistence" everywhere in the world. Again, the INR was not promising anything the Johnson Administration was not eager to deliver.

Obviously, the idea of a Moscow-Washington partnership had to be odious to Peking, and it reacted accordingly. In December, 1963, the Red Chinese had harped on Khrushchev's "obsession with summit meetings between the Soviet Union and the United States," and the Soviet Politburo's advocacy of "peaceful coexistence as the general line of foreign policy." Three years later, Washington's intelligence campaign bore more fruit when Peking charged that Moscow had joined with the U.S. "to betray peoples' revolutions and dominate the world."

The charge was in a warning to Hanoi that the North Vietnamese regime was being duped by the Soviet Union, which posed as a friend even as it was plotting with Washington to enable the U.S. "to occupy South Vietnam permanently." Besides getting in licks at Moscow, the diatribe also was intended to warn Hanoi that it was living dangerously in attempting to play Russia and Red China against each other to reap support for its war effort. Soviet economic and military aid to Hanoi had increased significantly within the past several months and there were reports that Peking's prestige was diminishing.

To feed the Mao regime's paranoia, State's intelligence planted with Red Chinese spies, through cooperative neutral diplomats, the story that a 1967 mission to Hanoi by the Soviet troubleshooter Alexander Shelepin was part of President Johnson's peace offensive. Peking fell for this rather heavy-handed gambit, duly reporting that Shelepin had urged Ho Chi Minh to "score a propaganda triumph" by announcing he was ready to go to the peace table.

Indeed, Peking charged that Shelepin's mission was to "get more of a say for the Soviet Union on the Vietnam question," a circumstance that could only be achieved if Hanoi agreed to settlement of the war by negotiation. The Russian leadership, said Peking, "want to find a way out for U.S. imperialism on the Vietnam question" in order to "strike a political deal with it."

Periodically, during the next two years, the Red Chinese Government launched new attacks on what it called "encirclement" of China by the Soviet Union and the United States. It charged that Moscow, Washington and India had formed a united front against Peking, and said discussions between Soviet and Japanese officials were part of a "Soviet-U.S.-

Japanese alliance to oppose China, (North) Korea and the peoples' revolutionary struggles in other parts of Asia." Both *Red Flag* and *People's Daily* attacked Soviet books on foreign policy as having described Presidents Eisenhower, Kennedy and Johnson as belonging to the "sober and sensible" category of American leaders.

Peking also retaliated by trying to whip up a military confrontation between the United States and the Soviet Union. Intelligence reports reaching the State Department in December, 1967, warned that Peking's strategy sought to involve the two countries in a possible war between India and Pakistan.

At the time, Red China had just wound up a series of negotiations for a new round of "economic" aid to Pakistan. The intense secrecy that surrounded these talks was penetrated by INR operatives, who claimed the aid would be mostly military.

Of the three powers contributing to Pakistan's economy, only Peking had continued to supply arms. Both the U.S. and Russia had cut off military aid, and Washington was offering Pakistan only spare parts for old hardware. U.S. experts thus saw highly political ramifications in Peking's new round of aid. Pakistan at the time was determined to bolster its defense against what its politicians described as Indian "invasion plots." They pointed to India's growing military strength and a new aggressiveness among Indian leaders, especially the extremist Hindu elements, concerning the dispute over the status of Kashmir.

Peking had long supported Pakistan's claim to this Himalayan state, and recently there had been an increase in Chinese demands that India bow to Pakistan's claim. Chinese-Pakistani "cultural associations" in major Pakistani cities hammered daily at the Kashmir issue. As State's intelligence people saw it, Peking was doing everything possible to incite an all-out war between India and Pakistan, as a means of weakening both nations and thus making Peking's expansionist path that much easier. Moreover, an Indian-Pakistan war would pose the possibility of intervention by either the United States or Soviet Union, or both, and a U.S.-Russian confrontation would be frosting on Peking's cake.

In these tense circumstances, it was small wonder that Soviet United Nations Ambassador Nikolai Fedorenko in

1967 gave the most perfunctory endorsement to UN membership for Red China. Federenko spoke only ten minutes, and
spent part of this time vigorously urging the seating of East
Germany. Such pallid support for Peking in an international
forum would have been unthinkable a few years before, and
it gave weight to the argument that the Sino-Soviet split was
irreparable. If so, the State Department's urbane and courtly
"super spies" could take some credit.

13

East to Amman, South to Havana

Spying on a locked-up country like Communist China is a considerable achievement which would not have been possible in the casual old days before World War II, when American military attachés were chosen for their ability to look handsome in a dress uniform at an embassy reception. It is possible today only because the United States has come of age in the intelligence field and demands a great deal more of its attachés. And, of course, America's spies no longer depend exclusively on the gossip picked up by these uniformed brilliants on their social rounds, but hire specialists for their necessary dirty work. In any event, both the attachés and the specialists now are required to undergo a rigid matriculation in espionage techniques before they are entrusted with serious employment.

The Defense Intelligence Agency and, to a lesser extent and for different purposes, the State Department's Bureau of Intelligence and Research train spies at special schools operated by the DIA in the United States and in certain foreign countries. Both Americans and foreigners attend these schools, whose faculties include experts in everything from judo and pistol shooting to the techniques of sabotage and the spoken nuances of Mandarin. INR people, or individuals under contract to the INR, concentrate exclusively on languages and the study of history and geography as they relate to modern foreign policies, with occasional side courses in such fascinating subjects as how to determine whether a given individual will be receptive to a bribe.

Recruits from college graduating classes, experts in certain fields and young officers and enlisted men from the Army, Navy, Air Force and Marines make up the DIA's own student body. A select number of the military men are assigned abroad as military attachés; the others wind up as secret agents in foreign countries or as technicians sitting behind desks or working in laboratories. The DIA is said to boast that it carries on its payroll the world's foremost expert on knife fighting and a man who knows as much about nuclear weapons as anyone in the Atomic Energy Commission.

DIA spy schools for the most part are located at various military establishments in the U.S., such as Fort Benning, Georgia, although in the sixties some were established in friendly countries abroad. At least two of these schools offer courses conducted in the atmosphere of Russian and Chinese towns. Only Russian or Chinese is spoken in these towns, and the students live in surroundings reconstructed as closely as possible to resemble those in which they will ply their black trade.

Students who will work abroad undergo thorough physical training conducted by tough military noncoms; there are those who claim this "combat course" is more rigorous even than that given the famous Green Berets of the Special Forces. All must take a polygraph, or lie detector, test, answering such questions as "Have you ever had homosexual relations?" and "Are your sexual relations with a member of the opposite sex normal?" The students also are subjected to running psychological tests during their training. That is, they are appraised during their daily routine to determine how they react to verbal abuse and kidding, and are rated on the quickness of their tempers. They are marked on their capacity for withstanding physical discomfort, such as rain, snow, cold and heat, and on their behavior in the dentist's chair.

Recruits specializing in languages spend six hours a day in cubicles listening to tape recordings. Within two months, a student usually can read a newspaper in the language he is studying and can carry on a simple conversation in that language. Some students achieve spectacular heights; one Air Force officer whose college marks were only ordinary became fluent in fourteen languages and dialects over a period of four years of study.

Students are taught how to read maps in several foreign languages, not only because they might find themselves some

day in one of those foreign countries but because at a desk
in Washington the latest map might tell them something significant—the relocation of a highway in a region believed
to shelter a radar station, for example. Foreign telephone
directories are stocked in the libraries as one means of keeping in touch with a politician or military officer in, say, Sofia.
If his name is missing, it might indicate a shuffle in the power
structure. Translation computers render foreign texts into
English at the rate of 35,000 words an hour.

Emphasis is placed on the little things. Students study dos-
siers on officials of Communist countries and are required to
pass memory tests on what they have read. They must re-
member, for instance, that a certain minor Rumanian bureau-
crat has a relatively inconspicuous deviated septum—a minor
nasal deformity—that his voice has a whining quality when
he is nervous or aroused, and that he has a small mole under
his left eye. They study reports of American doctors who
have diagnosed the illnesses of Chinese officials from information supplied by agents in the field and from their own personal knowledge. All such reports are used to update
identification of officials who seek anonymity.

A spy assigned to a Communist country is given a new
identity which he must memorize so fully that he becomes,
in effect, a different man. Several times during his training
course, he is awakened in the middle of the night and asked
a question about his identity—"How many children did Aunt
Grzdgxygx have?" He must be able to speak familiarly about
his new birthplace, the schools he attended and some of his
schoolmates in the Communist country of which his passport
says he is a native. He is trained in European eating habits
(keep the fork in your left hand) and must know his way
around a city he has seen only through maps and the tutelage
of his instructors. Often, he must keep a complicated code in
his head for communicating with his contacts.

Sometimes an agent, usually a foreigner who has a business
or diplomatic reason for being in a Communist country, is
assigned to strike up a friendship with a government official.
His object may be to try to pry secrets out of the man, but
more often than not his superiors just want to keep their
dossier on the official up to date on the chance he is headed
for bigger things. The agent must know everything possible
about the man, including the name of his mistress, the fact

he is a horse player and his relationship with a secret police official who lives in the same apartment building. If the agent does his job well, he can provide the "home office" with periodic baskets of goodies about the personalities of the government's ruling clique and the dissensions and conflicts among its members.

Such a DIA agent, patrolling a beat in the cutthroat political alleyways of Jordan's capital city of Amman, did much better. Because he was on intimate terms with a high Jordanian official who had his own private spies operating in Israel, the agent was able to inform Washington that Israel was planning a surprise air attack on Egyptian airfields on or about June 4, 1967. The attack was made on June 5.

Sergio is not the man's real name, but it will have to do here. He had been set up in business by the DIA four years earlier, and he traveled regularly from Amman to Cairo and Baghdad. Fluent in the Arab tongue, as well as in Yiddish, Hebrew and Italian, Sergio made friends because he had an outgoing personality, and yet was never suspected of blabbing what he knew. Arabs and Jews grew to trust him because he faithfully lived up to his credo, which was to turn a good profit while refusing to get involved in the Byzantine politics of the region. In Amman, in Cairo and in Baghdad, people told Sergio secrets and he kept mum. He also made money, which he banked in his own name, in accordance with his DIA contract.

For four years, Sergio offered the DIA no intelligence of any substantial value. That was in his contract, too. His job was to cement his relationship with the Jordanian high official so that some day the Jordanian would tell him something worthwhile—or let drop something important.

Sergio ate with the Jordanian and drank with him and womanized with him. He gave the Jordanian official tips on the stock market, furnished by DIA experts, that made him richer. He fed him morsels of political and diplomatic information he had picked up on his travels throughout the Middle East. Once, he even accepted a commission from the high Jordanian official to go to Saudi Arabia and purchase for him a female slave whose charms had been recommended to the Jordanian by an Iraqi policeman. By May, 1967, Sergio and the Jordanian were as close to bosom pals as the suspicious Middle East permitted.

Thus, it was perhaps predictable that when the Jordanian received Sergio in his home one night during the last week of May he should feel a need to confide in his foreign friend. The official from Amman had attended that afternoon a solemn meeting of Jordanian military officers, presided over by no less a personage than King Hussein. The Jordanian was in a state of furious depression, and he told Sergio dramatically, "Tonight I shall get drunk." They sat around for two hours, while Sergio's friend gulped Scotch, and got drunk. He also told Sergio that the meeting had been called to discuss an intelligence memo submitted by a spy in Israel which said the Israelis were completing mobilization for the air attack on Egypt.

The attack, the Jordanian told Sergio, would take place on June 4. He said he had absolute faith in the memo, because he knew the spy who submitted it personally. The spy, he said, was an Israeli with impeccable connections within the Israeli government.

Most intriguing of all, the Jordanian informed Sergio that King Hussein himself, the day before, had passed on this intelligence to President Nasser of Egypt, and "the goddamn fool" wouldn't believe it.

The Jordanian passed out in the arms of one of his girl friends shortly after midnight, and Sergio went home to bed. Next day, Sergio checked on the credentials of the Israeli who had submitted the memo and found them sound. He also made some discreet inquiries among other well-placed pals in Amman and learned that there was considerable disquiet in high circles over a possible Israeli-Egyptian conflict. By means known only to Sergio and the DIA, he passed on this information to Washington. He gave June 4 as the date of the aerial attack, then added that in the Middle East it was always wise to allow for at least a 24-hour delay even in important military matters.

The DIA's investment in Sergio paid off. No one in the official know was surprised when the Israelis attacked on June 5 and found the great bulk of Egypt's Soviet-supplied air force trapped on the ground. Indeed, in the meantime, President Johnson had had time to let the Israeli Government know that he was aware of its plans and to warn that it could expect no support from the United States if the Soviet Union rushed to the support of the Arab states. Johnson also had reached an understanding with Soviet Premier Aleksei Kosygin via the hot line between Washington and Moscow that neither of the two nuclear powers would intervene to an extent that might force the other to take military action.

Betweentimes, Sergio had sought out an Iraqi diplomat in Amman, who confirmed the projected attack and expressed the personal, expert opinion that Nasser's forces would take a clobbering. Sergio quoted the Iraqi as saying the war would be "a picnic for Israel." Later, Sergio picked up from the Jordanian official the tidbit that Nasser had admitted by radiotelephone to King Hussein that his charges of Anglo-American air assistance to Israel were unfounded, but that they made "good propaganda."

The success of agents like Sergio bolsters the arguments of those in the U.S. intelligence community who maintain that it is more profitable to employ foreign spies, for money, than American-grown products. "Let's face it," said one military intelligence officer, "Americans are suspicious characters all over the world these days. Besides, they don't blend into foreign environments as well as other nationalities do. I guess Americans haven't been around enough in this dodge to feel really at home when they're abroad."

At any rate, foreigners in the pay of U.S. intelligence have earned their pay in various other parts of the world, including Africa, Southeast Asia and Cuba. In all these areas, both the State Department and military intelligence agencies have shown a substantial profit by employing so-called "fast buck" foreigners in their espionage activities.

For example, it was a Nigerian agent for State's Bureau of Intelligence and Research who offered the first hard intelligence, in the summer of 1968, that black guerrillas captured in Rhodesia had been supplied with arms by the Soviet Union. The Nigerian infiltrated a guerrilla band and returned with a packet of photographs showing the guerrillas armed with Soviet Antonin-K assault rifles, Simonov semiautomatic carbines and RPD light machine guns.

Although the United States had joined in a United Nations resolution imposing economic sanctions on the Rhodesian Government for refusing representation to its black majority, some U.S. diplomats had argued that this was playing into Russian hands. The photographs of Russian arms in the hands of black guerrillas gave considerable support to this argument, and President Johnson ordered a new study of "foreign influences" in the black majority movement.

Shortly after the outbreak of civil war between Nigeria and the secessionist Biafrans in July, 1967, the DIA dispatched a Portuguese agent from Kenya to the Nigerian capital of Lagos to "cover" the conflict. The Portuguese, a school-teacher and trader, used carrier pigeons among other means to transmit his information to American contacts in other African capitals.

He also managed to spend a considerable amount of time among the fighting Ibo tribesmen of Biafra, and by the fall of 1968 reported back that the Biafrans were determined to keep on fighting a guerrilla war for years, even if their leaders were forced to sign a capitulation to the Nigerian federal government. Earlier, he had reported that the Biafrans were plan-ning to seek aid from Communist China in their struggle for independence because of the failure of the United States and Britain to mediate an end to the war that would assure Bia-fran independence.

Official diplomatic reports to both London and Washing-ton confirmed these findings. In mid-October, these reports said the Lagos regime was convinced the Biafrans would fight on, and expressed fear that the federal treasury would be unable to stand the financial strain of a long guerrilla war. And at about the same time, Lieutenant Colonel Odumegwu Ojukwu, the Biafran leader, dispatched a 450-word letter to Red Chinese Party chief Mao Tse-tung in which he appealed for Chinese "cooperation" against "Anglo-American imperi-alism and Soviet revisionism." (Russia had supplied Nigeria with jet bombers and fighter planes.)

In Southeast Asia, both the DIA and the State Department have done profitable business with French agents, many of whom have lived in that neighborhood of the world for two generations. It was from a French planter, given the pseudo-nym Louis, that the DIA and State first learned, in the fall of 1967, of an underground port in Cambodia from which arms shipments were transported to Communist forces in Vietnam.

Louis claims, probably with complete justification, that he was the first foreign agent to visit the little fishing village of Ream, in Southeast Cambodia, fifteen miles by dirt track from the major Cambodian port of Sihanoukville. It was there, in the summer of 1967, that Louis discovered that arms from Red China and East European countries were being transferred from freighters to motorized fishing boats several miles off Ream, and then brought to the village for transfer to trucks for the trek to the South Vietnam border.

The arms, Louis reported, were mostly small weapons and ammunition, for use by the Viet Cong and not by North Vietnamese troops. By shipping the arms to Ream, he said, Communist sources told him they avoided the long trip from Hanoi and other North Vietnamese points over the Ho Chi Minh trail through Laos to South Vietnam. In Ream, Louis said, people treated as a joke the cover story that arms shipments were being made without the knowledge of Cambodia's Prince Sihanouk, who had repeatedly denied that the Communists were using his country as a transshipment depot.

Louis also discovered, probably not for the first time, that spying in the boondocks of Southeast Asia can be a dangerous pursuit. Driving along a road between Ream and the South Vietnam border, his car was stopped at a roadblock and he was taken prisoner by a band of armed peasants clad in the black-pajama uniform of the Viet Cong.

He was taken to a nearby village, where he was interrogated by a man he described as a "Chinese" officer who smoked long, Russian-type cigarets and gestured with a submachine gun. Dissatisfied with Louis's answers to his questions, the officer turned him over to a squad of soldiers who took Louis to a hut and tried to get him to talk more frankly. Among other things, they stuck a tube down his throat and took turns urinating into it, crushed his testicles with pliers, forced motor oil up his anus, set fire to his hair, and wound up by dosing him with a quart of castor oil. Curiously, however, they set him free that night and he made his way through the jungle back to Ream, where he spent two days with a friend and then took a bus to the Cambodian capital, Phnom Penh.

Louis told his story at a "safe house" maintained in the Phnom Penh suburbs by the American embassy. He was also examined by a physician, who corroborated Louis's story of his mistreatment at the hands of the men in the black pajamas. Other DIA agents checked on Louis's tale of arms shipments through Ream, and verified that they had been taking place at the time he reported them.

After a leave spent in Bangkok, Louis went back to work and in the late summer of 1968 was again in Cambodia, where he was the first to discover that the Viet Cong were using the area around Bathu, abutting the South Vietnam border, as a supply and staging area. He reported that large amounts of enemy weaponry, including 122-mm. rockets used to shell the South Vietnamese capital of Saigon, had passed through Bathu along Communist supply routes.

Louis, described by one DIA source as "the village gossip type," spent a lot of his time chatting with Viet Cong officers and soldiers. From these conversations, he learned that Cambodian troops often supplied Viet Cong forces with rice and other food in exchange for money and ammunition. He quoted one Viet Cong officer as saying the supply unit he commanded was frequently stopped by Cambodian troops and forced to make payoffs in money and weapons before they were allowed to move on. Other sources verified these reports and, three months later, Louis's revelation that the Bathu area was the site of three Viet Cong field hospitals, a plant for manufacturing grenades and mines, and several military brothels.

*   *   *

The adventures of Louis and Sergio reflect the more glamorous and often dangerous side of espionage, but intelligence is also pure brain work—involving the ability to appraise the significance of the bits and pieces of information supplied by spies in the field. The accomplishments of those who do this heavy thinking rarely make headlines. They are for the most part faceless scholars sitting at desks in the State Department, the Pentagon and the CIA, whose judgments are contained in the daily, and sometimes hourly, memoranda used as working papers by their bosses assembled in the National Security Council. They are collaborators at what might be called the cerebral level with the agents in Amman and Sihanoukville; they make sense—or try to—out of what the agents tell them.

One of the best examples of this intelligence think tank in action was provided during the months leading up to the Cuban missile crisis in the fall of 1962. Nikita Khrushchev obviously was casting about for an opportunity to make geopolitical capital of Fidel Castro's establishment of a Communist dictatorship in Cuba. He wanted to use Cuba as the means of blackmailing the United States.

Castro had been demanding missiles as protection against the American imperialists. He was the Russians' pet stepson, the man upon whom the Russians pinned their hopes of extending Communist power in the Western Hemisphere. Installing some of their medium- and intermediate-range missiles in Cuba would be a stopgap measure which would give the Soviets an offensive weapon ninety miles from the United States while they sweated to produce a more sophisticated ICBM system at home. If the move succeeded, Castro's hand would be strengthened and the Soviet Union would be enabled to deal its hand in the international game of politics from added strength. It also would encourage other Communist guerrilla leaders in Latin America, by weakening the American position as defender of South America. All these considerations were expressed in INR intelligence memos in the spring of 1962.

By the early summer of 1962, both the INR and American military intelligence reported that sites were being cleared in Cuba for what looked like missile installations to both U-2 planes and diplomatic informants on the ground. What was not known at the time was that the Soviet Union planned to send both defensive missiles—twenty-four batteries of surface-to-air weapons—and offensive weapons—IL-28 light bombers and medium- and intermediate-range missiles. There also would be four battle groups of ground troops armed with tactical nuclear weapons for support purposes.

First arms shipments began arriving in Cuba in late July, 1962, and were so reported by the DIA, and a bit later by the CIA. INR sources on the island emphasized the high degree of secrecy surrounding the deliveries. Castro used only a few ports, whose docks were guarded by high fences and Russians in sports shirts and slacks. The Cuban Army summarily evacuated Cubans living in the dock areas. Roger Hilsman, then director of INR, prepared a long memo to President Kennedy which told of Russians doing much of the unloading, always at night, and superintending transport by road, also at night, to "sites readied in remote areas, naturally screened by hills and woods, whose population had been evacuated . . . con-

crete arches used for constructing buildings were prefab-
ricated—made in the Soviet Union and shipped to Cuba."

All this looked to the INR as if Russia was sending much
more than conventional arms to Fidel Castro. Hilsman's intelligence memos to Secretary of State Dean Rusk bristled
with warnings that Moscow probably was shipping, or about
to ship, fairly sophisticated missiles into Cuba. In one case,
a diplomatic source from a neutral country swore he had had
a chat with a crew member from one of the missile-carrying
vessels.

Moreover, the INR reported that all its studies indicated
Khrushchev was determined to force a showdown with the
youthful President Kennedy by adopting the "high-risk policy"
of arming Cuba with missiles clearly aimed at the American
mainland. Among other things, Hilsman noted that recent
public utterances by Khrushchev and other members of the
Russian Politburo had emphasized the "immorality" of American missile bases in such countries as Turkey and had hinted
at retaliation in kind.

"Providing the Castro regime merely with antiaircraft guns
and fighter planes would not seem to offer the means of such
retaliation," Hilsman remarked. Hilsman also reported the
arrival of between three thousand and five thousand Soviet
personnel, many of whom were military technicians connected with installing the equipment. None of the Russians
was in uniform.

Ten days later, pictures taken by an Air Force U-2 showed
that the crates had been opened and that they contained
surface-to-air missiles (SAMs) similar to the American
NIKE missile. The pictures also revealed the arrival of radar
equipment and several motor torpedo boats armed with
guided missiles having a range of fifteen miles.

Air Force Intelligence U-2 flights over Cuba on August 29,
September 5, and September 17, showed surface-to-air missile
sites being erected around the perimeter of the island in the
central and western areas. They also showed a ramp in the
port town of Banes, fitted with what looked like a robot airplane with stubby, swept-back wings. It was identified as a
launching platform for shore-to-ship missiles, with a probable range of forty miles. No sweat—yet.

That, at least, was the conclusion of the United States
Intelligence Board when it convened on September 19 to

consider the situation. CIA operatives and analysts had come up with no hints that the Soviets were planning installation of offensive missiles in Cuba. Moreover, CIA's political thinkers disagreed with the INR warning that Khrushchev was in a mood to force a showdown with the Kennedy Administration. Taking its cue from the CIA, the estimate looked into the Soviet mind and decided it would be uncharacteristic of the Russians to give Castro offensive missiles. The board noted that the Russians almost surely realized the Americans would have little difficulty in discovering the missiles and that the reaction would be vigorous. It also harped on the Russians' previous unwillingness to trust their most strategic weapons to the safekeeping of other nations, including even their Eastern European satellites. It spoke of Russian concern over Castro's instability, and of the dangers inherent in transporting such sophisticated missiles halfway around the world to a little country especially vulnerable to American attack.

On September 19, therefore, a national intelligence estimate—adopted unanimously—recommended an intelligence alert but said there was little danger of the Soviet Union placing offensive missiles in Cuba.

Allen Dulles's often-stated stricture that espionage is worthless without assured communications now struck home. On the night of September 12, a CIA operative in Havana spotted a truck convoy carrying missiles much too big to be SAMs. He dredged up enough informed gossip to mark them for what they were—offensive missiles. But Castro's police network, which had stepped up its security operations when the first missiles arrived on September 8, prevented the agent from transmitting his intelligence for several days, and it did not reach the CIA until September 21, two days after issuance of the national estimate. At about the same time, a report from a DIA operative in Cuba quoted Castro's private pilot as boasting that Cuba now had long-range missiles.

Curiously, these two reports caused no change in the Intelligence Board's collective mind. Neither was any particular concern felt when Castro's chief of staff, Che Guevara, wound up a visit to Moscow on September 22, by joining with the Soviets in a communiqué which stated that Moscow was sending "armaments and technical specialists" to train Cuban servicemen.

But by this time both Secretary McNamara and INR Director Hilsman were convinced offensive missiles had been delivered to Cuba and probably already had been installed. In high Administration councils, there were clashes between McNamara and Hilsman on the one side and CIA Director John McCone on the other. McNamara at this stage was not necessarily pressing for an American response. He argued that it didn't matter whether missiles were in Cuba or in the Soviet Union. "A missile is a missile," he said. "It makes no great difference whether you are killed by a missile fired from the Soviet Union or from Cuba." But he insisted vigorously that American policy makers "face the fact" that offensive missiles either were in Cuba or were being shipped there, and not "turn your back" on the intelligence provided by DIA agents of the "highest quality."

Hilsman argued in favor of drafting an immediate "contingency plan" for an American response and for a strong and immediate protest to Moscow, coupled with a warning that the United States would not tolerate the continued presence of the missiles only ninety miles from its shores. McCone insisted we were not sure the missiles had been emplaced, or even delivered, and cited a flood of conflicting intelligence from CIA agents and from refugees. The United States, said McCone, "should not go off half-cocked," but should wait for confirming evidence from overflights of the U-2 spy planes.

No member of the intelligence community downgraded the effect on the balance of power between the Soviet Union and the United States if there were, indeed, offensive missiles in Cuba. The type reported could deliver an initial load of forty missiles, each with a warhead of from three to four megatons. The bigger missiles could hit American ICBM bases in Wyoming and Montana and could reach every major city but Seattle. The smaller missiles could strike at our manned bomber bases in the South and Southwest. With these missiles in Cuba, the Soviet leaders could just about close the real "missile gap"; that is to say, they could increase by 50 percent the explosive power with which they could hit American targets.

The confirming evidence CIA's John McCone was waiting for came on October 14. A U-2 overflight which had been postponed four times because of bad weather finally was made. The pictures it took showed the installation of a battalion of Soviet medium-range ballistic missiles at San Cristobal, in western Cuba.

What happened in that crisis was that the intelligence thinkers were in conflict, and the wrong side won. The scholars at the DIA and INR almost from the very beginning had correctly judged the intelligence evidence and concluded that the Kremlin was embarked on a most audacious course. In effect, the CIA thinkers dismissed this judgment as unnecessarily alarmist and succeeded in selling their own appraisal to President Kennedy. Had Kennedy heeded the DIA-INR counsel, he could have acted much sooner and probably with less risk in calling the Russians' bluff.

History records, of course, that it all came out all right in the end, but the disagreement within the intelligence community revealed the perils inherent in America's sprawling and costly espionage system. Unfortunately, the difference of opinion during the Cuban missile crisis was only one of many similar examples of intellectual friction which stirred our not-so-close-knit family of spymasters in the sixties.

A look at some of those conflicts is mandatory in any serious study of America's spies. But before taking that look, it is important first to consider some of the other problems that plague the nation's multi-billion-dollar spy shop. They are the problems concerned with a special species of personnel—more than sixty thousand human beings of temperaments more varied and complex than those of any other body of Government workers. Spying is a tense profession, and the tension sometimes causes crackups among the varying temperaments engaged in that profession. They constitute the tiny minority—the defectors and thieves.

14

The Defectors

Appropriately enough, the performance was staged in the theater of the House of Journalists in Moscow. There under the glare of television lights on September 6, 1960, William Hamilton Martin and Bernon Ferguson Mitchell told the whole world all the intelligence secrets they had learned during their three years as cryptologists in the Office of Research and Development of the super-secret National Security Agency.

Among other juicy morsels, Martin and Mitchell revealed that the NSA had broken the codes of more than half of the world's nations then possessing them—about forty. Martin ticked off some of them: "Italy, Turkey, France, Yugoslavia, the United Arab Republic, Indonesia, Uruguay—that's enough to give the general picture, I guess." It certainly was, especially since some of these countries were American allies, and Yugoslavia and Indonesia were counted among the touchy "non-aligned" governments.

Their revelations climaxed more than a month of apprehension in the United States. As the House Committee on Un-American Activities noted in the introduction to its report on an investigation of the Martin-Mitchell defection, "There was uneasiness in the minds of millions of Americans when, on August 1, 1960, the news broke that two employees of the National Security Agency were missing and unaccounted for, having failed to return from a *vacation* trip they had taken together. Uneasiness deepened into shock as, in the days immediately following, it was learned that they had purchased one-way airline tickets to Mexico City and then to Castro's

Cuba. There was no relief for the anxiety of the people of this country in the Department of Defense's statement of August 5, 1960, that 'It must be assumed that there is a likelihood that they have gone behind the Iron Curtain.' " (Italics added.)

Martin and Mitchell told the world they had defected and accepted Soviet citizenship because of "dissatisfaction" over some of the practices used by the United States in gathering intelligence information. They were "worried about the United States policy of deliberately violating the air space of other nations," and its practice of "lying about such violations." There was irony here; they might have been talking about the Soviet Union, which since its creation as a Communist state had led the world in violating any national space, and national rights, that lay open for violation.

A second irony was found in one of the reasons they gave for choosing Russia. This, they said, was that the Soviet Union encouraged "the talents of women. . . . We feel that this enriches Soviet society and makes Soviet women more desirable as mates." Full-scale investigations by the FBI and the Defense Department as well as the House Un-American Activities Committee stated bluntly that Martin and Mitchell were homosexuals.

To most Americans, however, the crowning irony was that Martin and Mitchell had slipped through the security defenses of the NSA, which had been hailed by NSA itself and Congress as the most rigid of any member of the American intelligence community. A look at their backgrounds puts their defection in the category of things that couldn't happen.

Both were bright boys from typical, backyard-barbecue American families; Martin was twenty-nine, Mitchell was thirty-one. Martin was found scholastically qualified to bypass high school and enter the program for gifted teenagers at the University of Chicago but his high school principal ruled he was too immature and not socially developed enough to manage it. Martin finished high school in three years in Ellensburg, Washington, then spent a year at Ellensburg's Central Washington College of Education before enlisting in the Navy. There, Martin met Bernon Mitchell in a cryptologic section to which both were assigned.

Mitchell, who grew up in Eureka, California, was a science bug in high school, a kid who drove the neighbors crazy by exploding hydrogen-filled balloons in airbursts over their houses. He spent a year and a half at the California Institute of Technology before joining the Navy. Mitchell called himself an agnostic, and his favorite reading was books on the philosophy of mathematics.

Neither Martin nor Mitchell dated girls much, although both were handsome and athletically built. Both had few friends, although Mitchell was an accomplished poker player. Martin's chief after-hours interest was chess; he won the chess championship of the Northwest at the age of seventeen. He also was interested in psychology and hypnotism.

After his Navy tour of duty, Mitchell returned to the United States to study mathematics at Stanford University. Martin stayed on for a while to do cryptologic work for the Army before returning to the U.S. to study mathematics at the University of Washington. They were hired separately by the NSA as mathematicians in February and March 1957, and went to work on July 8, 1957, at $6,000 a year. NSA's security investigation of both men in retrospect seems most casual.

Mitchell, a barbell, physical culture enthusiast, had posed for nude color slides seated on a velvet-covered stool. Under a lie detector examination, he admitted that he had engaged in "sexual experiences" with dogs and chickens when he was an adolescent, but this was not considered a basis for denying him final security clearance. It later was revealed that in May, 1960, Mitchell began visiting a psychiatrist for what were called "intellectual discussions" of homosexuality.

The security investigation of Martin revealed that as a boy he had tended to be overbearing, especially with adults, and was a master of the gratuitous insult. Friends and acquaintances called him an "insufferable egotist," who was not wholly normal and inclined to be somewhat effeminate and rather irresponsible. With one exception, his former superiors declared they would not think of hiring him again, but only one questioned Martin's loyalty to the United States.

By January, 1958, Mitchell had been granted final security clearance, and the two men reported for duty as cryptologists in the Office of Research and Development. Martin's final clearance did not come through until May 12, 1958; it has never been explained why this lack was waived in January. The two men lived in separate bachelor apartments in Laurel, Maryland, and apparently neither was a good housekeeper.

At any rate, the orderly Allen Dulles later wrote that "Their living quarters were a shambles of disorder and slovenliness. Something must be wrong with people who lived as they did."

Martin did well in Research and Development. He was approved for an NSA scholarship at the University of Illinois, and later the one-year scholarship was extended to two years. He enrolled at Illinois in September, 1959, to study Russian and work toward a master's degree in mathematics. Mitchell stayed in Washington.

Investigations after their defection dredged up the information that both Martin and Mitchell joined the Communist Party in February, 1958. They also were described as having expressed "strong anti-American political feelings." They were opposed to the secret U-2 flights over the Soviet Union and went so far as to drop in on Representative Wayne Hays, Democrat, of Ohio, to protest the flights and to warn Hays that they constituted "great dangers" to the United States. Incredibly, the two friends traveled to Communist Cuba in December, 1959, despite an NSA directive specifically banning such travel.

When the House committee and governmental investigative agencies went to work on the case they discovered that personnel procedures within the NSA were hardly what were expected of an agency created to protect the nation's security. Personnel were employed and put to work on sensitive material before getting full clearances under emergency regulations put into effect during the Korean War, when there was a manpower shortage, but whose temporary character had been ignored. One NSA employee was hired after three other Government agencies had refused him employment on grounds of homosexuality and Communist activities. Twenty-six other NSA employees were revealed to be sexual deviates, and discharged.

More fantastic still, NSA's Director of Personnel, Maurice H. Klein, and its Director of Security, S. Wesley Reynolds, were charged with utterly lax procedures. Klein admitted he had falsely stated on his own employment forms that he had been graduated from Harvard Law School instead of a New Jersey law school, and that he had attempted to conceal this by correcting and falsely dating his records. Reynolds, a former FBI agent, knew about this but decided that it "did not have security significance." Both men resigned.

Investigators for the House committee reported that Klein also had concealed a change in his name, had listed several dates for his birth, and had supplied an employment history "which was not factual." The committee also furnished the NSA with what it called "startling facts" about Martin "which were unknown to the Agency's security office until after they had defected." It said Martin had associations with members of the Communist Party during his matriculation at the University of Illinois in 1959, and that he was "in fact, a masochist." Both Martin and Mitchell, the committee said, had made statements "complimentary of the Soviet way of life and critical of the United States. This was known by several dozen employees of the NSA. . . ."

Klein's "making of false statements on official Government documents," said the committee, "should have been a bar to his continued employment as Director of Personnel in such a sensitive agency."

Meanwhile, Martin and Mitchell arranged their escape to the Soviet Union in a fashion that reflected unusual solicitude on the part of their supervisor. In June, 1960, shortly after Martin had returned to Illinois, they applied for annual leave from June 24 to July 1 to visit their parents on the West Coast. Their supervisor authorized them to extend their leaves to July 18 in case they needed more time for their family reunions. This must have furnished a laugh for the two men as they bought their one-way airline tickets to Mexico City, for which city they departed from Washington June 25. From Mexico, they flew to Havana on July 1, and then sailed for the Soviet Union on a Russian trawler, bringing with them the secrets that would cause unknown numbers of governments to change their secret codes and force the United States temporarily to suspend the electronic transmission of intelligence.

Martin and Mitchell, of course, were cryptologists and thus in an excellent position to steal NSA's secrets. But an employee need not be a scholar or a technician to attract the attention of the Russians in their search for classified information. They also did a profitable business with a Navy yeoman first class and a first class sergeant in the Army, from whom they received top-secret information on United States Navy intelligence and on American estimates of the wartime capabilities of the Soviet armed forces.

The yeoman, Nelson Cornelius Drummond, was sentenced

to life imprisonment for selling secrets to the Russians.* The sergeant, Jack Edward Dunlap, a decorated combat veteran with a clean record, solved his problem by committing suicide.

Until now, details of the Dunlap case have been blurred. They are of a fantastic piece with the story of Martin and Mitchell. Again, NSA's personnel security program and its investigative techniques would seem to have assured that Dunlap couldn't get away with what he was doing, but he did. He peddled secrets to the Soviet Union for four years, from mid-1959 to July, 1963, and earned about $60,000 for his treason, although he never held a job higher than clerk-messenger.

Dunlap went to work for NSA as part of an Army Security Agency unit in April, 1958, when he was assigned as chauffeur to Major General Garrison B. Cloverdale, NSA's assistant director and chief of staff. Within a few months he was promoted to clerk-messenger. Several months later, the Russians made their first contact with him and Dunlap agreed to sell them whatever bits and pieces he could lay his hands on.

An FBI man, understandably piqued that his agency had not been called in until after Dunlap's death, later dismissed the NSA investigators as "Those flatfeet in Brooks Brothers suits," and suggested bitterly that the NSA sleuths "couldn't catch a thief if they were locked in the same room with him." Certainly, the agency's detection department seemed incurious about Dunlap's way of life. The sergeant had two Cadillacs, a baby-blue Jaguar sports car, a 30-foot cabin cruiser, and a 100-mile-per-hour hydroplane. He was a big spender in saloons from Laurel, Maryland, to Miami; he was lavish in his gifts to his blonde mistress, and occasionally even bestowed gifts on his wife.

Only when Dunlap was dead did the NSA detectives discover that Dunlap had told friends an assortment of stories to explain his affluence. One was that he owned land on which certain valuable minerals had been found. Another was that he had inherited "a package." He also said his father, who was a bridge-tender, owned a plantation in Louisiana. He told his mistress that he had a "bookkeeper" who periodically turned over "profits" to him—in cash.

---

* For details of the Drummond case see Andrew Tully's *The FBI's Most Famous Cases* (William Morrow and Co., Inc., New York, 1965).

Dunlap drove one of his three expensive cars to work, under the noses of NSA security. When he was hurt racing his hydroplane, the NSA had him transferred from a local hospital to the Army hospital at Fort Meade because the authorities feared the local doctors would administer pain-killing drugs that might cause him to talk about his job.

Although no one really knows, the assumption is that Dunlap smuggled out top-secret documents under his clothing, since personnel are not frisked. He apparently turned the documents over to the Russians at regular intervals, probably at rendezvous in Washington and Baltimore. Again, no one knows what kind of material he pilfered, but it is significant that when the case broke the authorities admitted he probably could have taken his pick of a treasury of sensitive stuff.

Dunlap's downfall was not the result of any detective work by NSA; it came because he was determined to continue doing business with the Russians. In early 1963, the sergeant's tour of duty was nearing its end and Dunlap made application to be separated from the Army and then kept on at NSA as a civilian. Military personnel are not subjected to lie detector tests, but civilian employees are, and when they sprung the polygraph on Dunlap they discovered that he had engaged in some petty thefts and was guilty of what NSA described as "immoral living."

Still, apparently, no one took any action—for two long months. Meanwhile, Dunlap stayed on his job and, presumably, continued to commit treason. It was not until a further investigation revealed that the sergeant obviously was living far beyond his income that he was transferred to a minor Army job where he had no access to secret papers.

That tore it for Dunlap. On July 23, 1963, he committed suicide by inhaling monoxide gas in one of his cars. (The NSA was unaware that he had made two unsuccessful attempts to take his life.) A month later, his widow found a package of highly classified NSA documents among her late husband's effects.

Dunlap's suicide was one of two blows the NSA suffered on the same day. Also on July 23, 1963, a former NSA employee, an Arab who had changed his name from Hindali to Victor Norris Hamilton, had a letter published in the Soviet newspaper, *Izvestia*, in which he revealed another bagful of NSA secrets.

In the letter, "Hamilton" identified himself as a former "expert on the Near East Sector in the office designated ALLO, which means All Other Countries . . . The duties of my colleagues in ALLO included the study and breaking of military ciphers of these countries, and also the deciphering of all correspondence reaching their diplomatic representatives in any part of the world . . . I knew for a fact that the State Department and the Defense Department systematically read, analyzed and utilized in their own interests the enciphered correspondence between the United Arab Republic embassies in Europe and the U.A.R. government in Cairo."

Hamilton gave one important example: "I had in my desk all the deciphered communications between Cairo and the U.A.R. embassy in Moscow relating to the visit of the U.A.R. mission to the U.S.S.R. in 1958 for the purpose of purchasing petroleum in the Soviet Union. NSA sent all these communications to the State Department. . . ."

The letter also said that American authorities "take advantage of the fact that the United Nations headquarters is located on American soil." The United States Government, it said, was so "high-handed" that enciphered instructions of the governments of the U.A.R., Iraq, Jordan, Lebanon, Turkey and Greece to their missions at the UN "fall into the hands of the State Department before arriving at their proper address."

A graduate of the American University at Beirut, Lebanon, Hamilton married an American woman he had met in Libya. They came to the United States shortly thereafter, and Hamilton got a job as a doorman and bellhop in Georgia; he said the color of his skin barred him from other employment. Recruited by a retired American Army colonel, Hamilton went to work for the NSA on June 13, 1957, as a research analyst engaged in solving Arab cryptosystems. He resigned by request two years later after Defense Department officials said he was "approaching a paranoid-schizophrenic break." Hamilton said he was fired because he wanted to try to contact some relatives in Syria. At any rate, he found asylum in the Soviet Union, in exchange for betraying his former employers.

Like William Martin, Bernon Mitchell and Sergeant Jack Dunlap, Hamilton's treachery was motivated by selfish interests—political asylum or cold cash. Their cases were of the stuff of tragedy, despite the unattractiveness of their personalities. The case of Joseph Sidney Petersen, Jr. is sheer pathos. Even a Justice Department spokesman has said privately that Petersen was the victim of his own eagerness to help a friend.

During World War II, Petersen worked for the Army's Signal Intelligence Service, which did such a spectacular job of breaking the Japanese diplomatic and military codes. He became friendly with one Colonel J. A. Verkuyl, a liaison officer for the Royal Netherland Indies Army, who sat at the desk adjoining Petersen's. Petersen and Verkuyl used to dine together often, and eventually Verkuyl introduced Petersen to Giacomo Stuyt, communications officer at the Dutch embassy. Their mutual interest was cryptology; they rarely talked about anything else.

When Verkuyl returned to Holland after the war, Petersen wrote him long letters full of ideas about instructional methods to assist his friend in setting up a cryptologic department. Inexplicably, since Petersen never testified, Petersen also showed Stuyt, who had remained in America, copies of top-secret notes containing details of how the United States broke the Netherlands' code during the war. Verkuyl later said he was positive Petersen was merely trying to help his friends tighten up their government's code against the assaults of other prying nations.

Petersen's arrest on October 9, 1954, came as a shock to his associates and superiors. At the time, Petersen was working for NSA as a cryptologist, having been transferred to that agency from the Armed Forces Security Agency (AFSA) when it was abolished in 1952 and its strategic communications-intelligence functions taken over by the brand-new NSA. Petersen was highly respected for his competence, and well-liked by everyone who knew him. On his own initiative, he had organized an instruction school for AFSA employees which had become the basis for NSA's own instructional program in 1953.

But after FBI agents found various notes and documents in Petersen's apartment, the Justice Department and Pentagon had no choice but to prosecute. They were, however, anxious to avoid a trial which would expose too many secrets to public—and Communist—view. Petersen was desperately eager to make amends for the damage he had done. There was talk in official quarters that the Government had promised the defendant a light sentence, or even probation.

In any case, Petersen changed his plea from not guilty to guilty. But his hopes of getting off lightly were dashed by Federal District Court Judge Albert V. Bryan, who said he was not interested in what Petersen stole but only in the fact that he did steal records from the NSA. He hit Petersen with a seven-year prison term, and Petersen served four years before being granted parole.

The argument about whether Petersen deserved better at the hands of the government he had wronged probably will never be resolved. Under the circumstances, however, it does seem he deserved at least something approaching the second chance given an imaginative rascal named Georges in Vietnam, about whom more later.

Meanwhile, the military-diplomatic espionage community has been constrained to tighten its security. As noted earlier, Congress in 1964 gave the NSA the power to fire at will any employee when such action is considered to be in the interest of the United States. In the other agencies, the director—or, in some cases, a supervisor—may suspend an employee without notice if he is the subject of derogatory information. All agencies now deny conditional employees access to sensitive material until their clearances have been completed, and in no cases may an agency director delegate authority for granting final clearances. (In practice, of course, the director does not review every clearance paper, but he may not shrug off the responsibility for approving it.) Supervisors must notify personnel and security offices within two hours (three in State's INR) of the unauthorized absence of an employee. Security services have been expanded and given more authority to initiate investigations. Throughout the community, more psychiatrists are being used to check on applicants for employment.

Observing these sometimes hastily instituted measures by "the people across the street," the Central Intelligence Agency could assume an infuriating air of complacency. Since its birth in 1946 as the Central Intelligence Group, the CIA has never suffered a major defection.

15

Trouble in the Family

On the official, on-the-record level, there is a reluctance among the tribal chieftains of the American intelligence community to discuss or even admit the existence of an undercover agent who may as well be called Georges, although not in deference to the journalistic axiom that the innocent should be protected. Georges is a thief whose thievery was exposed, but he is still doing odd cloak-and-dagger jobs for the Defense Intelligence Agency—in the language of the law courts, making restitution.

There is no official estimate of how much money Georges stole from the DIA, and thus from the American taxpayer, but expert governmental sources have placed it at between $100,000 and $200,000. Either figure would not be a bad take, because the swag was accumulated in just under five years' time. American captains of industry have launched their careers on a much more modest scale.

Georges, son of a French father and an Irish mother, might be called a retired captain of industry. He lives comfortably in Argentina off the income of a piece of a small steel plant in France, bought with the money he siphoned off from the "Confidential Cash" entrusted to him as a spy. In the national interest, prosecution of Georges is out of the question; it would reveal too much about the operation of which Georges was a part. But Georges was not an ingrate. He agreed to run some minor espionage errands for the U.S. to atone for his peculations, and his work has been satisfactory.

The story of Georges' rise to infamy and fortune opens in the spring of 1961 when he was hired by a DIA representative to pass on bits of intelligence about the activities and thinking of the French colony in Saigon, South Vietnam. U.S. Intelligence had always felt that some French businessmen in the Vietnamese capital and in the rubber plantations in the countryside did occasional and profitable business with the Communist Viet Cong. Georges was an accountant in a French firm in Saigon, a handsome six-footer with Gallic black hair and blue eyes inherited from his Irish mother. He did so well that within seven months he was earning $1,000 a month, and was put on the Confidential Cash list.

Confidential Cash is the label applied by the Defense Department to monies disbursed secretly through a series of "fronts" for various payoffs to informers and other part-time employees, such as saboteurs. Its expenditures are concealed in order to protect the high Defense officials who approve them for operations which would not pass muster with, say, a particularly high-minded archbishop, and to frustrate attempts by other nations to connect the United States with international shenanigans of a more sordid nature.

No one outside the White House and the Pentagon knows how many millions of dollars are spent in this manner, but some estimates go as high as 20 million a year. In any event, there are many hiding places for these transactions in an annual Defense budget which has grown to enormous size— 72 billion dollars in fiscal 1969.

At any rate, Georges was approved to receive and disburse sums of varying amounts to those who supplied him with information, bribed public officials to obtain this information, or engaged in assorted acts of sabotage against both the Viet Cong and the North Vietnamese. He was a good operator. He almost invariably delivered the goods, and he had a built-in army of contacts as a result of his connection with a French company. Intelligence finance officers soon were entrusting Georges with cash boodles running as high as $15,000 a whack.

Georges dutifully paid over some of this money to his fellow spooks, and kept the rest, carefully depositing it into a numbered bank account in Switzerland. (It has been said by some intelligence cynics that Switzerland would be plunged into bankruptcy if all the Georges of the world suddenly withdrew their money from its banks.) In the meantime, *this* Georges tooled up and polished his acquaintanceships in the cozy little half-world of the business underground. This was the milieu of the hustler in the silk suit, who skimmed a furtive share of the cream off foreign aid (Agency for International Development) funds pouring into South Vietnam and assorted contracts and purchases entered into by the Saigon Government. It was the world of the black marketeer, of the peddlers and buyers of import licenses, and of the fast buck made by bribing corrupt Saigon officials.

Georges started small, picking up walking-around money as an intermediary for fathers with cash in hand to buy their sons exemption from the draft. But he soon branched out into bigger stuff, as a "businessman." He traded in import licenses, and from the contacts made in that sphere he was able to invest some of his savings in enterprises with a facade of legitimacy.

It was a far-ranging pursuit of wealth. Georges did business with merchants and assorted expediters in Hong Kong and Singapore as well as in Saigon, and was not averse to speculating in rice shipments he knew were headed for Hanoi. Within two years, he had amassed enough capital—and enough influence among the more important rascals of both business and government—to set up his own trading and import company, with a former opium runner as his front man.

Now Georges could expect to keep more of the profits from his extracurricular activities. There were still bribes to pay, of course, and they made up a sizeable part of his budget, but the Confidential Cash was still rolling in; and he had enough capital to take advantage of various opportunities available to those with ready money.

With a bought-and-paid-for import license, Georges brought in a shipment of an indigestion remedy which he sold to the Army of South Vietnam for American foreign aid dollars. The remedy cost Georges three cents a bottle, but he bribed the Army's purchasing agent to pay him one dollar a bottle for the stuff. Not content with that profit, he split the remedy with plain bicarbonate of soda and licorice flavor and doubled his take.

Georges also bought pieces of other shipments of medicine, paying for them partly in cash and partly in services rendered —that is to say, in his expert knowledge of the bribery market. In a country where few transactions with the Government were possible without bribes changing hands, Georges' specialty was a valuable item of merchandise.

From medicine, Georges bought his way into the U.S. surplus property racket in Laos. Under the terms of the program designed to make such surplus equipment as trucks, tractors and bulldozers available to have-not countries, the equipment is shipped to those countries and then local contractors are signed up to perform the necessary repairs on it. Georges did business with the repairmen.

First, Georges arranged for the awarding of fat contracts to these firms in exchange for a flat percentage of the contract gross. Then he hit on the idea that the profits would be bigger if the contractors spent as little money as possible on the repairs. He had no trouble persuading the contractors to give the equipment only the most superficial overhaul, and bribed the inspectors to award the equipment their okay. Naturally, Georges drew another commission from the savings realized by the contractors.

Back in Saigon, meanwhile, Georges took over a number of sidewalk vending stands specializing in black market items from American post exchanges. There was a two-way profit accruing to him from this enterprise. He bought the merchandise from the PX's at bargain prices for cash, then sold it to his own vending stands at a fat markup, and eventually took a second share from the retail sales. Often, Georges bought PX merchandise right off the docks, thanks to selective bribery of port officials.

It may seem incredible that Georges could have got away with this profitable double life for so long. But after all, intelligence people are well aware that the foreign Georges they hire in cities around the world are not the stuff of which Eagle Scouts are made, and an agent is left alone so long as he delivers. Any investigation or surveillance is aimed at checking on the foreign agent's competence and trustworthiness as a spy, not at his private or business life. There was nothing unusual about Georges' associations. Moreover, there was no evidence that he was embezzling Confidential Cash. Periodic checks were made of Georges' little helpers to whom he made disbursements, and without exception they verified their signatures on the receipts Georges turned in. They had no choice, of course. They took what Georges was willing to pay them, or did without altogether. Squealing on Georges would merely kill their golden goose. Besides, Georges regularly paid them little bonuses from his various business ventures.

No one is saying just how the DIA caught up with Georges, but a comely Vietnamese lass was taken into custody with him and its seems reasonable to conclude that the girl either messed up an assignment or did some loose talking. Since no charges were lodged against either of them, for reasons of security, there is no way of knowing what mischievous role the girl played. Georges, however, did not take her with him when he departed, a richer man, for Argentina.

There have been other foreign nationals who have used Confidential Cash to build up their personal bank accounts, but none ever operated as successfully as Georges. One agent salted away enough U.S. dollars to buy a brothel in Naples, another paid his way through law school in Ireland, and a third—a woman—set herself up as proprietor of a beauty parlor in Lyons, France. In all these cases, no more than $10,000 was involved. Meanwhile, there has been only one case—involving three officials of the Defense Department—in which Americans were accused and brought to trial on charges of embezzling Confidential Cash.

The three men were James R. Loftis, an administrative assistant to the then Secretary of Defense, Robert McNamara, with direct responsibility over the Budget and Finance Bureau of the Office of the Defense Secretary; John A. Wylie, Director of Budget and Finance in the Office of Secretary of Defense; and William H. Godel, Deputy Director of the Advanced Research Projects Agency (ARPA).*

All three were indicted by a grand jury in the United States District Court in Alexandria, Virginia, on December 16, 1964. Wylie and Godel were charged with being involved in a conspiracy to siphon off Confidential Cash funds through falsification of documents and diverting money to their personal accounts, acts which the Government charged resulted in the embezzlement of more than $60,000. Loftis was named in six counts on charges of embezzling $3,873 and making false statements.

* All information concerning these cases is taken from investigative reports and court records, notably the appendices of appellee and appellant in the case of the United States of America, appellee, versus William Herman Godel, appellant.

Loftis was acquitted on all counts. Wylie and Godel were convicted on charges of false statements and conspiracy, and Wylie also was convicted of embezzlement. They drew five-year prison terms. Both men appealed, but Wylie later dropped his appeal, went to prison and turned Government witness in the Loftis trial. In November, 1966, the United States Supreme Court denied *certiorari* in the Godel appeal and Godel was ordered to serve his sentence.

The three cases pointed up the dangers inherent in a system under which substantial amounts of cash are disbursed almost willy-nilly, with no meaningful independent check into the uses to which these funds are put. It is a system full of loopholes, for the most part dependent for its honest administration upon lower-level Pentagon auditors who are not eager to challenge the word of higher-ups. As in all matters involving national intelligence activities, the independent watchdog General Accounting Office is barred from poking its inquiring nose into the affairs of the Defense Intelligence Agency or those of any of the intelligence branches of the armed services.

In the Defense Department, and almost surely in other intelligence units, Confidential Cash is paid out only by a relatively few men, who are accountable directly to the Office of the Secretary of Defense. This looks more impressive on paper than it is. Hundreds of persons are attached to the so-called "personal" suite of the Defense Secretary; it may be a private club but it is one with a big membership. The supervision from the top is supposed to be close and personal, but in such a huge organization supervision is a relative word.

At any rate, Confidential Cash is drawn in cash or in checks by high-ranking officers known as "Class A Agents." The money comes from the Finance Officer of the DIA or one of the services, and the Class A Agents distribute it to a variety of "fronts." These "fronts"—organizations or business firms or individuals—then disburse the funds to buy certain adventures in skulduggery designed to advance the national interest. The accounting system calls for periodic statements of funds received from the Finance Officer, the amount of cash or checks on hand in the Class A Agent's office, and hand receipts from those to whom advances have been made.

Obviously, the system is an invitation to such operators as

Georges to feather their own financial nests. Hand receipts can be made out for more cash than was advanced, or signed by fictitious names. On the whole, however, intelligence people insist the system has worked quite well, perhaps due to the continuing checks made of the hand receipts.

But in the fall of 1963, there was a shortage of about $2,000 in the one acount. It was quickly covered by John Wylie. This puzzled Joseph P. Welch, director of audit operations in the Office of the Secretary of Defense. Welch didn't understand why Wylie would use his own money to balance the account of a Class A Agent. Welch decided to conduct a surprise cash count of all Class A Agents within the Office of the Secretary of Defense (OSD).

The cash count disclosed that several thousand dollars were outstanding against receipts signed by Wylie. Welch and one of his auditors went to Wylie's office and demanded access to all of the Class A Agent accounts in Wylie's possession. Wylie asked for a little time to put his account in order. Welch agreed, but insisted upon remaining in the office while Wylie prepared his records for an audit. Wylie, of course, was a big wheel in the Defense Department, while Welch was a faceless auditor, but Welch stood his ground. Eventually, Wylie walked into the office of his budget officer, Carl Fisher, and returned several minutes later with a brown envelope. Welch and his auditor assistant then accompanied Wylie to Loftis's office, where Wylie said he was accountable for $9,800, and produced the envelope and $200 in cash. The envelope contained $5,600 in cash and a check for $4,000 made payable to Wylie and his wife, Harriet W. Wylie.

Welch was both dissatisfied and mystified. In the first place, he had believed Wylie was accountable for only $7,400. It seemed strange that Wylie should produce more money than was required. Besides, the rules suggested there was something irregular about accounting for funds with personal checks or personal cash. Welch turned the case over to Loftis and Morris Landman, Assistant General Counsel for Financial Management, and asked for an investigation by the Inspector General.

A few days later, Welch found more grist for his investigative mill. He checked the account of a major in the Marines, William Corson, and discovered therein receipts from Wylie for $550 and $1,000, and a $3,031 receipt from William Godel. Major Corson was directed to turn in his records and when he did so, Welch told him—with Loftis in the room—that he would have to get $1,550 from Wylie and $3,031 from Godel to redeem the receipts by 2:30 P.M. that afternoon of November 5.

Wylie handed over $1,550 in cash to Major Corson at 1:30 P.M. It took Godel a little longer to raise his money. At lunch, Godel sold his car to a business associate for $2,195, but by the time the transaction was completed the banks had closed, and Godel was unable to convert the $2,195 check to cash. He then went to the David Mann Jewelry Company in the Pentagon concourse, where Richard Mackedon, the manager, wrote his own check for $2,000 and—a man of some ingenuity and influence—cashed the check at a side door of the bank. Mackedon accepted Godel's check for $2,000 in return. Godel then returned to his office and took $1,031 in cash from the safe to complete the payment to Corson.

But neither Wylie nor Godel were out of the woods. The investigation continued, and before it was concluded the FBI had collected enough evidence to press for indictments charging the embezzlement of more than $60,000 in Government funds. Loftis was implicated in the conspiracy by Wylie, who testified that Loftis knew of the irregular handling of the Class A Agents' funds, that he loaned money to Loftis from the funds and that he purchased various gifts, including cases of Scotch whisky, for Loftis out of the funds.

The investigators were especially interested in a $10,000 advance given to Godel for special combat training work in Vietnam. Godel, it was charged, endorsed $3,000 of the fund to Wylie, and converted $2,500 to traveler's checks and $2,500 to a cashier's check, all payable to himself. Godel also submitted a voucher for expenses of $10,000 for a trip to Vietnam in June, 1961. He did not itemize the expenses, but noted that "the documents necessary to support this transaction are on file in the Office of the Secretary of Defense, Budget and Finance Division." Investigators were unable to locate the receipts.

Wylie was notified in January, 1964, that he would be suspended from his job, but on February 4 he was permitted to apply for disability retirement and remain on the Defense

Department payroll. The Civil Service Commission granted the disability retirement in April, and on June 12 Wylie started drawing total disability retirement benefits of $516 a month.

Loftis's job was abolished, because of a "reduction in force." Then only fifty-two years old, Loftis promptly went on a Government retirement pension of $735 a month.

But they threw the book at Godel. At first he was suspended, as Wylie had been notified he would be, but on August 24 he was fired. Thus Godel was ineligible for retirement benefits such as Wylie and Loftis received. He did apply for a refund of $13,199.40 he had paid into the retirement fund, but the application was denied pending a decision on his possible indebtedness to the Government for loose handling of Confidential Cash.

All this happened, of course, before the indictments were handed down against the three men, and the developments puzzled one of the Senate's most indefatigable and accomplished muckrakers, John J. Williams, Republican of Delaware. Williams wrote to the Civil Service Commission demanding a full explanation of the circumstances under which Wylie and Loftis had been granted their pensions. The CSC eventually replied to Williams, detailing the size of the Loftis and Wylie pensions and the extra benefits they received as a result of the higher pensions they were permitted to take.

In the meantime, Williams also had written to Defense Secretary McNamara for information on "financial irregularities." He received a cool letter from David E. McGiffert, Assistant to the Secretary for Legislative Affairs, stating that Wylie and Loftis were within their rights and that Godel had been "removed from his position . . ."

Williams held his fire until after Wylie and Godel were convicted in late May, 1965, on charges of conspiracy, false statements and embezzlement. (Loftis was granted a severance, and stood trial later.) Then Williams took the floor of the Senate to wonder aloud about why Wylie and Loftis, "rather than being fired," were permitted to "claim immediate retirement benefits far beyond what they would have been eligible to receive had they been routinely separated."

Assuming that the two men reached the age of seventy-seven (the normal life span), Williams declared that Wylie

and Loftis together would collect additional retirement benefits of around $120,000 over and above what they would have
received under normal circumstances. He noted that Wylie,
a convicted embezzler of Government funds, "will collect an
additional $39,204 as a result of being carried on the payroll
after the embezzlement was discovered until he could be
classified as disabled." Loftis, said Williams, was "the second
employee to get kid-glove treatment after being suspected of
embezzlement." He added that after laxity and crime were
discovered in Loftis's office, a "special arrangement" was
made under which Loftis "will be able to collect an additional
$77,400 over what he would have received under a normal
pension."

A few months after Loftis's acquittal on all counts, he was
hired by the Communications Satellite Corporation, a quasi-
official, Government-created corporation, as director of organization and manpower planning at a salary of $25,000 a
year. Loftis carried a letter of recommendation from Deputy
Defense Secretary Cyrus Vance, who said Loftis's acquittal
had wiped the slate clean for him. Vance admitted, however,
he had not read the Loftis trial record or examined the Justice
Department files on the case. Vance said, "I don't think he
[Loftis] was a very good manager," but he replied "Not in the
least" when he was asked by James McCormack, chairman
and chief executive office of the Communications Satellite
Corporation, if the hiring of Loftis would adversely affect
relations between the Defense Department and the corporation.

Both Senator Williams and Representative H. R. Gross,
Republican, of Iowa, had a few words to say about Loftis's
new job.

On the Senate floor, Williams pointed out that Loftis had
bettered his income: "Here we have a man who under charges
of embezzlement two years ago left a Government position and
a $20,000 salary and is now drawing a total of $33,820 per
year—a $25,000 salary from Communications Satellite Cor-
poration and an $8,820 Government pension."

Gross took the House floor to declare "It is almost impossible to believe that the No. 2 official in the Department of
Defense . . . would help clear the way for the appointment of
J. Robert Loftis to a $25,000 a year job with the Communica-
tions Satellite Corporation. If he is not a good manager

Pentagon at $20,000 a year, what reason would there be to think he would be a good manager on the payroll of Comsat at $25,000, plus a Government pension of $8,820 a year, compliments of Defense Secretary McNamara?"

16

Needed: A Nosier Congress

Despite the sometimes loose handling of taxpayers' money within the American intelligence community, Congress has been notoriously reluctant to meddle with the budgets of the various agencies making up that community. Part of the reason is Capitol Hill's inbred reverence for the espionage trade and its admitted ignorance of the subject. Moreover, the CIA, the military spy outfits—especially the National Security Agency—and J. Edgar Hoover's FBI have powerful lobbyists within the Congress itself. Only the INR, possibly because it is a part of that eternal whipping boy, the State Department, is without a constituency in the nation's legislative halls.

It made news, therefore, when the House Appropriations Committee in the summer of 1968 slashed the Pentagon's operations and maintenance account by a hefty 987 million dollars and offered some strong suggestions as to where savings could be made. Military intelligence, said the committee, was overstaffed and undermanaged to the point that "useless information is collected, and useful information is ignored or not understood." The committee called for a sweeping reorganization of military intelligence agencies, and declared that "A realignment of operations is clearly needed."

There is little doubt the committee had become seriously concerned with both the quality of some of the intelligence on the Vietnam war and the frequent conflicts among members of the intelligence community arising from differing interpretations of that intelligence. The committee had been strongly influenced in its deliberations by certain members of the House Armed Forces Committee who were in a position to know about some of the arguments that had raged among the intelligence chieftains over such diverse items as the civil disorders in France that spring and the economic sanctions imposed by the United Nations on Rhodesia. What triggered the blast at military intelligence, however, was the committee's belated discovery that the Pentagon spooks had all but won the Vietnam war, on paper, three years earlier. Somehow, a reassuring document that reached President Johnson's desk in late September, 1965, had come to the committee's attention.

The document was a detailed intelligence estimate on the war in Vietnam compiled by the Defense Intelligence Agency from in-depth reports of the intelligence branches of the three armed services, and its gist was that the end of the war was in sight. The tide was turning as the result of the infusion of large numbers of American troops earlier in the year, the estimate said, and added that the Communist Viet Cong and their North Vietnamese allies had been thrown off balance. There was a strong possibility that the United States could begin a "leisurely" withdrawal of its troops "within a year."

For Americans old enough to have been in on the beginning, this secret report—had they been permitted to peruse it—undoubtedly would have been hailed as overdue. Washington had started pumping money into Indochina in 1950, during the second administration of Harry Truman, to help the French Army in its war with Ho Chi Minh's Viet Minh. Two years later, the United States had shipped the French 222 warplanes, 235 naval vessels, 775 combat vehicles, 1,300 trucks and 200 shiploads of war material. By that time, the United States had paid one third of France's Indochina war bill and its financial support was running between 350 and 400 million dollars a year.

In all, the United States spent nearly 4 billion dollars supporting the French war effort in Indochina. Eisenhower had dispatched 1,000 American military advisers to train the South Vietnamese Army. In the fall of 1961, President Kennedy increased this "advisory" force to 15,000 men, costing 1.5 million dollars a day. By the middle of 1968, more than half a million American troops were fighting a full-scale war in Vietnam.

Such an eventuality obviously seemed preposterous to American intelligence in September, 1965. With the American force then totaling some 140,000 men, the DIA estimate on President Johnson's desk "suggested" that the U.S. manpower buildup in Vietnam would go "as high as" 200,000 men. Certainly, no greater increase would be necessary because the United States "no·longer is losing the war on the military front."

Part of this flagrantly optimistic viewpoint was based on what the DIA called the "psychological shock to the enemy" of the "massive buildup of American manpower in Vietnam." In DIA's view, the Communists had not expected such a "retaliatory" buildup when in the fall and winter of 1964-65 their leadership made the "vital and possibly bad decision" to shift the weight of their fighting from small guerrilla units to their main forces. Until then the enemy had fought a kind of "neighborhood war" with guerrilla bands of no more than forty or fifty men, and loosely organized militia-type provincial forces. This Communist shift, said the DIA, was just what the American military strategists had ordered. They believed they could defeat the enemy in a war of main forces, fought in a series of conventional battles. Moreover, DIA gloated that the shift posed certain serious problems for the Viet Cong and its North Vietnamese allies. The rose-colored estimate continued in a fashion that must have had Lyndon Johnson rubbing his hands in gleeful anticipation of a quick victory:

With their decision to emphasize their main forces, the Communists were forced to change their system of logistical support. Previously, they had relied heavily on captured weapons; now they had to maintain a conventional logistics organization designed to provide a flow of weapons from North Vietnam, Red China and the Soviet Union. In particular, they needed heavier artillery to protect their larger battalion- and regimental-size units. They needed more of everything, and everything had to be bigger and better. In addition, they had sacrificed their flexibility by switching to a war of main forces.

There were other immediate problems. Previously, the Viet Cong units had operated in their home territory, in familiar surroundings. This developed a camaraderie, an *esprit de corps*, because they were "fighting for their homes." Moreover, a guerrilla's life was a relatively pleasant and leisurely one; he engaged in perhaps two or three well-rehearsed operations a month and took it easy the rest of the time. But now the Communist leadership was yanking men out of the guerrilla units, giving them a few days of crash, perfunctory training, and moving them into the larger forces, with no time to get adjusted to the stiffer discipline. The guerrilla's war was no longer a kind of violent picnic. He was far from home, fighting alongside people he didn't know. Those guerrillas who had had a modicum of prestige and authority back in their jungle lairs suddenly found they were faceless parts of a big machine. Defections had risen to 1,000 a month.

American air power had proved "amazingly effective," and Washington's decision to bomb North Vietnam came as a "real shock" to Hanoi, which "seriously misjudged" American determination. In the battlefield areas, the U.S. had built a "roof" of air power. Defectors complained of the "terror" of air attacks and said that for weeks they hadn't been able to sleep more than two or three nights in the same place. It was true the air strikes weren't producing as many casualties as the civilian might have expected, but casualties were only one of the objectives of air war. The air strikes had thrown the Viet Cong off their planning and reduced their effectiveness. They had planned "major operations" during the summer of 1965, but they didn't come off because American air power had disrupted their timetable.

All this, of course, was of the stuff that makes pleasant reading for a Commander-in-Chief. To Lyndon Johnson, it must have seemed momentarily certain that the Vietnam war would be over long before the 1968 election. At that stage, he may have been unhappy at the thought that the United States might have to increase its troop commitment in Vietnam to as many as 200,000 men, but there seemed to be a little light at the end of the long tunnel.

Fortunately, Johnson had other intelligence advisers to whom he always gave equal time, and they pricked the DIA bubble. Secretary of State Rusk said he couldn't understand how the DIA could be so optimistic. His own INR, he said, had gathered information from informants in both the Far East and Eastern Europe that disagreed almost *in toto* with the DIA's rosy picture. Bluff, hearty Admiral William F.

(Red) Raborn, director of the CIA, pronounced the DIA estimate preposterous, and he was backed up in more polite language by his assistant, Richard Helms—who later succeeded Raborn. Helms said in effect that North Vietnam's decision to stand and fight a conventional war could only mean a conflict whose end could not be foreseen at that particular time. Obviously, Helms said, the Communists believed they could handle a conventional war or they would not have shifted their strategy. Raborn added that every report received from agents abroad indicated it would be a long time before judgment could be pronounced on the North Vietnam decision.

Even Defense Secretary McNamara expressed doubt about the DIA estimate. He agreed with its conclusion that the United States had stopped losing the war, but said the overall situation continued to be serious, and suggested that someone was guilty of wishful thinking. He was constrained to point out, however, that the estimate was the product of a great deal of work by military intelligence teams in the field and long hours of analysis by intelligence scholars. The question McNamara left unasked was how the intelligence community could be in such deep disagreement over a subject that had received so much expert study. Undoubtedly, the question was asked later, but any answer it evoked was not made public.

One fact that did come out was that both Air Force and Naval Intelligence disagreed with the DIA's estimate, but were overruled in a private Pentagon session before the estimate was submitted to Johnson. The disagreement no doubt was sincere—and more important, accurate, as it turned out —but it also reflected the resentment on the part of the service intelligence branches of their subordination to the DIA.

Before McNamara created the DIA, the service spy branches had had a voice in discussions by the United States Intelligence Board. McNamara made the DIA the sole military representative on the Intelligence Board. The viewpoints of the service branches were heard only in sessions with the DIA; they were not allowed to air their dissents at the highest levels. In the case of the DIA estimate on the Vietnam war, the services had argued in vain that they be permitted to submit a minority report.

Moreover, the DIA director, Lieutenant General Joseph

Carroll, was suspect among the old hands in service intelligence because his experience had been as an investigator (for the FBI and the Pentagon), and he had no background as an intelligence analyst. Before he resigned as CIA boss in late 1961, Allen Dulles also was inclined to be critical of Carroll's credentials, and CIA people referred to the general as "that cop."

Curiously, the military bosses had some unkind words for the CIA's Raborn, who took over from Dulles's successor, John McCone. Although Raborn was a retired vice admiral and was given most of the credit for the development of the Polaris missile, his onetime Pentagon associates dismissed him as an amateur in the fine art of spookery, and poked fun at his ignorance of the language of the trade.

Perhaps understandably, the intelligence community has never been one happy family. The esoteric nature of its work lures prima donnas who nurture a high opinion of their own talents (usually justified), and cooperation among the assorted tribes was once described by President Kennedy as "an armed truce." A characteristic of the average intelligence expert is that he believes he or his agency can do a given job better than a competing agency, and never mind a lot of jazz about rules and regulations.

As has been seen, the CIA has frequently meddled in purely military business by mounting para-military operations abroad, notably in Cuba and Guatemala. The DIA, in turn, has branched out into foreign policy intelligence with its poking about in the political jungles of Europe and Asia. State's INR has not always been satisfied with the information gathered by the CIA, and so it has worked through the department's diplomats abroad to obtain certain specialized data. INR people shrink from calling their spies by name; they are always "informants." And J. Edgar Hoover's FBI has plowed its own intelligence fields through the agents it stations in numerous American embassies overseas under the cover of "legal attachés."

All this activity has resulted in charges and countercharges of "interference" by the various spy agencies. Under all its directors, the CIA has been privately critical of FBI operations abroad, and was especially upset when President Johnson dispatched a passel of FBI agents to the Dominican Republic during the unpleasantness of 1965. CIA men also have complained that the DIA's spy schools are duplicative and wasteful. The Pentagon has never forgiven the CIA for taking command of the abortive Cuban invasion in the spring of 1961.

On the more violent flaps in the community arose in the summer of 1965 when the "Camelot" scandal erupted and the State Department landed with both feet on the military for what one spokesman called "dangerous meddling with American foreign policy." The brouhaha offered an illustration of what can happen when intelligence's right hand fails to let its left hand know what's going on.

"Camelot"—hardly a felicitous choice of a cover name for such a project—was the name given to a study sponsored by Army Intelligence to determine the factors involved in promoting and inhibiting revolution in Chile. G-2, of course, called it a study of "political instability." A special fund estimated at close to a million dollars was allocated to the project, and it was placed under the directorship of a sociologist. A number of consultants were engaged to assist in the research, one of them an expert on revolution from a small "neutralist" country.

In due time, the "neutralist" decided that the study was a plot by the Pentagon and the CIA to organize a people's guerrilla army to take over Chile by force. He carried his opinion to the Chilean Government, which lodged an understandably strong and angry protest with the American embassy. The U.S. ambassador was shocked, in part because he had not been informed of the project, and complained to the State Department.

Both Secretary Rusk and INR Director Thomas Hughes hit the roof. In conference with President Johnson, they charged that the Army had "contaminated the atmosphere" in Latin America by sponsoring a project with such pronounced "political colorations." The State Department, they said, must in the future be authorized to pass judgment on all research projects which might affect foreign policy. Snapped Hughes: "Research is designed to be part of the solution, not part of the problem" of a given foreign policy situation.

There was also an angry scene between Rusk and Hughes on one side and the DIA's General Carroll on the other. Rusk complained that the evidence showed Carroll "hadn't bothered" to inform himself about the project, and wondered aloud about the Pentagon's "casual approach to serious matters." Carroll accused the State Department of suffering from pique because it had not thought of the study.

That was in June. On August 2, President Johnson canceled the project, noting that Federally-supported social science research could "raise problems affecting the conduct of our foreign policy," and directed Rusk to set up procedures for reviewing such contracts in the future. He agreed with Rusk and Hughes that there was danger in the intelligence practice of setting up research studies abroad which might incur foreign policy risks, and noted with surprise that the State Department seldom had the opportunity even to comment "in a timely manner" on the risks inherent in such projects.

New procedures went into effect on November 18, 1965; the State Department can work fast when it wants to. They set up regulations for three categories of research.

The first category consists of projects which must be submitted to the State Department for approval. These are projects involving foreign travel or contacts with foreign nationals which are sponsored by military and foreign affairs agencies—the Department of Defense, the United States Information Agency, the Agency for International Development (AID), the Arms Control and Disarmament Agency, units of the State Department itself—and the freewheeling CIA. Including CIA in the list probably represented State's biggest victory over that agency, after years of seeing its complaints about CIA's foreign policy meddling airily dismissed by a succession of Presidents.

Projects in this first category were described as those "most likely to pose problems of political sensitivity." Under the new regulations, they required action by the State Department which must be communicated to the sponsoring agency within fifteen days after the Department receives the information.

Category 2 consists of projects on which the "clearance office" within the agency decides whether or not the projects need to be submitted to the State Department for clearance. The projects include unclassified studies sponsored by military and foreign affairs agencies but not involving foreign travel or contacts with foreign nationals, and those financed by domestic agencies and requiring contacts with foreign nationals. But if the sponsoring agency decides the project does not require State Department clearance, it still must dispatch a brief summary of data to State, which has the right to seek more information and/or review the project.

Category 3 includes projects that must be submitted but do not require specific State Department clearance. Typical is the project which is classified but which is conducted entirely in the United States without contacts with foreign nationals. Information on them must be furnished to the Department either just before the project is undertaken or in a quarterly report. Again, State can demand more information and may review the project.

An indication of the magnitude of the nation's intelligence research program is found in the statistic that during the first year the new rules were in operation, the State Department reviewed more than 10 million dollars' worth of contract research sponsored by fifteen Federal departments and agencies.

Except for the rather lavish expenditures of the taxpayer's money, this proliferation of studies undoubtedly poses less risk to American foreign policy now that Foggy Bottom is authorized to withhold approval of them. (Although intelligence community gossips still chew over the embarrassment caused Washington by a sociological look-see into the sex life of Englishmen sponsored by the CIA. Curiously, the project was conducted at desks in CIA headquarters in Langley, Virginia, and required no field work abroad and no contact with foreign nationals—according to the CIA.) The pitfalls for the most part are to be found in such cases as the DIA's goof on the Vietnam war situation in 1965 and, on a later day, an appraisal of the 1968 civil disorders in France.

In *l'affaire Française*, the undisputed fact is that in early June one estimate of the situation, presented in the most positive terms, was that the French Communist Party was poised for a coup aimed at taking over the Government by force. Some details of the estimate are available. But intelligence sources were in firm disagreement as to where it came from.

One report was that the estimate was based on information supplied by a labor attaché at an unnamed American embassy in Europe. (Labor attachés are an excellent source of intelligence, especially in countries with strong unions.) A second report said it was a digest of the findings of an FBI agent somewhere overseas. In any event, the estimate was replete with details that had the ring of authenticity.

Among other things, it told of a secret meeting of Communist leaders, including the No. 1 French Red, Waldeck Rochet, attended by an American agent who had infiltrated the Communist organization. At this meeting, Rochet supposedly reported that the Communist strategy of initially remaining aloof from the demonstrations staged by students and workers was paying off. This restraint, Rochet said, had impressed the French people and had won new supporters among the working class. The party had even made contact with certain French businessmen, who wanted to restore order by any means, Rochet added. The American agent further quoted Rochet as saying that the party's plans were progressing and that with patience the Communists should be able to put together a coalition with the students and workers and seize power.

On the surface, the estimate sounded plausible. Rochet had refused to let his membership take to the streets in support of the rebellious students and, later, the striking workers. Not until the general strike became an accomplished fact which paralyzed France did Rochet move smartly to assert the party's leadership of the rebels. Many Frenchmen had applauded the Communists' restraint, and anti-de Gaulle sentiment was building. Moreover, Rochet and his labor union leaders had urged the workers to limit their demands to bread-and-butter issues, which added to the party's new aura of respectability.

Ironically, the Frenchman at his labor bench had long distrusted his own non-Communist unions for dallying with Big Business in arranging deals which frustrated the workers' demands. In the meantime, the Communist unions had consistently campaigned for higher wages, a 40-hour work-week and such fringe benefits as cheap life and health insurance. Behind their back, Rochet now apparently planned to strengthen his own position by the same kind of undercover liaison with Big Business.

Rochet's machinations aside, the estimate set off a brawl within the intelligence family. CIA Director Helms denounced it as "the worst kind of alarmist foolishness, unworthy even of an unlettered country constable." The DIA's

General Carroll agreed with Helms, although he said some of the reports he had received indicated that the Communists were gaining strength, and added that Washington should not dismiss the possibility of a Communist "move" if the situation in France was prolonged. The INR's Hughes commented dryly that he thought the estimate was "overblown." Some official observers of the intelligence scene later found it significant that J. Edgar Hoover defended the findings as being worthy of serious consideration. But their opinions were weakened by the fact that the uncompromising Hoover over the years had always been sniped at by the more scholarly spooks. At any rate, only the chiefs knew where the estimate came from, and they weren't talking outside chambers. Indeed, it was not until after de Gaulle's France had survived the summer of 1968 that it became possible to learn something about the much-discussed estimate on an "imminent" Communist coup.

With hard decisions to be made almost daily, it perhaps is no wonder that our temperamental espionage bosses sometimes fight among themselves. Personal slurs, often imagined, are reported to associates in what the intelligence crowd calls "the outside," giving the impression that their high-level discussions are spiced with the same sort of cattiness found at a female tea party.

In the privacy of their own organizations, the spy chiefs refer to their counterparts by derisive nicknames. Within the CIA and among some members of the INR, Hoover is known as the "Chief of Police." Military men call the CIA's Helms "Princeton oo," and his predecessor, Admiral Raborn, "Admiral Malaprop." The legend is that Raborn had a hard time pronouncing foreign names and once asked General Carroll what the word "oligarchy" meant. Carroll replied icily that the word described about two thirds of the governments the United States dealt with daily. At the Pentagon, Hughes was always known as "The Professor," a title military men do not use as an expression of admiration. Rear Admiral Eugene Fluckey, former head of Naval Intelligence, was referred to in CIA corridors as the captain of a "sinking ship." FBI men are unimpressed with the whole lot, although they get along fairly well with the military types. They have always referred to the scholars in the vineyards of the CIA, INR and the National Security Agency as "high-domed theoreticians."

Special interests sometimes seem to influence intelligence attitudes. Thus during a discussion of the sanctions proposed by the United Nations on the white-supremacist government of Rhodesia, DIA's General Carroll spoke up vigorously in opposition to what he called a campaign to harass "a good friend of the United States." Carroll was supported by the INR's Hughes and by Secretary Rusk, whereas Carroll's boss, the then Secretary of Defense McNamara, favored sanctions. Reports from both DIA and CIA agents in Africa stated flatly that neighboring black republics planned to join forces and invade Rhodesia. That was in 1965, and by late 1969 the invasion had not materialized, although "foreign" black guerrillas were causing Rhodesia considerable concern.

Both military intelligence and the FBI have been openly critical of some of the more professorial projects undertaken by the INR. There were reports that both the DIA and FBI leaked information to certain friends in Congress about some of these projects. At any rate, at a Senate hearing in 1965, the quiet, low-key Hughes was given a hard time by Senator John McClellan of Arkansas when Hughes testified that a Professor Louis Alexander of the University of Rhode Island was helping the Office of the Geographer of the State Department in producing International Boundary Studies.

After discovering that the five studies cost the Government $2,641, McClellan—Main Street-like—wanted to know: "Why do we have to do that? Do they not know their own boundaries? What is our function? Where do we come into the picture?"

"We could come in in any number of ways," replied Hughes. "In Africa alone, for instance, the boundary questions are so unsettled that Algeria and Morocco recently had a war over one; Somalia and Ethiopia at the moment are also contesting a boundary. . . . We have to take a position, or play a role as mediator, or work behind the scenes for a solution of the problem, or decide whether we are going to contribute to a United Nations action. . . ."

McClellan was skeptical. "What can we do about it?" he asked. "What purpose do these studies serve?"

Replied Hughes: "All I can say, sir, without being specific in a classified way, is that the United States finds itself involved on almost a daily basis in other peoples' problems."

McCLELLAN: What would be classified about that? How

do we get involved in disputes between other countries on their boundary lines? I don't quite understand it.

HUGHES: We are asked to intervene by the parties concerned. We have to make up our minds whether we want to intervene. . . . Let's stake the Sino-Indian boundary, several thousand miles long. There are all kinds of international pressures building up on both sides of this question. China and India fought a slight war over this in October, 1962. . . . There are pressures coming toward Washington from Pakistan and from India and from the Colombo powers, who are all trying to mediate the Sino-Indian border problem.

McCLELLAN: Asking us to do what?

HUGHES: Intervene one way or another.

McCLELLAN: Where is our responsibility for intervening in these boundary disputes all over the world?

HUGHES: There is no responsibility, except the general one that we do not want wars to break out.

McCLELLAN: I wish you would prepare a statement showing what you are paying out to give us something so that we can see the picture when we look at it. I am not opposing this necessarily, but I am concerned that we do not have a lot of duplication and go out and hire professors, universities and others to write up a lot of things to throw up on the shelf, to catch dust, rust and never be of any service.

Hughes wound up by reminding McClellan, in effect, that in its role as a powerful mediator the United States has been forced willy-nilly to assume the responsibility of trying to keep everybody happy, or at least out of one another's hair. In the INR view, boundary studies, with emphasis on disputes over frontiers, help to alert American policy makers to incipient problems which the United States may decide it must try to solve in the name of world peace.

But McClellan remained unconvinced. "After all," one INR official noted waspishly, "John had been briefed by those guys at the FBI and the DIA. Hughes didn't have a chance."

That apparently is the way it has to be in an intelligence community which employs some sixty thousand persons, engaged in doing roughly the same thing, and directed by human beings of strong convictions, admitted high talent and temperaments that would have been the envy of Sarah Bernhardt. Some foolish things are done and more foolish things are said, but this gigantic spying machine *does* work. The question the tax-paying American public has a right to ask is whether it might not work just as well if it was cut down to more manageable and less duplicative size. Certainly there would be fewer personality clashes among the tribal chiefs if there were fewer chiefs, and perhaps the United States would get into less trouble.

Project "Camelot" was an example of intelligence trying to do too much simply because it had the money and the manpower. So was the faulty estimate predicting a Communist coup in France. In the fall of 1968, the influence of intelligence on foreign policy was shown again when the United States announced it had dispatched a team of thirty Special Forces advisers to train Argentine troops in anti-guerrilla warfare, although others in Government warned that such a move might easily lead to another Vietnam. Intelligence, and military intelligence in particular, convinced President Johnson that sending the advisers was "in the national interest."

Over the years, Congress has shied away from looking too deeply into the finances, activities and influence of the intelligence community on foreign policy, on the grounds it should not hamper or compromise these secret practitioners of the second oldest profession. But in embracing this philosophy of courteous avoidance, Congress has abdicated its duty (in the Senate) to advise and consent on matters of foreign policy and to inquire (in the House) into the uses to which the taxpayer's dollar is put. Indeed, a Congress dominated by the military's constituency on Capitol Hill has been loath to act even when exposures of delinquency made headlines.

Surely, the defection of the Army sergeant, Dunlap, with its indications of lax security procedures within the National Security Agency, suggested a Congressional investigation. But both houses declined to inquire into a case in which an NSA employee had sold vital secrets to the Russians while obviously living beyond his means. At the State Department, INR people grinned wickedly at this example of legislative restraint, noting that had the scandal broken at Foggy Bottom "we'd have had cops all over the place."

Even during its investigation of the Martin-Mitchell defections, the House Un-American Activities Committee treated the NSA with unwonted gentleness. It did not "attempt to learn the details of [NSA's] organizational structure . . . feeling it had no need for [such] knowledge . . ." the committee's report admitted. Over the years, Congress frequently has given the military spy agencies and the FBI more money than the agencies requested; in 1965, for example, the lawmakers on their own initiative increased from thirty-five to fifty the number of scientific posts for which salaries were increased to $15,000 a year. And only a few years after the NSA built its new 35 million-dollar home, Congress approved another 10 million dollars for a nine-story annex.

But the criticism of military intelligence by the House Appropriations Committee in the summer of 1968 had an almost immediate effect on Pentagon spending—immediate, that is, for Washington. Early in 1969 the Defense Department launched a program to reduce by 33 percent the number of personnel in United States military missions ("milgroups") in Latin America. The cut was scheduled in two phases, which would reduce the number of men in the forty-three Army, Navy and Air Force missions from more than 700 to less than 500 by fiscal 1971.

Moreover, President Nixon told Defense Secretary Melvin Laird he was dissatisfied with the size of the projected reduction and ordred Laird to study the matter further and come up with a bigger cut.

Pentagon estimates at the time reported it cost $20,000 a year to maintain a milgroup member in Latin America. Other experts put the figure at $25,000. Whatever the cost, the milgroups had been an abject failure at gathering intelligence, one of their major, though hush-hush, functions. Jeremiah O'Leary of the Washington *Star* quoted one diplomat as saying, "You can't use the missions for intelligence purposes. They are often the last to know what the Latin military is doing, even though they have their offices right in the army, navy and air force ministries."

Again, the Defense Department was guilty of too much bigness in its intelligence efforts. Its admitted premise was that if it assigned enough men to intelligence it would find out what was going on. But O'Leary quoted other authorities as rejecting the milgroups as "expensive boondoggles," used as dumping grounds for officers who didn't measure up for important commands. Indeed, few of them spoke the language of the country to which they were assigned.

The question of whether the proliferation of spy agencies

has made America more secure is a difficult one to answer from the outside. Certainly, more information is gathered, and that has to be a plus. In the business of espionage, it is still unwise to suggest that less information is as good as more information. Moreover, no responsible examination of the American spy empire can overlook the advantages to the trade of today's highly expensive electronic gadgets—and their highly expensive technicians. There is no doubt that spying is a much more thorough operation than it was in the days just after World War II. The use of space alone makes it so.

But there is also the question of whether the country can have too much of a good thing. This proliferation of spy agencies means that more people know what the intelligence community is up to. It trifles, therefore, with Allen Dulles's stricture that information should be shared with as few people as possible, and that the number of those granted the "need to know" should then be reduced again.

The intelligence community also suffers, willy-nilly, from the weakness of its bigness. The bigger the operation, the more plagued it will be by the little inefficiencies that are inherent in bigness. In its 1968 report, the House Appropriations Committee stated the problem tersely—"useless information is collected and useful information is ignored or not understood." It is a problem of the *quality* of information used to help guide United States foreign policy. Too often, too many cooks have produced information and estimates whose quality has been poor to useless.

Congress's role here is clear. Carefully, and with prudent regard for the fragility of national secrets, it should launch a major examination of the intelligence community with the twin aim of reorganizing its structure and realigning its operations. This is a role Congress in the past has always shirked. On Capitol Hill, the subject of spying has always been regarded, in the words of former Senator Leverett Saltonstall of Massachusetts, as "too scary." The legislators shrink from knowing too much about this esoteric and not-quite-respectable profession. Quite simply, they don't want to get involved in what they fear is a dirty business. They do not yearn to open Pandora's Box.

Thus, the legislative branch must shoulder a large share of the blame for the high cost of spying by the United States.

The Republic may not have too many spies, and it may not be spending too much money on their activities, but no one in authority seems interested in looking into the matter. Certainly the public will never know whether its espionage money is being spent wisely until its representatives on Capitol Hill, at the very least, examine the balance sheets a little more closely.

Index